So happy
it
huRts

ALSO BY ANNELIESE MACKINTOSH

Any Other Mouth

So happy it hurts

ANNELIESE MACKINTOSH

JONATHAN CAPE
London

1 3 5 7 9 10 8 6 4 2

Jonathan Cape, an imprint of Vintage Publishing,
20 Vauxhall Bridge Road,
London SW1V 2SA

Jonathan Cape is part of the Penguin Random House group
of companies whose addresses can be found at global.
penguinrandomhouse.com.

Penguin
Random House
UK

First published in the United Kingdom by Jonathan Cape in 2017

penguin.co.uk/vintage

A CIP catalogue record for this book is available from
the British Library

ISBN 9781910702543

Designed by Two Associates
Printed and bound in Great Britain by Clays Ltd, St Ives PLC

Supported using public funding by
ARTS COUNCIL
ENGLAND

Penguin Random House is committed to a sustainable future
for our business, our readers and our planet. This book is made
from Forest Stewardship Council® certified paper.

MIX
Paper from
responsible sources
FSC® C018179

ONE

Happiness is the meaning and the purpose of life, the whole aim and end of human existence.

Aristotle

Text Message to André

Tues 31 Dec 22:41
You're married and IM FED UP
dont bother contacting me ever again
Except when I see you at work godddmamt

Text message to Mina

Wed 01 Jan 00:41
Fusk it Andrje, istill wa<3nt you,
SEX EMOJIZZ! 💧💧💧

Text message to Mina

Wed 01 Jan 00:48
Oopppss sorry sister,, that text was meant fr my boss.
Haaaapy neyear! Hope things get batter4 u in 2014
Vodka is nott my friendxxx

Advert on the Chemotherapy Day Services Noticeboard

All over the world, for a whole month, people are staying off the sauce.

In the USA there's Dryuary, in Finland there's *Tipaton tammikuu* and in the UK there's Dry January, also known as Janopause, Dryathlon and Banuary. Whatever you want to call it, the results are the same: quit drinking for the first thirty-one days of the year and you'll transform into a **healthier, happier you.**

Whether you are doing it to lose weight, lower your cholesterol, get a few good nights' sleep, or make some positive changes in your life, there's something in it for everyone!*

Also, did you know that cutting down on alcohol helps to reduce nausea and oral problems during chemotherapy and radiotherapy?

Speak to Linda at reception and find out how you can sign up today!

* If you think you might be dependent on alcohol, DO NOT TAKE PART without consulting your GP. Going cold turkey could be life-threatening.

Recovery Meeting Transcript

PATIENT: My name's Ottila. It's O-*double* T-I . . . Yeah, that's right. Bit of a weird one. My dad used to call me Hun because my name sounds like the barbarian leader.

THERAPIST: Can you talk to me about what's brought you here today, Ottila?

PATIENT: I'll try. I don't know where to start.

THERAPIST: Anywhere you want; take your time.

PATIENT: Okay. It's something that happened a week and a half ago. It was just after New Year. I'm in a sort of, I don't know, a sort of relationship with my boss. I work in the Maggie's Centre, at The Christie.

THERAPIST: Sounds rewarding.

PATIENT: It is. And Maggie's is great. You don't have to have cancer to go there. It's for anyone who's affected: friends and family. Originally I went there to get support after my . . . Just for a few weeks, to get my head straight. Now, two years on, I work there. Marketing and Communications Officer.

THERAPIST: And what about your boss?

PATIENT: He was one of the people who helped me when I first started going, but then I got this job last October, and a couple of months ago we . . . I tried so hard not to let myself do it. Something about him being married though. I don't know. I've always been attracted to chaos.

Just before Christmas, without any warning, he left his wife. And all that excitement and *risk* has just disappeared. But every time I end it, I get drunk and stuff happens again. Seeing André is wrong on so many levels. Not just because he's my boss. And not even because he was my grief counsellor before that. He's also forty-four and a card-carrying Tory. He goes on zorbing holidays.

THERAPIST: It sounds as though you and André have both been quite vulnerable. But given that he's your boss –

PATIENT: He gave me a disease.

THERAPIST: A disease?

PATIENT: Well, an infection or something. Bacterial vaginosis. Can you catch that from a man? Well, I got it, and it's disgusting, and I'm blaming him.

THERAPIST: Did you see the doctor about it?

PATIENT: Yes, of course. I had to. The smell is . . . And that's the problem. I got this medicine. Metro-thingy-zole, and she said to me, the doctor, she said I wasn't to drink while I was taking it, *under any circumstances*, for at least ten days.

THERAPIST: Did she explain why?

PATIENT: She said it's like Antabuse, the medicine alcoholics take to help them stay sober. Basically, if you have a sip of alcohol, or even put a drop of perfume on your skin, it's game over.

THERAPIST: It wouldn't be quite that –

PATIENT: Well, I'd been trying – and massively failing – to do that Dry January thing. I saw an advert on the noticeboard at work and figured it was a good idea. I'm thirty now. I can't keep this up forever: making myself ill, dating terrible guys and accidentally sexting my sister. It's ridiculous. But the problem is I didn't tell anyone I was trying to do it, especially not Grace –

THERAPIST: Grace?

PATIENT: She's my best friend. I just kept caving in and going out drinking with her. Or, if I'm honest, staying in and drinking *without* her, too. When the doctor told me that I shouldn't drink on the medication, I was like, okay, this is it. I'm going to have ten days sober, whether I like it or not.

THERAPIST: How did it go?

PATIENT: The first evening my palms were clammy and my heart was racing, but I forced myself to stay in bed and wait it out. I hid under the covers and watched cartoons from when I was a kid: *Count Duckula* and *Captain Planet*. One of the worst nights I've had in ages.

The next day I went to work. It was tough spending the day working with André, and I was still feeling grim from the BV, so when I got home and saw there was a bottle of wine in the fridge . . . The wine was Laurie's. He's my flatmate. He was out.

I threw up so violently my ribs ached. I called an ambulance, but I couldn't remember my address.

They found me in the end, prodding me with needles and tubes and questions. Laurie came home just as they were loading me in to the back of the van. He nodded at me and said 'get well soon', then went inside. I passed out after that and woke up in a hospital room, attached to a drip, hungover, hating myself.

THERAPIST: Sounds like a scary experience.

PATIENT: I phoned in sick the next day. Told André I had an STD.

He immediately went to get tested, and I'm almost annoyed he didn't have anything. [*Pause.*] I'm sorry, do you mind if I have a glass of water? [*Muffled noise. Tape switches off and on. More noises.*]

THERAPIST: Here you go.

PATIENT: Thanks. I'm sorry.

THERAPIST: Not a problem. So, was it the experience on antibiotics that's brought you here? That's made you want to quit drinking completely?

PATIENT: It started with that, yes, but it's everything. It's the cuts that I scratched into my calves to punish myself for drinking Laurie's wine, the cuts that are only just healing. It's the fact that I realised, while I was lying in that hospital bed, that my friends were too busy getting trashed to come and see me. It's the fact that really, deep down, I know that Dry January's not enough for me. I need to go so much further. Dry Forever.

THERAPIST: You want to take control of your own life, instead of letting the alcohol control you?

PATIENT: I want to remember who I am. Every morning, I've been trying to do something that'll make me feel better. Eat a banana, meditate, look at photos of cirrhosis. Sometimes I scream into my pillow.

THERAPIST: Does it help?

PATIENT: I don't know. If I could properly end things with André then . . . Maybe I'm just trying to sabotage my own happiness.

THERAPIST: Your hands are in fists. Can you explain how you're feeling?

PATIENT: For the past few days, I've been thinking about something that happened while I was at university. It probably won't sound like a big deal to you, and maybe it'll make me sound like a spoilt brat . . .

THERAPIST: Go on.

PATIENT: At the end of their first year, students have to stop living on campus. You're meant to branch out and learn how to live like responsible adults. Well, me and my group of friends left looking for a place to live until the last minute. We had other things to worry about, like which nightclub should we go to on Thursday nights: the indie one, or the goth one? So we ended up having to take a place in a really bad part of the city. We'd hear gunshots in the middle of the night, and, one morning, when Beth left the house, she found blood on the doorstep.

It used to take two hours to walk to campus. I don't think I made it to one nine o'clock lecture that entire year. There was a bus, but it rarely turned up, and I didn't want to pay the fare anyway. I lived on 7p tins of spaghetti hoops, saving all my cash for Fosters and vodka-cokes. [*Barely audible exhalation.*] I hated every second of the walk to campus. I didn't like my degree either, and I felt bad about that. I knew it was a privilege to be there, at university. Mum and Dad were proud of me, my sister was getting worse, and I had to be the okay one, so I kept going.

THERAPIST: Is there a particular incident you've been thinking about?

PATIENT: This one morning – there was nothing special about it. Rainy, grey. But as I set off on the long walk to campus, totally hungover, past a street cordoned off with police tape, I thought: *Just make a decision, Ottila. Decide not to hate this walk any more. Decide to be okay with it.* And from that moment on, that's what I did. Don't ask me how it worked, but I never minded making that journey again. I even learnt to enjoy it.

I was thinking I could do that with my new booze-free life: decide to be okay with it. No more restlessness, looking for faults, cheating. Just decide to be okay with it. So that's why I'm here, talking to you today. Because I'm never going to have another drink, and I'm only ever going to have monogamous sex, and no affairs, from this moment forwards, forevermore. I want to be a good person. And I want to be happy. So happy it hurts.

I need you to help me with that.

To be happy you must be your own sunshine.

Charles Edward Jerningham

Little Book of Happy

Dear Happy Little Shit,

Who on earth called you the *Little Book of Happy* anyway? You know as well as I do that final adjective should be a noun. As soon as I saw your smug spine on the shelf, I knew I hated you.

Little Book of Happy. As if everything there is to say about 'happy' can be said in one 'little book'. And yet I couldn't help picking you up this morning and trawling through your pages, full of white space and moronic aphorisms. And I couldn't help putting you in my handbag and stealing you from work. Think of all those cancer patients who'll never know the secrets of how to reach nirvana because of me.

I guess I'm not that sorry I took you. But I am a bit sorry that I've started ripping your pages out. I'm doing it for a reason though – it's something I learnt at the Maggie's Centre, back when I was a service user. I'm making a grief scrapbook. Except that nobody's died. Not lately, anyway. I'm grieving for alcohol, though, and maybe that's enough.

It's going to take more than a shitty, happy book to bliss me out, so I'm going to upgrade you. Stick in some brand new pages and make you tell the story of my life for a while. By the time I'm finished with you, you're going to be the *Big Bulging Book of SO FUCKING HAPPY IT REALLY FUCKING KILLS*, and I'll have been sober for One Whole Year. Just you watch, little guy. Just you watch.

Ottila McGregor, who is about to turn everything around.

Twenty Things to Do Instead of Drinking

1. ~~Read a book~~ *can't concentrate*
2. ~~Go for a drive~~ *illegal*
3. ~~Exercise~~ *no*
4. ~~Dance like no-one's watching~~ *makes me want to drink*
5. ~~Stroke your cat~~ *dead*
6. ~~Call your mom~~ *busy*
7. ~~Read to a child~~ *creepy*
8. ~~Visit someone in an old folks' home~~ *creepier*
9. ~~Speak in rhyming couplets for an hour~~ *creepiest*
10. ~~Scrub the limescale in your bathroom~~ *um?*
11. ~~Make marmalade~~ *fuck off*
12. ~~Take a hike~~ *you said it*
13. ~~Listen to music~~ *makes me want to drink*
14. ~~Have a bubble bath~~ *bad for vagina*
15. ~~Make pickles~~ *who are you?*
16. ~~Visit a friend~~ *want to drink*
17. ~~Do your nails~~ *want to drink*
18. ~~Write a poem~~ *want to drink*
19. ~~Do some laundry~~ *YOU ARE MAKING ME WANT TO DRINK SO BADLY*
20. (Develop a new crush)

Name Badge

THE CHRISTIE HOSPITAL STAFF

Thales Sanna

Trainee Coffee Shop Assistant

Maggie's Centre

Maude is eighty years old, with rheumatoid arthritis and a grade-three brain tumour. She strides into the room like none of that matters. 'Morning, *ulubieńcu*,' she says, sticking the kettle on.

Maude is not Polish, but her husband was. He died years ago – I don't know how it happened, but Maude left Poland and returned to the UK in the mid-nineties. I've only ever heard her mention her husband once, but he comes out in her *pierniki toruńskie* and her scattered Eastern European words. Although her memory's got worse since the tumour, it's the Polish words that she never struggles to find. Sometimes I think she uses them to hide the fact she's forgotten the English equivalents.

Today, Maude hasn't brought any gingerbread with her. In fact, this must be the first time in months I've seen her arrive without a Tupperware full of cake. While waiting for the kettle to boil, she stoops, unzips her trolley and retrieves a small package wrapped in white tissue paper.

'What do you reckon that is, eh?' She puts her hands on her hips and looks at her audience. Actually, there are only two of us here. I'm on my morning break and a new guy called Rajesh is over on one of the sofas, reading a leaflet. I saw him crying ten minutes ago though and he's been re-reading that leaflet ever since.

One of the great things about Maggie's Centres is how well designed they all are. Lots of windows, natural timber and, most importantly, open space. There are private areas if you need them, but for the most part, walls are taboo. It means that you never feel alone, even if the only other person here is at the opposite end of the building. In other jobs I've had, I've always been eager to get as far away from work as possible in my breaks. Here, I often feel better in work than out of it. At least, I did until André happened.

'I've no idea what it is,' I say, picking up the package and giving it a light squeeze.

Maude winces. 'Ooh, I wouldn't do that! Cup of tea?'

I put the package on the table. 'I'd love one.' I feel as though I should be offering to make the tea, but I know Maude would tell me to rest my tootsies if I tried, so I stay put.

Maude pops teabags in cups then takes off her coat and puts it on the back of a chair, smoothing out its creases with a contented sigh. She walks over to Rajesh and sits on the sofa beside him. 'I'm Maude,' she says. 'Good to meet you.'

Rajesh looks up from his colon cancer leaflet.

'Cup of tea, *przyjaciel*?'

He shakes his head.

Maude takes his hand between her palms and pats it. 'Well, I'm here if you need me, chuck.'

It's easy to forget that Maude isn't a staff member. She's our longest-running service user; she's been coming here for the past seven years. She had breast cancer back in 2007, and a double mastectomy sorted that out, but she kept coming to the centre, giving support and encouragement to others. And then, two years ago, she was diagnosed with the brain tumour. It's not fair the hand some people get dealt. Although I suppose fairness doesn't really exist. Everyone suffers.

Maude makes her way back to the kitchen, rubbing her temples. 'Now tell me, Ottila,' she says, sorting the teas then sitting at the table with me. 'Have you spoken to that chap yet? The one in the main building, in the cafeteria?'

I look around, making sure André's not nearby. Secret conversations are difficult in open plan, so I let my blush and nod tell the story.

'Atta girl. And do you know if he has a *dziewczyna*?'

'I've bought four sandwiches this week, trying to find out as much as I can.' I've managed to learn a surprising amount about my new crush in our few brief exchanges. Thales writes films in his spare time. I told him I used to write stories and plays, and he said his favourite writer is Pessoa. I don't even know who that is, which I find exciting. Yesterday I managed to get my morning break to coincide with his, and we sat in our duffel coats in the sunshine, talking like old friends. I mentioned my problems with alcohol, and he was really sweet about me opening up. Made everything feel normal and un-awkward.

Also, in a totally non-creepy way, I know where he lives and it's very, very, close to me. Not that something like that matters, of course, because *if* we were dating – and I know I'm getting ahead of myself – but if we were dating, I'd trek across the whole of Greater Manchester to see him. But it just so happens that he lives in Chorlton, three streets away from me. When I look out of my living room window, I can almost see the roof of his building. And, even better than that, there's an alleyway that runs from my street, past Chandos Road, past Ellesmere Road and straight onto Egerton Road North, directly opposite his place. I tested the walk last night and it took exactly four minutes.

'He's recently broken up with someone,' I explain to Maude. 'I spent days figuring out the right way to say *are you single* without being blatant. In the end he told me without being prompted. His girlfriend moved out of his flat recently and took half his stuff with her.'

'Oh well, it doesn't sound like the competition's too stiff. Now you can ask him on a date.'

'I don't know, maybe he needs some time.' Actually, I'm thinking about André. Maybe *I* need some time. I still haven't officially ended things with him, even though I've been very maturely ignoring his texts for the best part of a week. And I know it's not exactly the feminist way, finding a nice new man to save me from all my problems. But this feels different somehow. Perhaps it's because I've been speaking to him since I've been sober, but our conversations are actually *fun*.

And really, getting to know Thales has been so much more than a distraction from drink. I can tell I'm smitten because I've been muttering his name under my breath for the past few days. His parents are Greek. I've always had a thing for Greek people. Thales was named after a philosopher, one of the Seven Sages of Greece. The philosopher's name is pronounced *Tal-ees*, but Thales is sick of people getting his name wrong so he pronounces it *Thal-ess*.

'Psh, poppycock. Go to that cafeteria and get to it. Life's way too short, more's the pity.' Maude looks over at Rajesh. He's put the leaflet to one side and his head is in his hands. One of the support workers, Mairi, will be coming down soon to have a chat with him. She's got a very soothing way about her; hopefully he'll be all right.

'I might ask him out face-to-face. Or I might write something down instead. I don't know. An invitation to go on a date but, like, in the form of a story or something.'

'Sounds like the coward's way out.' Maude blows onto her tea then takes a sip. I wonder what she would think if she knew about my problems with drink. If she knew that every night, when I go home, I bite my knuckles red raw, trying to fill the gap that hungers for whisky and wine.

My eyes rest on Maude's hand as she grips her mug and I notice how tight her wedding ring looks. Her finger has swelled around it, and the ring is getting lost between folds of flesh. Then I look down at the table and remember the package. 'So what's in there, Maude?'

'What? Oh yes! Of course.' She picks it up and cradles it lovingly in her arms. 'Did anyone see *Naked and Marooned* on the Discovery Channel last night?'

I'm not sure whether Rajesh is listening, but I shake my head.

'It's a survival programme, set on a *Pustynna wyspa* . . . what's the name for it? Desert island. This young chap gets dropped off on an island, starkers, and has to live there for sixty days.' She removes the tissue paper encasing the package and holds up a small cardboard box. 'Do you know what he ate while he was on the island?'

'Coconuts?' I hazard.

Maude plucks a lizard out of the box and throws it into my lap. 'A gecko!'

I jerk my chair back, its legs screeching on the timber floor. The creature drops to my feet.

Immediately Maude bursts into peals of wicked laughter. 'Gotcha!'

The lizard is, of course, a toy.

'I played that trick on my granddaughter this morning and she was just the same as you!'

I look over at Rajesh, hoping that he has been just as gullible as me, but I notice something far more wonderful: he is laughing too.

Burns Night

Thales, you sexy thing. I know we've only chatted six times, or six and a half if you count the 'hello' I said to you outside the Melanoma Department, but you accepted my invitation to go for an ice-cream tonight and I think it's only fair that you know: I've got big plans for you, cafeteria boy.

This Saturday we're celebrating Burns Night. I've been researching the heck out of it, so here's the plan. First, we'll draw a Scottish flag in blue pencil crayon and Sellotape it to the wall, covering up the hole your ex – who I'm presuming meant absolutely nothing to you – punched into the plaster, under that poster (of a dog? Octopus? I can't remember!) you told me you won in a competition, inscribed with the words: 'A Good Day is Coming'.

Next, I'll find the raunchiest bagpipe music on Spotify and we'll listen to it while we cook. Now and then we'll stop slicing turnips and kiss, and the kisses will feel so good our lips will tingle. Once the food is in the oven, we'll raid your wardrobe and put on the closest thing you've got to tartan, which I imagine will be checked pyjama bottoms, and we'll parade around the living room like a pair of clowns.

Unfortunately, there's no table to sit at, because your completely inadequate ex-girlfriend took it with her, along with the chairs, the bed and the TV, all of which I am reliably informed officially belonged to you, but we'll sit on your sofa, with our cutlery on a crate, and clear our throats.

Everything will happen in the right order.

We'll begin with the host's speech. Since we're in your flat (to avoid sharing our special evening with my irritating flatmate) this makes you the opening speaker. I'm expecting something epic, something about our forefathers, the men they killed and the lassies they ploughed in order to make it possible for us to be here today. Something about the longing you feel for me in your *painch* and *thairm*, the tightening in your *hurdies*, the gushing in your *weel-swall'd kyte*. Something about the infinite, animal lust you feel for me, deep down in the trembling earth, all the way up to the twinkling stars. A simple 'thanks for coming' will also suffice.

We won't say the Selkirk Grace because we're not religious (or are you? It's not necessarily a deal-breaker), but we will say how much we like the word 'Selkirk'. I'll tell you it makes me think of soft, cobwebby threads, which sounds a bit pretentious but that's the way it is. Then we'll have a bowl of Cock-a-Leekie soup. It is our second date, this Burns Night supper, our second delicious date, and the Cock-a-Leekie will go down a treat. We will only make innuendos about cocks around half a dozen times; we'll be sensible. We'll put the cock in our mouths and we'll be sensible.

When you take away the empty dishes, I'll hear you whetting the *ceremonial dirk* (the least blunt knife you can find in the cutlery drawer), and then you'll bring it in, face puckered with concentration, along with a roasting tray laden with brown bits and white bits and yellow bits, which you'll set down on its *groaning trencher*, i.e. the crate.

As 'The Best Ever Rabbie Burns Bagpipe Medley' plays, I'll stand and clap and whoop a little too loudly. When I give you a hug, I'll briefly notice how warm your skin is underneath your jumper and wonder whether it's because of all the manly hair that I am ninety per cent sure adorns your chest.

We'll sit and look at the food. The brown bits will be haggis and the yellow bits will be neeps and the white bits will be tatties. It will *not* look tasty. It will look like insides. Insides is more or less what it will be.

Earlier that day, I'll have printed off the 'Address to a Haggis' on the work printer while my boss (who happens to be my kind-of boyfriend – um, my *other* boyfriend, which of course you're totally fine with because this is my fantasy and everything is perfect), wasn't looking. We'll read it out in terrible, possibly offensive, Scottish accents – I can never work out whether doing accents is racist or not – while the sheep guts go cold on the plate. On the line *His knife see rustic Labour dicht*, you'll draw the knife, and when I shriek *An' cut you up wi' ready slicht*, you'll slice the haggis from end to end. The steam will rise tantalisingly up from the offal and into our nostrils. We'll clink our glasses, which will contain alcohol-free ginger beer, since I'll have been sober for sixteen whole days, and then we'll eat.

It will be the best meal we've ever eaten.

As we dine, our conversation will roam. We'll start off talking about work, and very quickly we'll stop, because talking about working in a cancer hospital tends to get depressing. Besides, work is just something absurd that humans have to do in order to get money, which is absurd too, but we need it in order to pay for things like haggis suppers, which are not absurd – they're the whole point.

We'll discuss the things we want to do next weekend (go for a walk to the park with the chainsaw sculptures and get a £1.50 coffee from the petrol station shop for the journey), and the things we want to do for the rest of our lives (you, and I'm guessing here: stop working in a hospital, win the Palme d'Or; me: write a bestselling short story collection, become the new Marina Abramović), and briefly – very briefly – we'll talk about those we have hurt and screwed over, about your hideously deformed ex and the other guy I'm seeing, my boss (I'm working up to telling you about him in real life, Thales, I promise, and I'm working up to leaving him too), and how important it is we keep this night a secret.

'It's time to give my speech now,' I'll say, mouth full of oatmeal and spice. 'This speech is meant to be about Burns's life, his poetry, or legacy.' I'll look into your eyes and think about the first time we spoke, when I asked you for a BLT and a packet of Cool Original Doritos. 'It's known as the Immortal Memory.'

I'll start to tell you about the girl that Burns fell for when he was sixteen. He was out in the schoolyard measuring the altitude of the sun when he spotted her. For the next six months, he found a new sun to focus on . . . I won't know the details to be honest, because I always scroll down Wikipedia faster than I can read what's on the screen, but I'll make something up for you. Something about how this girl was engaged to another man, but her fiancé didn't set her heart alight. It was the bard, and the bard only, who could make her sun burn, burn, burn.

You'll thank me for my speech, steadying yourself as you get up, trying not to trip over the crate, being careful not to curse your flatulent, hunchbacked ex-girlfriend, and we will move on to the toasts.

You will tell me you have never met a woman like me. You will tell me that you have a strong, strong feeling about this.

I will reply that it is only date number two, but you are changing my life. You are so much *more* than a Thing to Do Instead of Drinking. You are exactly the type of person I want to be with when I'm sober.

I will stand beside you and take your hands in mine, then we'll dance around the living room to 'Auld Lang Syne'. It is only date number two and, although the bagpipes will be distorting my thinking, I will tell you, quite sincerely, that this is *exactly* what I want, now and always.

But today, Thales, it is just day one.

It is January 23rd and I am on the way to the hospital coffee shop to ask if you want to do something after work. We have not touched fingers yet. We have not let our breath mingle.

Today (I hope) we will walk to your house eating strawberry ice-cream, and then we will watch TV and chat. You'll show me your bookshelves and your signed copy of I don't know, something offbeat and intellectual like *The Mezzanine* by Nicholson Baker. I will tell you I have only read one Nicholson Baker book and did not enjoy it. You will recommend I try another before giving up on him. I will ask which one you think I should try next. You will reply. I will respond. You will smile, with teeth. I will smile, with teeth.

Today, we wait for everything to begin.

Receipt

FOOD SAVER

Wilbraham Road
Manchester
M21 0FT
0161 332457
VAT NO. GB 8224579

003867 POTATOES LOOSE.................................. 2.25
002458 TURNIPS LOOSE..................................... 1.21
001745 HAGGIS FLAVOUR CRISPS....................... 1.29
003875 GINGER BEER... 0.64
009122 DUREX 'SURPRISE ME' CONDOMS (20 PK)
.... 14.99

Items: 5

TOTAL DUE... 20.38
VISA DEBIT from customer............................. 20.38
Balance... 00.00

You were served today by: MARLON.
THANK YOU for your custom.

25/01/14
18:02

Of all forms of caution, caution in love is perhaps the most fatal to true happiness.

Bertrand Russell

Note Inside Tuna Mayo Sandwich Container

Surprise!

If you are the lucky recipient of this message, I managed to convince Naomi to take this to the Maggie's Centre and deliver it to you personally. Apologies if you aren't in the mood for tuna mayo. It was either that or cheese and RAW ONION, and *no one* likes that.

I just thought I'd tell you that I think you are cool, and I hope you're doing okay. I really enjoyed Saturday evening. Sorry I didn't have any checked pyjama bottoms, but I think we managed to make the evening authentic regardless. I've certainly never seen anyone fit eight crisps into their mouth in one go before: must be a Burns Night record. And don't worry about not finding any haggis; I'll survive without eating sheep stomach until next year. On a more serious note, I loved hearing about that story you wrote when you were at university. I know you say you've lost your creative spark, but I think it's still there.

We don't know each other very well yet, but I want to share something with you. I was going to mention it at the weekend but we were laughing too much and it never felt like the right time, so here goes . . . I am a recovering addict too. Until very recently, I was hooked on codeine. I used to go to seven different chemists across South Manchester, buying as much Paramol as I could lay my hands on. Great habit, no? Definitely not as rock and roll as alcohol. The truth is, I was numbing myself from depression with painkillers and food. I'm all right now, but coming off the codeine wasn't easy. Lots of 'stomach issues'.

Hope you enjoy your sandwich?

Thales x

P. S. Sorry I'm fat.

Text Message from André

Mon 27 Jan 11:05
Really digging that tartan skirt today, lassie. How about I get us a room at the Marriott tonight? special treat for our 3-month anniversary. by the way, this recent silent treatment has made me very horny.

Email to Grace

From: Ottila McGregor
To: Grace Shotts
Date: Fri, 31 January, 2014 at 19:12
Subject: Re: dude where are you?

Shottsy!

How are things? Hope you're doing well and that all's good in Hallé land. I saw a thing in the *Manchester Evening News* about a series of Strauss concerts. I think there was one at the Bridgewater. Are you involved?

I'm so, so sorry for going off the radar for a few weeks. The last time I saw you I was trying to convince some guy at Funkademia to swap jeans with me and you were lying under a pile of coats screaming out the lyrics to 'Pick Up the Pieces'. Hang on, was that before or after the four-way Frenchie in Walrus? You are outrageous, missus! Anyway, I'm sorry I didn't get a taxi home with you that night. I threw up out of my nostrils and the bouncer made me leave. I went home, put six burgers under the grill and stuck a drawing pin in my knee. Laurie found the burgers in the morning, slowly melting into the grill pan under a low heat. I woke up, fully-clothed, in the living room with a drawing pin and a load of bloody gunk in my leg. I guess we'd normally have a laugh about stuff like that. The truth though, the real truth, is that I can't keep doing it any more.

You seem to manage it somehow, I don't know how – you can go on a massive bender and then play the most searingly beautiful violin solo the next day, and no one would know you'd been doing a hedgehog impression coked up to the eyeballs at 3 a.m. that same morning. But me . . . I can't carry on like this. I need to be good. Have you ever noticed that all our old drinking buddies have stopped hanging around with us now? It's just me and you and Saz and sometimes Kameko, although even she seems to be settling down and getting all responsible now she's got that new haircut.

I don't know. I'm not sure what I'm trying to tell you. I'm thinking that I might try drinking less for a while, like maybe nothing at all for a bit. What do you think? Do you hate me and think I'm a loser? Can we still hang out and maybe go for a hot chocolate? Or roller-skating? Or to the cinema? I can hear you groaning from here.

It'd be good to see you. I've had so much going on lately. I tried breaking up with André (I know, I know, *again*) on Monday, because . . . well, because it's destructive and bad for me, but there's this other guy too . . . more on him in a sec. The break-up with André went totally wrong. I asked him if we could chat in one of the confidential counselling rooms, but as soon as he shut the door I knew that being in a confined space together was a mistake. This is going to sound bad, so brace yourself, but you know those headscarves people wrap around their head when they've had chemo and their hair's falling out? Okay, don't laugh, because it was actually awful, but there was a box of those scarves under the table – Delyth sometimes runs a fashion workshop teaching people ways to tie them that look cool – and . . . I guess I always thought I'd like being tied up. André really thought he'd win me back by trying to go all *dom* on me. It's hard to be a good dom when you're crying though. Seriously: there were tears in his eyes. He's having such a hard time at the moment. I feel so sorry for him, but I need to start having some self-respect. I don't know why I let it keep happening. Not that anything actually did happen. Not really. I mean, just some touching. It's so hard to find the strength to properly end things. I feel responsible for him somehow. He left Jennifer for me. For a while, it made me feel good trying to make him happy. Especially after Ben dumped me because I'm supposedly 'high maintenance'. It's been nice being the maintainer for a change. André is probably the only person in the world more pathetic than me, which is obviously a great turn-on. Plus, he's fit. But he's also a dick. Ugh. I'm meeting him tomorrow night somewhere public, on neutral territory. I'm going to end things once and for all.

I don't know. What do you think? Am I an idiot? Was life better when I just didn't care about all this stuff? And then there's this other guy I've met that I really, really like. He's Greek and clever and sweet. He works at the hospital too, in the coffee shop. I think maybe I could start something with him, as long as I don't do the thing where I focus on all his flaws until I talk myself out of it. Maybe I just need to stay away from relationships for a bit.

I'm so low, Grace. Honestly. It's like a deep, deep ache inside of me.

Bet you didn't expect such a downer from me after all this time! Promise when we meet up I'll be all puppy dogs and fireworks.

O–Dog x

Meeting André in a Public Place

'Ottila! Over here!'

André is already at the table, waving. He has a new shirt on, which is a bad sign. It's light blue with a geometric flower pattern. I'm hoping that staring at the shirt might help distract me from the eager expression in his eyes, but I'm wrong. It makes everything worse.

As we hug, his lips graze my cheek. I swerve my face away from him, pretending to look around at the almost-empty restaurant, and sit down.

'Thanks for coming,' he says, sitting opposite me, and I can smell the scent of him, the expectant cologne, probably called something like *Eros*, flying up my nostrils and attempting to bond with some attraction part of my brain.

'André, I . . . What happened the other day, in the one-to-one room, I . . .' I pick up my menu, and glance down at the list of grilled meats. 'It shouldn't have –'

'Look, Ottila, I know what you're going to say.'

His eyelashes are so dark, so moist. Has he been crying again? He looks good with moist eyelashes.

'We need to stop doing stuff like that,' he says. 'That's why I suggested the Marriott, a *four-star* hotel, but then we ended up in the counselling room. Not appropriate. I'm your boss. We need boundaries.'

'That's what I've been thinking too. You're my boss, and we shouldn't –'

'So work is work, and leisure time is *pleasure* time.'

'Pleasure time? That's gross, André.'

My awful, attractive boss grins and I remember the time his perfectly white teeth bit down on my clitoris and I screamed. It was his first time on what he calls Thizz, but the world calls Ecstasy. He wanted us to try it out before using it with Jennifer to rekindle any lost love they might be able to find before it disappeared entirely. He and Jennifer took white pills with lightning bolts etched into them every weekend for a while after that. *We just run our hands up and down the sides of each other's bodies,* he later told me as we fucked in the car park after work. *It's so spiritual. If you don't want me, then maybe Jennifer and I have a chance of making it work.*

André raises his eyebrows, and all I can think in that moment is: your real name is Brian. It doesn't matter how cute you look when you raise your eyebrows at me like that, because your real name is Brian and you're not French.

'Look, all I'm saying is, we're away from work now, on a date. Chillaxing, or whatever.'

I'm repressing an involuntary shudder when a waitress wearing a badge bearing the name 'Peggy' approaches us and asks if we're ready to order.

'I'll take the Hunters Chicken,' André says quickly. I bet he always has the Hunters Chicken. I'm pretty sure he's been eating here every night ever since he left Jennifer and moved into the Premier Inn. Honestly, our sex life has been all hotels and hospitals since getting together. Thankfully, this is our first date in the Little Chef.

'Interesting how there's no apostrophe in Hunters,' I remark. Nobody reacts. 'I'll have the vegetarian cottage pie.' I don't trust the meat here. Guess I'm a snob. Although I *do* seem to trust the meat at Chunky Chicken every Saturday after a night of mayhem at the Mint Lounge, so . . .

'No problem.' Peggy is so good at her job that she isn't even writing our orders down. She has a polite smear of blue eyeshadow over each lid, which becomes apparent as she memorises our requests. 'What would you like to drink?'

'Pilsner for me,' André replies. 'Ottila? Red wine?'

I turn over the menu. 'They do *drink* drinks here?'

The waitress laughs. Now I hate her. 'Yes. We do drinks.'

'I . . . I don't want . . .' Even reading the names on the menu makes me salivate. Carling. Pilsner Urquell. Merlot. Sauvignon Blanc. Why does alcohol have such alluring names? 'I'll have a Robinsons Fruit Shoot.'

André's jaw drops.

'What flavour?' asks Peggy.

'Tropical.'

'You not feeling well, birdie?' André asks as Peggy walks away.

I shake my head. 'Think I've got a migraine brewing. Wine would just make it worse.' Even saying the word 'wine' makes me want wine. There's something really satisfying about the way you have to draw you lips together, and then drag the sound across your teeth. Oh god, I miss wine. Wine would make everything much easier. I have no idea how I'm going to survive watching André put his lips to a cold bottle of Pilsner, imagining the bubbles fizzing on his tongue, the refreshing amber liquid flowing down the back of his throat . . .

'You're shaking, Ottila. Maybe we should just get some in a doggy bag and go back to my room? Snuggle up and put the telly on? I'll run a bath for you. I'll even let you have something from the minibar. They've got M&Ms for a hundred quid.' I've stayed in André's room a couple of times. He doesn't have a minibar.

A man and woman at a nearby table high-five each other. There are four people sitting at their table: mother, father, son, daughter. They all have red balloons tied to the backs of their chairs, the simpering white face of the Little Chef on each one. Clearly it's someone's birthday. Maybe they all have their birthday on the same day as each other – that's how perfect they are. These perfectly happy people, each with a slightly different burger for their slightly different personalities, are continuing to high-five one another and laughing in unison. What's their secret? How do they get to be like that, when I'm sitting here, like this? I close my eyes for a split second and meditate on my goal: simpering, gurning, throbbing, exquisite happiness.

'Listen, André, I need to tell you something.'

André holds out his hand, but I don't take it. I think about the time that hand stuck two of its fingers up my bum while we kissed in the Premier Inn lift.

'You and me,' I say decisively. 'I can't do it any more.' The carpet is a dusky pink, the same colour as Pripsen powder, which Mum used to give me and Mina when we had threadworms. It was meant to be raspberry-flavoured. It wasn't. Remembering its chalky, alkaline taste makes me feel queasy.

The waitress appears with our drinks. 'Fruit Shoot,' she says with gusto, handing me a piece of paper containing the outline of a fireman and a pack of crayons. 'The Fruit Shoot comes with these.'

André takes a big gulp of his Pilsner and I look back at the carpet. Pripsen powder worked by stopping the worms from being able to contract their muscles so they got dislodged from your gut and you'd shit them out, live and paralysed. I try to imagine that Pilsner tastes like Pripsen powder. It doesn't help; I'd drink worm medicine if it was alcoholic.

'What do you mean, Ottila?' he asks. 'You told me to leave

Jennifer. Said you wanted to fuck me as an old man.' His voice cracks. 'You said you wanted to run your fingers through my grey pubes.'

I close my eyes. *I've said so many things when I've been drunk. So many things, André.* I open my eyes and look over at the perfect family. They've stopped high-fiving each other but they're still laughing. 'Look, the fact is, André: I'm a lesbian.'

'Hot,' is his predictable reply.

'You know I told you about my past, about how I went out with a woman – Reatha – for three months, and she was the person I loved most in all the world?'

'I remember,' he grins. 'I remember when you told me all about how you and her used to use your desk chair to –'

'It's over,' I snap. 'I'm sorry you left Jennifer, but I think you should go back to her and apologise. I've met someone now, and she is my future.' I lift the plastic cap off my Fruit Shoot and suck tropical juice from its teat. 'I'll see you at work on Monday.' I stand up, realising I haven't even taken off my coat yet. I'm one of those women in movies who orders food and then leaves without eating any of it.

André takes another mouthful of Pilsner, and all his words wash away with it.

'Bye, André,' I say, and I walk out of the Little Chef.

There isn't much choice along this particular stretch of the A556, so I head for the BP garage, where I'll buy a (cheap, dirty, meat-filled) pasty and order a taxi home. As I walk across the forecourt, I say three short words under my breath, which fly out of me like sparks off a struck match: *I'm in control.* The sparks grow into flames and devour me, my musculoskeletal system blazing with victory.

Just then my phone buzzes. I take it out of my duffel coat pocket and see I have a Snapchat message. It's from my sister.

'Oi, love, put your phone away,' says a burly woman on the forecourt.

I smile and put my phone back in my pocket, deciding not to tell her that it's actually a myth that mobile phones shouldn't be used on forecourts.

I'm in control, I say again, and the flames incinerate everything in sight.

Snapchat from Mina

Today

TEENYMEENY

| I'm really worried about you, Tilly.

Email from Grace

From: Grace Shotts
To: Ottila McGregor
Date: Sun, 2 February, 2014 at 18:28
Subject: Re: Re: dude where are you?

rocket dawg, i am so effing hungover! can't believe you missed fuckademia last night. saz pulled two guys who turned out to be brothers, and i got chucked out for lighting up in the bogs. it was awesome. head hurts like a bitch today. you're so wrong about me not feeling it the morning after. i get hangovers, lady, believe. meant to be writing some bela bartok rip-off for a wedding marquee advert today, and no way is that happening, man! it's gonna be red dwarf, pjs and cheese on toast under the duvet all day long. she says, well aware it's evening now and she only got up 2 hours ago.

aw, wish you were here, dude. sounds like you're going through another one of your phases. i know what you mean about drink. once in a while i wish i could just stay in and watch a nice film and then, i don't know, like, go to the park and look at all the snowdrops the next morning or whatever, but then i'm like, i'm young. this is my time! your thirties are basically the same as your twenties these days. it's different for our generation, and anyone that says they're happier being all responsible or whatever in their thirties is lying, i swear. i mean, seriously, you've got plenty of time for all that stuff. have fun while you still can. unless of course you want kids, in which case, you might wanna sort your shit out, but you've probably pickled your ovaries by now. it's no biggie though because everyone in our generation is gonna be adopting, it's the next big thing.

omg speaking of fun, your rendezvous in the counselling room at work totally reminds me of this thing i had in the toilets at kro bar last week. there was this guy in there, like a totally normal emo type guy, cute and shy-looking, and he kept staring at me all evening while there was this poetry thing on. you'd have really hated the poetry. it was all these hipsters reading from their iphones, stuff about gumtree and one direction. i actually found it quite funny, but you know my sense of humour. it's basically anything a ten-year-old boy would laugh at. and i'm loud and proud! yeah, this guy, he was reading one of the poems actually, about wearing gloves for the first time and then the gloves start talking but they have the voices of ant and dec. i was pissing myself. wish i could remember more of it but i was on the ciders and you know how that gets me. anyway, this guy, he followed me to the loos in the break, and then he just pulled me into a cubicle in the men's bogs, ripped off my top and pushed his hands down my pants and told me he'd fucking kill me if i made a sound. i feel like that one night kind of realigned my brain. like, i got a part of myself back. everyone in the orchestra was just like, what is with you, man, cos i was grinning for two days afterwards.

i doubt i'll see him again. he's so beautiful i can hardly remember what he looks like. i gave him my number but he never called so i have no way of getting in touch. it probably wouldn't be the same next time anyway. you can only have that shock of like don't kill me, i want to fuck you, once, i think. after that it's just make believe.

i've been reading katherine angel's *unmastered: a book on desire*. she says you can be totally submissive and do nothing and just get fucked to smithereens by men and still be a feminist. at least, i think that's what she says. it's kind of arty and hard to read. i think you'd really like it. i can lend it to you when i next see you. and on that subject: you HAVE to get tickets for the 6 music festival next month! you should totally try not to drink until then, so you can get pissed on, like, half a pint and it'll be dirt cheap. lykke li, the national and and AND a silent disco. come on dude, it'll be amazing. even kameko and her new pixie cut are coming along. but in the meantime, yeah, a non-alcoholic thing sounds kitsch. we could go clubbing dressed as schoolgirls and drink lemonade all night and ask guys to slip vodka into our cups. norty!

omg I almost forgot to tell you: i ran into ben the other day. it was outside that tibetan street food place which looks amazing, but benny boy didn't have anything from there, he was just walking past. and not to piss you off or anything but he looked effing fit! he asked about you too. i hope you don't mind but i told him where you worked. i made it sound like you were doing really well these days, like all that shit about you being high maintenance was totally wrong. he seemed super chill anyway, he is still working at the insurance place. he's been doing loads of climbing and his biceps are maHOOsive.

ok this has already been way too much typing for my busted brain. time for a cuppa and some smegging red dwarf. everybody's dead, dave. not chen! everybody's dead, dave. they're all dead. haha!

miss you, crazy girl.

shotts x

Hand in hand, on the edge of the sand, they danced by the light of the moon.

Edward Lear

Little Book of Happy

Dear LBOH,

So far not one of your aphorisms has suggested that the key to happiness is sobriety. But I know I'm doing the right thing, even if I did break down in Marks and Spencer yesterday because those little cans of gin and tonic were in the same aisle as the salmon en croûte. Talk about a middle-class meltdown.

Thales was coming over to mine for the first time, hence the fancy dinner. I set the table with some scented candles (lime and bergamot: purifying and uplifting) and picked an early-blooming daffodil from the alleyway and put it in a vase.

I'd only just served our meat platter starters when Laurie walked in, fell onto the sofa and switched on the telly. We had to eat our salmon to the sound of Laurie slurping beer and watching *The One Show*. Thales was sweet though. He tried to make small-talk with Laurie, and Laurie must have liked him because he offered him a beer. And, drum roll please, LBOH: Thales refused! He hasn't had anything to drink in front of me yet. I wonder how I'll feel when he does. Will I be able to kiss him if he tastes of alcohol? Will it make me want to drink too?

I know I've daydreamed about it a lot but we haven't *actually* kissed yet. Not even a peck on the cheek. Maybe I cursed it by buying all those condoms on Burns Night. At first I thought it was because of André. I spilled the beans last week, just slipped it into conversation in this casual, this-is-the-kind-of-mess-I've-got-to-sort-out-now-I've-quit-drinking way. Thales surprised me with his bluntness, saying I should sort that out before anything happens between us. Last night's meal was a sort of 'I'm single' celebration, but still he didn't make a move. Dating people without booze is really difficult. Normally I'd just get pissed and throw myself at someone. I have no idea what sex is going to be like. I haven't had sober sex for ages. The last person was Ben, and it doesn't really count because we were together for two years and we were used to each other. Plus, we normally *were* drunk when we had sex. I don't think I've ever had my first time with anyone sober. Not even when I was fifteen and me and Dreadlock Dorian popped our cherries. (Do men pop cherries too? Do women even do that? Is the hymen supposed to be a cherry?)

I'm not going to give up on all this though, LBOH. I've started filling in this drink workbook thingy my therapist gave me, and I'm trying to think of it like learning a new language. It's not easy, but here's how I know I'm doing the right thing: in the morning, when I open my eyes, I don't immediately check my phone with a knot in my stomach. I haven't had a fried egg sandwich or tweeted that I want to die in weeks. I wake up with this really calm feeling, as if I could almost be a good person.

And that's enough to keep me going for now.

OM

Forgive Yourself and Move Forward

It's time to let go of all that guilt inside you. Feeling bad can stop you feeling good; it's as simple as that. You *are* capable of making a change. You *are* worth it. Now it's time to start believing that.

Let's expunge those demons so you can forgive yourself and move forward. Write about anything from your past that you feel shame about, let it all out, and then turn the page and start living your life.

kicking Dad / calling Mum at 2 a.m. to say I'm dying / making Mina smoke / missing lunch date with Saz / eating 'road pizza' / butterfly stitches on thigh / glass in hand drawing on face with marker pen before interview / bus sick / plane sick / work sick / missing graduation / sleeping in Piccadilly Gardens / dentist sex / broken ankle / mystery drug / kissing a fifteen-year-old / love bite at work / eating stuff in ashtray / kidney infections / gonorrhoea / RUSSIAN ROULETTE / supermarket sick / road sick / posting shoes through stranger's letterbox / prank calling / threesome with Grace / bed sick / driving sit-on lawnmower / whipped cream competition / wrinkles / eating disorder / lost purses / lost brain cells / lost time / depression

Snapchat to Mina

Today

ME

Don't worry about me! I've never been better! Here's a picture of the tattoo I'm getting tomorrow.

Note Stapled Inside Bereavement Leaflet

Oh ho, Thales, two can play at this game. You're not the only one who can send sneaky notes from one side of the hospital to the other, Mister. I mean, sure, I had to tell Delyth that your auntie had died of acute lymphoblastic leukaemia last week and you're having a hard time dealing with it, but yeah – as long as you don't mind reading up on cancer of the blood cells and attending the odd grief workshop for the next couple of weeks, then this method of communication is definitely worth it. Just kidding, you don't need to do any of that stuff. But Delyth really does think you're recently bereaved. I'll come clean with her about that at some point, I promise.

So . . . it's just a quiet day in the office and I'm thinking of you. André's been off all week which has made everyone a thousand times more relaxed. There was a baking session earlier, led by one of our service users, Maude. She's really fantastic. We have to supervise her when she uses the oven because she's got a tumour the size of a baby squid in her brain, which she takes great pride in talking about. Her son is a marine biologist, and she relishes the connection. Anyway, I've been smelling Paul Hollywood recipes all afternoon. It would happen to be on the day I decided to be good and bring a salad into work.

I went to the kitchen earlier to make myself a peppermint tea (the healthy man's choice!) and overheard some of the service users talking about their happiest moments. One of the women, Lena, whose sisters both died of ovarian cancer in the same year – it's really sad – said that her happiest moment was on Christmas Day. She'd just been out for a walk, and when she got back home, she found out she'd been burgled and all the presents had been stolen from under the tree. She said her family rallied together that Christmas like no other. Even though the burglar was never caught so they never got their presents back, it was a bittersweet happiness that she'll never forget. And you know what I thought? I thought: *bollocks*! That's not the sort of happiness I want! Happiness tinged with pain? No thanks! I want candy floss and bunny rabbits and perfection. Is that too much to ask? Do you fancy joining me in my quest?

The workshops are finished for the day now, and there are just a couple of service users in the kitchen drinking tea. Other than that it's dead in here. 'Dead' is the sort of word I would try not to use in front of the service users. Having said that, some of the most poorly people here have the best sense of humour. Better than I would have if I had a terminal illness. I would just curl up into a ball and moan until I expired.

I hope you are enjoying this romantic letter. Sorry. I think my mind has been a bit scrambled by this press release I'm trying to write for a Kids with Cancer activity day. I've spent the last two hours trying to find a stock image that says *I'm afflicted, but having fun!* When I first started working here, I used to cry several times a day. It still felt so soon after my dad died. I haven't really talked to you about that stuff yet. Maybe I will one day.

Change of subject: do you fancy hanging out at yours tonight? I could bring over some leftover baked goods and we could watch one of your Studio Ghibli films and, I don't know . . . maybe I could kiss you? If you want me to. If you don't want me to, Princess Mononoke and a slice of chocolate cake would be lovely all the same.

Ottila

Text message from Thales

Mon 10 Feb 15:12

I just got told off for taking too long on the coffees. All I want to do is infuse the espresso with a perfect crema. Is that so wrong? Yes please. To cake and kisses. T X

Amended Tattoo Design

Lupercalia

Let me tell you about Valentine's Day, Thales. Valentine's Day was invented by card companies, it was invented by happy couples, it was invented by sentimental saps, it was invented by randy teenagers and it was invented by socially inept, unimaginative nerds and dweebs.

Valentine's Day, years one to eleven: card from Dad, card from Granny Joyce. Valentine's Day, year twelve: Granny's given up, decided I'm too old, but Dad's taken it further. Not just a card, but a bracelet from Argos. Mum's jealous. Valentine's Day, year thirteen: nothing. Valentine's Day, year fourteen: nothing. Valentine's Day, year fifteen: pity card from Granny, plus a £10 voucher for Tammy Girl. Inside the card, the ominous instruction BUY SOMETHING PRETTY TO WEAR. I buy a pair of jeans, rip holes in the knees, and sew a Dead Kennedys patch to each butt cheek. Valentine's Day, years sixteen to present day: nothing. Reaction? A well-rehearsed diatribe on the evils of Valentine's Day and its consumerist ideologies, fooling no-one, especially not me, and still, every year, I wear my rhodium-plated feather bangle from Argos and wait by the letterbox with tears in my eyes.

But we're not going to do Valentine's Day this year, Thales. I'm not saying this as one of those if-you-really-like-me-you'll-ignore-me-and-get-me-a-card-anyway tests. I'm saying this because I've found something better. Something more romantic than exchanging pieces of coloured paper. And we're going to do it tonight after work.

There's an ancient pastoral festival, which took place between February 13th and 15th, believed to avert evil spirits and improve fertility (don't worry, I'm aware we've only just had our first kiss and I promise I'm definitely not rushing things). The festival was called Lupercalia, and was held in honour of Luperca, the she-wolf who suckled Romulus and Remus, the orphans who founded Rome.

Each year, the festival commenced when some men dressed in animal skins sacrificed two male goats and a dog. A couple of boys were then led to an altar, where they were smeared with sacrificial blood, and a feast would ensue. I don't know what would be eaten – possibly goat and dog, given it was freshly available – and then the animal skin men ran around the walls of the city, striking anyone who came near. Girls and young women lined up enthusiastically to receive lashes, which they believed would make them extremely fertile and have an easy labour. I guess getting a good lashing was just a bonus.

So that's my Valentine's Day plan: Lupercalia. Sounds a bit more interesting than a Forever Friends card and a bunch of flowers, doesn't it?

I don't know exactly how we'll manage it, given certain constraints, like we can't kill any animals with our own bare hands, due to ethical concerns, the law, etc. But I was thinking we could improvise. Get a goat curry from that Caribbean place in Oldham, and a carton of Rubicon juice, pomegranate, to simulate blood.

After the feast I'll take you home, Thales, to your home, because there are no flatmates to worry about, and I'll make you stand in your stairwell with your eyes shut, probably for quite a long time because I'm going to light a fifty-pack of tea lights and you've only got that one old screwy lighter since you quit smoking (which I'm glad about - don't take it up again, please, not for the sake of having better lighters), and then I'm going to lead you on an odyssey around your own flat, showing you the hastily tacked decorations on the wall: a photograph of my roaring new thigh tattoo, bleeding and swollen, snapped upon completion last week (my leg is still disfigured, but the pain was worth it and don't worry, I didn't get your name on there . . . in the end), a ripped-out page containing an aphorism on happiness (something about *unrepentant pleasure* by Socrates) and a picture of a Romulus and Remus sculpture, the one where they're drinking milk from a wolf's nipple, which, I'll admit, makes me inexplicably amorous.

After that, I'll lead you through to the bedroom, give you a glass of milk and then flick my tongue across your nipples. I'll ask you to strike me, gently at first, and then harder, until you're lashing me across the shoulders, the back and the buttocks and, with every smack, the pain of everything I did before I met you will fade. The shame about having fucked my boss. The horror of having my stomach pumped five weeks ago. The fears about being unable to conceive because of three months of untreated gonorrhoea. I'll fuck you and I'll get lashed by you, and occasionally I'll look down at the beast on my thigh and I'll lash you back, and we'll be fucking and lashing, fucking and lashing, fusing our bodies in the name of desire, dreaming of drinking macchiatos on a piazza, or sucking at the teat of a giant bronze wolf, and we definitely won't give a shit about any stupid fucking greeting cards or sickly sonnets or drunken nights of shame or exes whose lives we've ruined. We'll be wild and free.

Email to Thales

From: Ottila McGregor
To: Thales Sanna
Date: Fri, 14 February, 2014 at 17:13
Subject: Re: Somebody has sent you an Animated GIF!

André is making me work late to design the Culture Walk leaflet, even though the event's not happening until September. I tried arguing my point but I think he's determined to ruin me and my imaginary girlfriend's Valentine's Day plans.

Probably won't be done until seven-ish. I'll ring you once I'm on the bus. Happy Vee Day, and thanks for the *eely like you* fish gif.

O.

Recovery Meeting Transcript

THERAPIST: And so did it work? The Valentine's plan?

PATIENT: Kind of. We had Jamaican jerk chicken and I showed him my new tattoo.

THERAPIST: You managed to avoid alcohol?

PATIENT: We got grape juice because it's a bit like wine. And watched *The Simpsons*.

THERAPIST: Well, that sounds like a pleasant evening.

PATIENT: It was the episode where a psychiatrist suggests Bart channels his anger by playing the drums. Lisa gets upset because music was always her thing, so she starts a new thing, caring for sick animals.

THERAPIST: How are you feeling?

PATIENT: Okay, I think. Tired.

THERAPIST: Have you seen any of your friends lately, other than Thales? How about Grace?

PATIENT: She said she was up for doing something without alcohol, but I'm not sure she gets it. She thinks we'd be doing it as a joke or a social experiment. Anyway, I emailed her last week suggesting we go for a hot chocolate. I haven't heard anything back. Knowing her, she'd turn up drunk anyway. I don't think I could cope if she was slurring her words, with lipstick all over her chin and red-wine teeth. I never realised how disgusting drunk people are until I got sober.

THERAPIST: Perhaps you can find some new friends now you've stopped drinking.

PATIENT: Maybe. I'll put out an advert.

THERAPIST: You seem happier than last time I saw you, anyway. And you look better. Brighter. You've got colour in your cheeks.

PATIENT: I'm happier . . . I think. I mean, things with Thales are going well. We finally kissed after, like, *forever*. That was over a week ago. I was hoping we'd take things even further on Valentine's Day, but I was too nervous to make a move, and Thales is a gentleman. I have these daydreams, these intense daydreams, where it's like I'm talking to him, telling him all the things I want to do with him, to him, and we . . . I don't know . . . I'm just pouring all my energy into building up our relationship really slowly.

THERAPIST: How does that work?

PATIENT: I'm trying hard not to try too hard.

THERAPIST: Sounds a bit tricky.

PATIENT: What does?

THERAPIST: Taking it slowly, while putting all your energy into it at the same time.

PATIENT: Slowly doesn't come naturally to me. I get carried away.

THERAPIST: Just make sure you don't burn out. This is a time for you, not for other people. Generally, I recommend newly recovering addicts don't get into a relationship for at least a year after they get sober. The most important relationship is the one with yourself.

PATIENT: Thales told me on Valentine's Day he's decided he's never going to drink in front of me. He said he might even stop altogether, for moral support. He's good like that. He genuinely cares about me, and goes out of his way to make sure I'm okay. Men like that do exist.

THERAPIST: They're a rarity. [*Long pause.*]

PATIENT: I've been really missing my dad lately. I'm wondering if maybe I never did my grieving properly because I was always too drunk.

THERAPIST: You're certainly more likely to face up to things now you're getting sober. It will be much healthier for you in the long run.

PATIENT: That night – the stomach pump night – before I phoned the ambulance, I remember steadying myself at the sink between vomiting episodes, and catching sight of myself in the bathroom mirror. I realised that I was beginning to look like Dad when he was dying. I had the same black circles under my eyes. The same hollow expression. I found myself whispering my dad's last words: *Be good for me.*

THERAPIST: They were his last words?

PATIENT: I mean, I'm talking about his last words to me. I think his *very* last words were: *Dø, drittsekker!* That's Norwegian for: *Die, you bastards!* But the last words he said to me were in a voicemail. *Be good for me.* It's a ridiculous phrase. [*Sniffing sound.*] I wish I'd picked up the phone that day. I saw him calling, but was too hungover to answer. How stupid is that? [*Slight pause.*] I don't like myself for what I said to André. It was a cheap trick, playing the lesbian card. Especially considering I'm bisexual. There was no need to lie. I just can't seem to stop myself from doing it. [*Longer pause.*] I think if I'm going to find happiness I'm going to have to start being honest. One hundred per cent of the time.

THERAPIST: Sounds like a good plan.

PATIENT: No more secrets.

THERAPIST: As long as you handle the truth with care.

PATIENT: I will.

THERAPIST: And you promise you're going to find lots of time for yourself before our next meeting?

PATIENT: Yes. I might even go and visit Mum and Mina too. I'm going to be a good daughter, and a good sister, and a good person.

THERAPIST: Don't put too much pressure on yourself.

PATIENT: Baby steps. Honest.

Manchester Museum Visitor Comments Book

21 February 2014

The Egyptians were wicked.

Today I learnt that people used money even in the olden days.

The gint spunge is discusting.

250,000 fossils in one place? That's almost as many as you'll find at a Cliff Richard concert.

My brother chucked up and Lucy said he couldn't have a biscuit.

Woah! Molluscs!

I don't like the mummies they scary.

The café is ramshackle. Get yourself a 'queue here' sign and some rope.

Rocks are boring but skeletons are ok.

I have come here today with the most amazing woman. Thank you for letting our relationship blossom among meteorites and Ibeji figures.

I peesed myself by the snake tank.

The only joy in the world is to begin.

Cesare Pavese

Little Book of Happy

Dear Perkiest Book in Existence,

Imagine being so happy you died from laughing. I've checked online and it really happens. Some guy in Ancient Greece laughed himself to death looking at a portrait he'd just painted. It was a depiction of Aphrodite, and the old woman who commissioned it had insisted on being the model. Some other dude in Greece conked out while laughing at a donkey. Apparently it had eaten his figs. They must have had good retsina in those days, right?

Well, I'm still not drinking, and I've been laughing a lot. Starting a relationship sober is fun. And, LBOH, we are *definitely* starting a relationship. Thales officially 'asked me out'! He put on a smart shirt and was sweating profusely. It was very sweet. The best thing about going out with someone sober is that you can have running jokes that you *actually* remember between dates. And I haven't cried in front of him once. Even more amazing than that is . . . we had sex! While I was sober!

We'd been to Manchester Museum that day. We held hands the whole time, and then, as we stood in front of the Egyptian corpses, Thales told me he felt like he was falling in love with me. It was so romantic. I just smiled and nodded because I wanted to remain mysterious, but I was whooping inside. Five minutes later I cracked and told him I felt the same way. We went back to his place and ate chips with chilli and cheese, which Thales calls his Ultimate Comfort Snack, and watched some *Gardener's World*, and chatted about the meaning of the word 'deciduous', and *then*, when the inevitable couldn't be put off any longer . . . it happened! It was incredible: I felt in control of all my body parts. Even though we were both nervous and Thales was very shy about his body (he thinks he's fat and hairy, but to me he's a big, sexy bear), it was such an adrenaline rush.

I'm so happy right now it feels dangerous. This is one of those proper relationships I've heard so much about, with someone who's actually good for me. I don't know . . . everything feels so different at the moment. Sobriety feels like a drug. Or maybe it's oxytocin. That's the chemical that makes couples sexually aroused. It's an antidepressant too. What if it's addictive? Will I need to abstain from love as well? Am I just addicted to everything that's good? Does everything that's good become bad if you don't take it in moderation? What was that Julia Child quotation I ripped out of you the other day? 'A little bit of everything makes you happy.' Something like that. It made me feel better, anyway. I stuck it on the medicine cabinet.

I'm sorry about the whole tearing you apart thing. I hope you don't mind me replacing bits of you with bits of me. Perhaps I've been disrespectful. I remember an illustration in one of my old school textbooks: Mary Antoinette was kneeling beneath the blade of a guillotine on Place de la Révolution, about to have her head sliced off, and someone had drawn a speech bubble coming out of her backside saying 'guff'. I was horrified as a kid, but now it makes me giggle. Whoever drew that fart just added an extra layer of history.

Speaking of history, the museum was brilliant. It's easy to forget your troubles when you've got a chunk of Roman amphora in front of you. I spent ages deciding what to buy from the gift shop afterwards. Eventually I chose a mood ring: it has a stone that changes colour, informing you that your mood is 'thoughtful' or 'enhanced by having the mood ring' or whatever. It's meant for kids, so I have to wear it on my little finger and it hasn't changed colour since I bought it. I've been stuck on 'crazy in love' for days.

Actually, the ring is scarily accurate. After we had sex, instead of basking in the warmth of each other's bodies, Thales and I did something more unusual. I'm going to show you on the next page. Apologies for ripping out the sacred words of the Dalai Lama, but this is worth it.

Love from your Little Disciple of Happy

Proposal

Project Title
Our Love Began with a Coin Touched by Alexander the Great

Aim
To create an interactive, experimental, multimedia performance piece that will take place in Manchester Museum.

Method
In our performance piece, we will ask participants to witness the story of two friends who fall in love during an hour spent in the museum. The growing wonder that our protagonists feel for the exhibits colours their interactions, until they are permitted to hold a coin that has been, at one time, touched by Alexander the Great. As they handle the coin, their fingers meet, and their love begins. (We are wondering if it will be better if the couple fall in love while standing in front of the T-Rex, because everybody likes dinosaurs, but that's what research and development phases are for. We enjoy the feeling of not knowing what we are doing, and see it as a positive.)

Artefacts from the continuing relationship between the two friends will begin to replace certain exhibits in the museum, creating an exciting, engaging and unique piece of participatory promenade theatre. For example, among the fossils, there may be a paper cup, from the first time the friends went to the petrol station to buy coffee together. Or between the Predynastic vases, there might be a note hidden inside a sandwich carton.

The finished piece will include spoken word, video projection, audience involvement, visual art and object-handling. It will be funny and touching. But mainly funny. And transcendentally touching.

Artists
This project is an interdisciplinary collaboration between two Manchester-based artists. Ottila McGregor is a writer/performer with a strong background in wanting to get involved in community-based projects. Thales Sanna is a filmmaker interested in examining the relationship between sentient and

non-sentient matter. His film-in-progress, *Inanimate Objects*, is about the impact that artefacts can have on our lives. So far it contains a talking sofa and a kettle with Alzheimer's. This project represents a logical progression for his work.

Participants

We have identified the following target groups:

Regular museum-goers. Non-regular museum-goers. We will attract participants from both groups using the Twitter hashtag *#ourlovebeganwithacoin*. In the weeks leading up to the event, we will run an irresistible online campaign, inviting participants to send us artefacts from their relationships: letters, photographs, videos and audio pieces. The more private the better.

Outcomes

The evocation of wonder and joy will be our constant goal. To achieve this, we will present the museum exhibits in an inspiring way. Not that they are not already presented in this way. But we will present them in a different inspiring way.

We hope that our activity will:

- bring new visitors to Manchester Museum;
- allow regular museum-goers to experience the museum in a new way;
- be a valuable addition to the realm of site-specific theatre;
- provide us with an outlet for declaring our feelings for one another, because we are in the first throes of love and want everyone, everywhere, to know everything about it.

Email from André

From: André Marsh
To: Ottila McGregor
Date: Mon, 3 March, 2014 at 22:41
Subject: nice one

Just had a chance to look over the text for that culture walk leaflet.

Looks like you nailed it.

Good job.

How's things with the new bird?

Mantra of the Week

Ang Sang Wahe Guru

Rough translation: The dynamic and infinite ecstasy of the universe dances in every atom of my body. My consciousness fuses with its consciousness and we euphorically vibrate together as one.

Email from Mum

From: Alice McGregor
To: Ottila McGregor
Date: Mon, 10 March, 2014 at 17:32
Subject: No Need to Worry

Hi darling,

Just a quick one. Mina had a little accident this morning.

Nothing to worry about. She's fine, I'm fine, everything's tickety-boo. Nowhere near as bad as last time. She's been admitted to hospital, but it's only a sprained ankle and a bruised neck. Don't worry about coming down to see her. Visiting hours are rather tricky anyway because she's been sectioned.

Like I said, nothing at all to worry about. We'll get her sorted.

Mum xoxoxoxox

P. S. _Don't worry!_
P. P. S. Care workers' report attached.

Preliminary Report on Mina McGregor

The patient is being referred by the crisis team to Simiel Ward for immediate admission. Due to the complex nature of her case, we have been advised to collate this information for her care workers.

Current diagnosis:
Asperger syndrome, with concomitant obsessive-compulsive disorder, anxiety and persistent depressive disorder.

Previous diagnoses (no longer deemed accurate):
Depression; severe depression; schizophrenia; underactive thyroid; psychosis; borderline personality disorder; social anxiety disorder; cyclothymia; overactive thyroid.

Current support and medication:
Receives Disability Living Allowance (DLA) and the support category of Employment Support Allowance (ESA) with Severe Disability Premium (SDP). Currently the patient is taking 2 x 300 mg moclobemide (Manerix) for the depression; 4 x 150 mg chlorpromazine (Largactil) for antipsychotic effect; 5mg aripiprazole (Ablify) to combat lactation caused by chlorpromazine; 3 x 2.5 mg procyclidine (Kemadrin) to combat stiffness; up to 4 mg lorazepam (Ativan) as a tranquiliser; 7.5 mg zoplicone (Zimovane) for insomnia; olanzapine injection to be administered when in restraint.

Other medication taken since 1998 (do not repeat):
Fluoxetine (Prozac); citalopram (Celexa); escitalopram (Cipralex); paroxetine (Seroxat); lofepramine (Gamanil); sertraline (Zoloft); amitriptyline (Elavil); doxepin (Sinequan); clomipramine (Anafranil); imipramine (Tofranil); nitroxazepine (Sintamil); noxiptiline (Elronon); trimipramine (Surmontil); diazepam (Valium); temazepam (Restoril).

Most common side effects experienced:
Tremors; fatigue; blood blisters; weight gain; non-puerperal

lactation; nausea; blurred vision; sleep disturbances; palpitations; photosensitivity; dry mouth; bruising easily; constipation; diarrhoea; confusion; rashes; decreased appetite; frequent yawning; decreased libido; paraesthesia; restlessness; suicidal behaviour; suicidal thinking; depression.

Recommendations during in-patient stay:
Twenty-four-hour surveillance until further notice. Patient is fixated on hanging and cutting. Remain vigilant for ropes and blades.

TWO

Alternate Reality

There's an alternate reality out there somewhere in which I didn't bully her growing up. Where I didn't raise my hand to her face and smack her on the left cheek three times, just for saying hello to me at the bus park after school. Where I didn't tell her that a wicked old man lived at the end of the garden, hiding in the old, run-down caravan by the bonfire, waiting to puncture her flesh. Where I didn't force her to smoke a joint with me in the summer house. And where, after too many swigs of White Lightning, I didn't kiss the boy she fancied.

But then what are big sisters for?

It'll help you grow up faster, I'd tell her. *Toughen you up. Make you strong and confident like me. Besides, it'll help you deal with the* real *bullies when they come along. Because believe me, they will.*

How was I to know things would turn out the way they did?

I didn't understand the warning signs any more than my parents did. Why she lined up the toys on her bed in size order. Packed a bag every night in case there was a fire and we had to evacuate. Measured the position of her slippers on her bedroom rug with a protractor to ensure they were at a ninety-degree angle. Tried to strangle me to death whenever she felt afraid. I didn't know what that stuff *meant*. I didn't know there'd be a connection between that, and the stinking, red rags wrapped around her wrists, stuffed under the sleeves of her school jumper when she came home crying in the afternoon.

I had no way of knowing, either, that it would go undiagnosed for so many years. That there's something called *comorbidity*, which makes finding a diagnosis even more difficult, and in my sister's case, almost impossible.

But somewhere out there, in that magical parallel universe, things work differently. My sister walks up to me at the bus station after school, and she says, 'Ottila. Hi.'

And even though I might still feel that itch in my right palm, that tensing in my puny, fourteen-year-old bicep, that sharp rush of adrenaline preparing me to make the hit, in this reality, I don't do it.

I acknowledge my anger, but breathe through it. Remind myself that just because my sister has decided to attend this secondary school, it doesn't mean she's copying me and, even if she is, this isn't a bad thing. The fact that she wants to say hello to me after her very first day at a brand new school is *good*. She's probably looking for support and reassurance from her big sister. She's certainly not looking for a smack . . . or three. So my arm remains by my side.

'Hi, Mina,' I say. 'How was your day?'

'Okay,' she replies, her eyes shimmering with relief. 'There are seven Sarahs in my class.'

'Seven?' I say. 'Wow, that's a lot.'

My sister nods, looking up at me.

'Would you like a hug?' I ask.

I can tell from her grin that this was the right question. My arms encircle her, wrapped tight around the BHS jacket that Mum bought especially for today. I can feel her warmth, can smell her shampoo, despite the grit and fumes in the air. It is the same shampoo that I use, the honeysuckle Organics one, from the exact same bottle that I used this morning, in the shower I took just ten minutes after her.

'I love you,' I whisper into her ear. 'I'm so glad you're here.'

'Me too, Ottila,' she says. 'I'm glad I'm here too.'

We stay like this for a while, my alternate-reality sister and me, hugging, while the buses hiss and growl around us, the boys and girls in school uniform flirt and laugh and argue and swear, and everyone grows up, by just a fraction of a lifetime, moving one tiny step closer to finally understanding who we are and why we're here.

Snapchat to Mina

Today

ME

| Sorry to hear you're in hospital again, Meen. Hope that doctor who played Bananagrams with you last time is still there.

Email to Mum

From: Ottila McGregor
To: Alice McGregor
Date: Mon, 10 March, 2014 at 20:53
Subject: Re: No Need to Worry

Are you sure you don't want me to come down, Mum? I'm feeling kind of useless up here, when I could be down there.

Ottila xxx

An Early Memory

We're in the kitchen, heating up a saucepan of ravioli. The ravioli is from a tin. It's got that gristly meat inside it. Yum.

I've opened the can because Mina is scared of the tin-opener. She says it reminds her of dying. Now she's stirring the ravioli in a pan on the Aga. The Aga is what we call 'very swish'. It's dark green, the colour of a Christmas tree. In winter, we sit in front of it and press our backs against the cast iron until it burns our skin.

I can't remember who started it, but today, as we cook, we're singing a duet. The song contains only one lyric:

Ravioli!

We're belting out this exotic word in shrill Pavarotti voices. The 'r's are rolled and the 'a's are long extended warbles.

Raaaa-violi! Ravioli! Ravioli!

We don't know why, but we get like this sometimes. These moods where we're so euphoric we can barely breathe. So happy that we could commit terrible crimes against humanity.

Raaaa-violi!

The last time we got like this, we stood by the living room window, lifting our skirts and showing our knick-knacks to anyone passing by on the A363. Mum walked in on us and put us in separate rooms for the rest of the afternoon.

Today we're just singing about tinned food. No harm in that. Besides, Mum and Dad aren't home, so we can do as we please.

I pirouette on the kitchen floor, not spinning quite as elegantly as I'd like in my Donald Duck totes, which are tacky on the bottom and keep sticking to the wood. I pirouette past the bread bin, the microwave, the Delia Smith cookbooks and an old biscuit tin where Mum stuffs other people's family newsletters, but not until after we've guffawed at the pictures of precocious children we've never met, wearing bow-ties, passing their Grade 7 piano exams and making sand sculptures of St Paul's Cathedral on Porthkidney Beach. Privately, I think we all feel a little bit sad as we look at them, wondering if this family we barely remember, and only met once at a barbecue in Surrey, had more fun than us this year. Maybe Mum keeps the newsletters to remind us to try harder in the months ahead.

My sister stops stirring for a moment and puts her thumbs

and forefingers together on each hand, holding them out and gesticulating wildly as she sings her loudest *ravioli* yet. If she were a cartoon character, I'd see her scarlet uvula vibrating in the dark cavern of her mouth. Windows would shatter at the pitch of her voice. I am beaming with pride.

At the moment when her lips let out the final syllable, we hear a door creak at the end of the hall, where Dad's office is.

Our mouths clamp shut. We cling to each other. We live in a cottage in the middle of nowhere. Mum and Dad aren't home, so who's in our house? And how are they planning to kill us?

Next, we hear footsteps, and then, standing in the kitchen doorway, we see Dad's twenty-one-year-old employee. Costanzo helps Dad produce his quirky history textbooks, *Mad About the Past*, for primary and secondary schools. He is holding a mug and smiles awkwardly at us – the smile of someone only recently acquitted of murder – and then he presses the red button on the kettle. He puts a spoonful of instant coffee into his mug, and waits.

Our cheeks blaze.

The remnants of our song are splashed all over the room. There's ravioli all over the walls, dripping down from the ceiling. The kettle that is currently boiling – much, *much* more slowly than usual – is full to the brim with thick, tomatoey pasta.

I wonder whether to speak. I could tell him we're practising for a school recital, or we're making fun of someone at school, but the words stick at the back of my throat. Costanzo is Italian. (Oh god, *Italian!*) He's perfectly bilingual, and a whizz at copy-editing. He's the most handsome member of the opposite sex we've ever had in our house. I've never had a conversation with him; surely I'm not about to start now?

He opens his mouth. 'Hi,' he says.

I feel my sister's body tense beside me. She hunches her shoulders and bends over the saucepan, her nose about to dip into the subject of our song.

'Hi,' I reply. I want to run upstairs and hide. There's ravioli all over my face. It's in my hair and dripping down my neck, running down onto my rude bits.

I try to smile without showing my brace, then I yelp and sprint out of the room, as fast as my tacky totes will carry me. I hurry halfway up the stairs, then I sit on the seventh step in silence, listening to my thumping heart and the sound of my sister stirring.

Eventually the kettle clicks.

Costanzo pours hot water into his mug and leaves the kitchen. I hold my breath as he walks down the hall past the staircase, without looking at me, and then . . . he's gone.

When I go back into the kitchen, my sister is sitting on the floor. 'You left me,' she sobs.

'Sorry. I didn't want to talk to him.' My voice sounds like I'm crying too, but I'm not. 'He's weird.' I sit beside her. 'Do you think he heard us?'

Mina looks up, a sudden greyness in her cheeks, a glint in her eyes. 'You're evil,' she whispers.

'Shut up.' I look at the kitchen door to check Costanzo is definitely gone.

Mina opens her mouth, baring her teeth like a lion, and then she bites down on her hand, hard.

'No! Stop it!' I try to grab hold of her wrist. When I finally manage to pull her hand away, there are teeth marks on the skin, white and fierce.

She growls and pushes me onto my back, then pounces on top of me and rests her knees on my chest. My top has ridden up and I feel the scratch of a splinter working its way into the thin skin over my spine.

'I hate you.' Mina grits her teeth.

Her knees jab my sternum. She hoists my arms over my head and pins them down one-handed. With the other hand she holds my neck, fingers curled, and she starts to squeeze.

'You're not even real.'

The arteries on either side of my neck strain under her grip.

'You have to die now.'

My forehead is throbbing. My eye sockets are stinging. I manage to free one of my hands and clutch her arm. I try to shout for help, no longer caring if Costanzo witnesses this embarrassing display, but Mina's thumbs are crushing my vocal cords. I'm making this curious gurgling noise, as if I'm drowning in my own bodily fluids.

My sister smiles, her tears dripping onto my face. Her sharp fingernails dig into my neck, slowly piercing the flesh. Her thumbs press into the dermis until they reach subcutaneous tissue, and she keeps on pressing, all the way down, tearing a ragged hole in my throat. Her nails snag the carotid artery, and my neck is a fountain of blood. But she doesn't stop. Her hands delve further, and I hear the crunch of cartilage. She rips out the trachea and lifts it high into the air.

The last thing I see, before I pass out, is that my insides look like ravioli.

Text Message from Thales

Mon 10 Mar 22:30

Do you fancy being locked in a small, dark room, where you have to solve a brutal murder? This place is opening in a few weeks and might be fun! Or, it might be wretched. https://breakoutmanchester.com/

Snapchat from Mina

 Teenymeeny 〉

Today

TEENYMEENY

That was a care worker. Not doctor.
His name was Pradeep. He's left.

Maggie's Centre

At Maggie's, there's colour inside and out. Doesn't matter what season it is; the garden has been designed so that something is always blooming. My mum would know the names of the flowers, but I just notice the shades. Currently, the garden is scattered with yellows and whites. As spring dawns, the purples will creep in, and then summer will be heralded by a fanfare of pinks and blues. Autumn is the best, though, because that's when the oranges and reds make our workplace glow like evening sunlight.

Today I'm on my way back from seeing Thales in my lunch break and I notice a figure on a bench in the garden, next to my favourite wintertime tree, whose yellow flowers burst along the branches, tiny fireworks. The figure is wearing a black anorak, and is hunched in a pose we see quite regularly at the centre. Normally I wouldn't intervene. As we're often reminded in our staff training, there is nothing wrong with our service users openly expressing their grief.

For that reason, I feel okay about starting to walk past whoever it is and heading straight for an afternoon at my desk. Besides, I've had a funny sort of lunch with Thales. We went to a deli in Didsbury, and Thales seemed different somehow. Really over-protective. Since he told me he loves me, I get the feeling he wants to be my handsome prince, rescuing me from the tower I've been imprisoned in for so many years. That damsel in distress stuff grates on me. For one thing, I'd make a shit Rapunzel. My hair is short and full of split-ends. But, if by some stroke of luck, I did happen to have long, strong locks of luscious, blonde hair, I'd immediately wrench it out of my scalp and use it to abseil down the side of the building by myself, thank you very much. I don't need a man to rescue me.

So, when we were buying our sandwiches and I grabbed a piña-colada-flavoured soft drink from the fridge next to the till, I didn't appreciate Thales swooping in, grabbing the bottle out of my hands, and saying: 'Are you sure you should be drinking this?' I swear the young guy at the till thought it was because I'm pregnant, and I blushed. I switched to a fizzy water after that because, well, I had to.

As I pass the hunched figure to go into the building, though,

I hear my name. I look more closely at the face under the anorak hood and see it's Lena. Lena has been coming to the centre for the past year or so. For the first few weeks, I don't think I ever saw her *not* crying, but this is the first time I've seen her upset in ages.

'Hi, Lena.' I hover in front of her awkwardly. I'm not sure whether to sit, or if that crosses an invisible boundary. Lena shifts towards the edge of the bench, so I consider my question answered and plop down.

'Can you tell Delyth I'm not going to make it to the craft session this afternoon please?.'

'Of course,' I reply. 'What's the matter?'

'Nothing, really.' Lena wipes her eyes. 'It's my sister's birthday today.'

Lena's sisters both died the year before last. 'I'm sorry,' I say. Since my dad died I've been reasonably comfortable with conversations like this. I always really appreciated people being able to talk openly to me when I was a mess, so I ask: 'Which sister?'

'Alix. The younger one.'

'The one who did Punch and Judy shows for a living?'

Lena nods and chokes back a laugh. 'Yes, that's her. She would have been forty-three today. Friede and I always used to make such a fuss of her on special occasions. Our baby sister.'

I surreptitiously check the time to see how long I have. I love this watch. Dad chose it for me. A Viking timepiece. Not the luxury watch brand – the face has just got a cartoon picture of a Viking on it. He's wearing a horned helmet, and Dad was very careful to tell me when he gave it to me that it's actually a myth that Vikings wore hats like this. But it's cute anyway. The horns are the hands of the watch. The perfect time of day is ten to two, as that's when the positioning of the horns is best. Right now it's quarter to one. Thales and I must have said goodbye much earlier than usual.

'What did you used to do for Alix's birthday?' I ask.

'Oh, we did all sorts. Hot air balloon, Segway racing, a behind-the-scenes tour of *Cats*. Alix was ill a lot when she was younger. She missed out on a few birthdays and Friede and I felt it was our duty to make it up to her.' Lena rubs her hands together; they're red with cold. 'But now Friede isn't here, and my parents aren't here. I'm running out of ways to celebrate all these anniversaries.' She takes a few, quick gulps of air, then pulls a handkerchief out of her pocket and blows her nose. 'Sorry, you need to get back to work.'

'It's okay. I'm glad to be here.' I glance over Lena's shoulder and spot André walking out of the building. I still get butterflies when I see him. I think it's because of how much intimacy we once shared. I shouldn't have lied to him about having a girlfriend. It's difficult to undo a lie with the truth. The right thing to do, but difficult.

'Listen,' I say to Lena. 'Why don't you go to Delyth's craft session this afternoon? Make something to honour Alix? I don't know – a finger puppet?'

Lena belly laughs as if I've just suggested she go and climb Mount Everest, but says: 'That's not a bad idea.' She pats my hand. 'Thanks, Ottila.'

'Not at all,' I say, feeling a small surge of happiness.

Snapchat to Mina

≡ Teenymeeny 〉

Today

ME

| That's a shame. Maybe someone else will play Bananagrams with you?

Letter to Thales

17 March 2014

Dear Thales,

Since it's your day off and I'm sitting in the café, your café, watching Jim make the coffees (badly) instead of you, I thought I'd put pen to paper.

It's weird working in a cancer hospital, don't you think? We spend our days hanging out with people with discoloured skin, missing limbs, scabs, alopecia. But even though there's so much death here, there's so much life too. So many people fighting, loving, laughing, sticking two fingers up at the Grim Reaper and getting on with it. Right now, there's a laryngectomy patient two tables away from me – a man in his late-forties, early-fifties, I'd say – eating a bowl of soup, with a hole in his throat, wearing a T-shirt bearing the slogan: *I Was Born Ready*.

I wish I was that fucking fearless. I wish *I* was born ready. Not only ready to take on a terminal illness, of course. I'm talking about the whole shebang. Rejection. Conflict. Love. They're all the same. They can all destroy you if you're not careful.

Have you ever heard of a *snekkja*? The smallest longship the Vikings used in battle. Ever since my dad told me about *snekkja*s when I was a girl, I've imagined manning one of those graceful, hardy little boats as a metaphor for navigating the choppy waters of life. When I'm sailing alone, I can just about maintain balance and control. As soon as someone joins me, navigating the ship becomes unpredictable. What if our rowing is out of sync? Or we disagree on which direction to travel in? The boat could easily be upended, or get crushed to pieces on a rocky *skær*.

There's something I haven't told you yet.

My sister was sectioned a week ago. I don't know why I haven't been able to say that in person. I think I was hoping you and I could have a relationship (sorry, that word sounds so severe right now) that wasn't governed by family drama. That's the way all my last relationships seem to have gone. It would have been nice if this one was different. But there you go: that's the long and short of it. I told you Mina's ill, but the full story is she has been sectioned. I haven't been told much more than that. Mum never shares the gory details with me. I do know *why* they sectioned her though: she lined up all her soft toys at the top of the stairs, tied a piece of wool around her neck, and then the banister, and threw herself off the highest step. The banister broke and she's fine. Something about bloodshot eyes and a bruised larynx.

It's quarter to two already. Back to work in a mo. And I haven't even got to my point yet. The main point. The real point. The problem is, Thales, I can't be with you any more. Things are too precarious right now, and I need to get myself sorted. I'm not ready to let anyone else in this little boat of mine. I'm sorry that I'm being a coward by putting this down in a letter rather than telling you in person. But saying it here stops me from chickening out. I need to figure out where I'm travelling on my own. For now, I think I'm heading off to do some good in the world. Mina needs me, and Mum needs me, and I'm going to go and help, in any way I can. Before you and I crash on the rocks and there's nothing left.

Well, there's a woman standing near my table now and she doesn't look too well, so I'll stop here and clear up. Make room for someone else.

Your fragile friend (I hope we can be friends?),

Ottila x

Email from Mum

From: Alice McGregor
To: Ottila McGregor
Date: Tue, 18 March, 2014 at 7:12
Subject: Re: Re: No Need to Worry

Hi sweetie,

You wouldn't believe how busy I've been, trying to sort Mina out, carting a load of stuff back and forth to her every day – she's requesting the strangest things! She wanted me to bring her two toothbrushes and a bag of ice cubes yesterday. I shouldn't really indulge her – I just hate to think of her in there, lonely and scared. Thanks for offering to visit us, darling, but really, there's not much you can do at the moment. It'll only upset Mina to see you doing so well. You know how jealous she gets when she sees your arms aren't covered in scars.

Try not to worry yourself over it for now, but you can stay on orange alert if you like, and I'll let you know if/when things worsen.

Be good to yourself. And don't worry!

Love Mum xox

Page 41 of the FoodSaver Guide for Wine Buffs 2014

Tempranillo is a black grape variety, native to the north of Spain. The word *tempranillo* is the diminutive form of *temprano*, meaning 'early'. It refers to the fact that the fruit ripens several weeks earlier than most Spanish red grapes. This variety has been grown on the Iberian Peninsula since the time of the ancient Phoenicians. The Phoenician word for wine was cherem. Cherem was considered an acceptable offering for gods and kings.

The pleasure
which we most
rarely experience
gives us greatest
delight.

Epictetus

Little Book of Happy

Dear Little Book of Platitudes,

I've been tearing out your pages at an alarming rate. I ripped one out just now: a Winnie the Pooh quotation about how balloons can never fail to cheer you up. Bullshit. Balloons are evil. If you don't believe me, do a Google Image search for 'scary clown balloon sculptures' and you'll see what I'm talking about. Not good.

I'm currently having a wobble.

So far, the wobble has entailed buying a bottle of wine. It's a Chilean red: *Casillero del Diablo*. It means 'devil's cellar'. I went to Morrisons looking for a Tempranillo after something I read in the FoodSaver guide, but then I saw the Satanic logo on this bottle and bought it instead. Plus, it was on offer, so.

I don't think I'm going to drink the wine. And buying it has nothing to do with breaking up with Thales. Really.

I miss the ritual, you know? Scanning the labels, imagining backpacking to each country of origin, selecting the perfect (cheapest) bottle, carrying it home like a newborn baby, placing it on the sideboard, getting out the corkscrew, realising the bottle's a screw-top, pouring the wine into a mug because the glasses are all dirty, draining the rest straight from the bottle, going out to buy a four-pack of lager because that wasn't enough, throwing up. Yeah . . . maybe I don't miss the *whole* ritual. But buying the wine today felt good. I felt like a teenager buying my first illicit drink, wondering if I'd get away with it.

You're probably wondering why I broke up with Thales, LBOH. I'm wondering that a little bit too. My longest relationships have always been with people who were bad for me. The good guys, the guys like Thales – I ditch them.

I felt so ashamed this morning that I called in sick. Couldn't face any chance encounters. I know I've asked Thales to be friends, but he hasn't replied to my letter yet. I'm an idiot for posting it to him second-class. I don't know how long it's going to take to get there, and in the meantime I'm ignoring his texts. What a wimp. But it keeps me strong. I know how vulnerable I am. I've always been so easily thrown off balance by other people. Look at what's happening with Grace. If I can't handle being around my best friend any more, why did I think I could let myself get close to a virtual stranger? I need to take care of myself.

I need to take care of my sister too. Mina was sectioned nine days ago. I know we've been here before. It's the third time she's been in psychiatric hospital. The first time she was in for six days. The second time she was in for three weeks. What if this time it's even longer? What if it's a whole month? I can't bear thinking about her in there, surrounded by madness and misery. When I visited her in hospital two years ago, I was terrified. One of the women on the ward kept going into Mina's room and pissing on her stuff. Another stood rigidly by the front door, naming serial killers under her breath. Some days I feel like there's such a fine line between them and me.

I've just noticed that my mood ring has finally changed colour. It's turned mauve. I've lost the chart, so I don't know what it means. Motivated? Melancholy? Moronic?

In a minute or two I'll pour the wine down the sink, and I'll carry on with life as usual. The devil's not tempting me to hell just yet. Not today, LBOH. Maybe tomorrow, but not today.

From Your Ottila of Very Little Brain

Recovery Meeting Transcript

PATIENT: Of course I didn't drink it!

THERAPIST: What did you do with it?

PATIENT: I watched it.

THERAPIST: For how long?

PATIENT: I don't know . . . an hour? Ten minutes. Two hours?

THERAPIST: What were you thinking about while you looked at it?

PATIENT: I was thinking about that feeling on my tongue. Velvety and tingly. The feeling of a mouthful of red wine.

THERAPIST: Did you try filling in some of your Recovery Workbook? That's what it's there for.

PATIENT: No.

THERAPIST: So what did you do?

PATIENT: I poured the wine down the sink, then I washed the sink with Flash, then I washed the wine bottle with Flash.

THERAPIST: And then?

PATIENT: I put a candle in the wine bottle. Thought I'd make it into a decoration.

THERAPIST: Oh. Did that help?

PATIENT: I'm only kidding. I wrapped the bottle in newspaper, put it in a carrier bag, and threw it in the bin.

THERAPIST: And how did you feel after you did that?

PATIENT: Guilty.

THERAPIST: Guilty?

PATIENT: Yes. I should have recycled it. I always recycle. Did you know that for every thousand tonnes of recycled glass we melt down, we save over three hundred tonnes of carbon dioxide?

THERAPIST: I didn't know that.

PATIENT: I Googled it.

THERAPIST: That's a lot.

PATIENT: It takes up to a million years for a glass bottle to break down in a landfill site.

THERAPIST: Do you feel guilty about the fact you didn't recycle, or is this really about the fact you bought the wine?

PATIENT: [*Long pause.*] It's about the fact I didn't recycle.

THERAPIST: That's the only thing you feel guilty about?

PATIENT: I didn't drink the wine.

THERAPIST: No, you didn't.

PATIENT: I always used to put my glass in the brown bin. Even when I was hungover. Every morning, on the way to work, smash, smash, smash. *There goes Ottila, doing her recycling, en route to the office. What a good little lush.* I associate the sound of breaking glass with 8 a.m. nausea.

THERAPIST: Why are you touching your abdomen like that?

PATIENT: I didn't realise I was.

THERAPIST: Whenever you talk about alcohol, you place your hand over your liver. Did it used to hurt there?

PATIENT: [*Patient mumbles something incoherent, then her voice cracks.*] It's the International Day of Happiness today.

THERAPIST: [*Pause, then brightly:*] I'm going to suggest starting you on some Campral.

Email from Thales

From: Thales Sanna
To: Ottila McGregor
Date: Fri, 21 March, 2014 at 18:39
Subject: Got your letter

O,

I got home from work half an hour ago and trod on your letter, which was lying on the doormat. I'm going to respond to it in just a minute, I assure you, but if you don't mind allowing me this brief indulgence, I'll begin by backtracking.

It's been a funny sort of day for me. This morning, Kerrie gave me a new badge. I'm no longer a trainee; I'm now officially a Coffee Shop Assistant. I suppose, ordinarily, that news would have delighted me, but I was preoccupied, worrying that you haven't replied to my texts all week. Goddamn the iPhone for showing me that you read my messages almost immediately after I sent each one. I even saw those three dots appear at one point, informing me that you were writing a reply, but then the dots disappeared, and with them went all contact.

This afternoon my uneasy feeling didn't diminish, but I was a little distracted from it due to a staff training day in which we were taught how to fill in a HACCP chart. HACCP stands for Hazard Analysis and Critical Control Point and it is basically a system for the most obvious, mundane, important things you need to know in the food industry. It involves anticipating every possible hazard that could occur in the workplace, and coming up with measures that prevent the hazard from becoming, well, hazardous. Kerrie, my line manager, printed off a certificate for each of us on parchment paper, with the HACCP initials making an acrostic poem spelling out Healthy And Careful Café Personnel, with a Clipart picture of an interracial handshake. Kill me now, somebody, please; just let me leave my job and spend my days building a beautiful rock garden.

83

Then I got home and saw your letter. Since reading it, I've paced around my flat a few times, eaten two packets of Wotsits and a chocolate Hobnob, and now I'm lying in bed, curled protectively around my laptop, writing you this reply.

First of all, before I say anything else, I want to say this: I am so, so sorry to hear about your sister. I've had problems with my sister in the past – she's a bit of a firecracker and prone to temper tantrums and the occasional stunt that's scared the life out of me and my parents – but the stuff you're going through with Mina is *immeasurably* tough. I had hoped that I would get to meet her one day, but I completely recognise why you need some time to yourself now, and why you feel that perhaps a relationship (that wretched word) isn't right for you at the moment.

Which leads me onto my next point. Really, Ottila, I am not upset with you at all. People don't possess one another. They don't have any claim over anyone else, and they're free to enter and exit relationships whenever they please. Basically, I believe that ownership of any sort promotes despotism and coercion at an individual and a societal scale. It doesn't matter how married you are, or how many decades you've been together. If you want to go, then go. You can't fill out HACCP charts for relationships, you know. You have to let the hazards play out, and react accordingly.

I'm not saying that because I'm a commitment-phobe or a polyamorist, because I'm definitely neither of those things. When I'm with the right person, I'm very loyal. Actually, when I'm with the wrong person I'm very loyal too. But what I'm saying to you, O, is that if you want to break up, I understand, and if you want to stay friends, that's fine by me. We should probably stop timing all our breaks to coincide with one another, though, and I don't think I could handle hanging out together outside of work too often. But I'd like to stay in touch and be able to chat from time to time. I feel like you could use a friend, and, to be honest, I could too. It's been a strange few months for me, and I'm going to spend a while hibernating, eating snacks, until I emerge, finally, a new man. Maybe even the sort of man who goes to the gym three times a week, and throws his junk food in the bin.

I'll see you at work on Monday then, friend? Have a good weekend and drink as many non-alcoholic piña coladas as you like without this old muttonhead interfering. I still feel bad about that, and I apologise.

T

Letter from Manchester Museum

21 March 2014

Dear Ottila and Thales,

Thank you for your application for a Dynamic World art commission at Manchester Museum. We had a huge response to the advertisement and we were delighted by the calibre of the applicants and their ideas.

We have looked carefully at each submission and unfortunately yours has not been successful on this occasion. We are unable to give detailed feedback, but comments from the judges' notebook under your project read: 'We do not understand this.'

Enjoy being in love though! Sounds wonderful.

Best wishes,

Ellen Prickle
Project Manager

If you would like to keep up to date with our work, you can subscribe to our newsletter or you can follow us on Twitter via the links below!

Text Message to Grace

Fri 21 Mar 19:51

What you up to, Shottsy? It's Friday and I'm feelin ♫ lonesome tonight ♫

Text Message from Grace

Fri 21 Mar 20:22

get your ass over here, rocket dawg. it's free mixers at the liars club then saz and i are crashing a mate's table at baa bar. cocktails, baby! hadron colliders and woo woos all night long.

Memory of Grace

Grace and I liked drinking in the afternoons the best. 'It leaves you with so many possibilities,' Grace would say, already on her third pint by three o'clock, the corners of her eyes pink and sleepy.

And Grace was right, of course. Drinking in the afternoon left the evenings wide open for adventure. Come seven o'clock, we'd be tap-dancing on the steps of the People's History Museum, or buying twenty packets of raspberry jelly, or snorting coke out of a stranger's navel in Levenshulme. Yes, evenings were unpredictable except for one thing: total intoxication.

One of our most memorable nights began with a Saturday afternoon drinking session. 'You okay, mate?' Grace asked me as she poured Sex on the Beach from a flowery teapot. We were in a chintzy bar in the Northern Quarter, and Grace found the idea of going for afternoon tea – but with cocktails – hilarious.

To say I'd had a rough week would have been a gross understatement. My dad had phoned me on the Tuesday morning to tell me he had been diagnosed with lung cancer. I didn't even know he was going in for tests. *They say it's stage four*, he told me. I could hear him wheezing. *It's amazing, because I feel so fit and healthy. Just a bit tired and short of breath is all.*

I really wanted to say something in response, but words eluded me.

I'll be alright, he said.

I'm going to fight this thing, he said.

I saw a documentary last night, he said, *about a woman who had what I've got, and she managed to exceed her life expectancy three times over by eating apple pips.*

Finally, I managed to speak, but my voice was hoarse: *What was her life expectancy?*

A year, he said at last. *I love you, Ottila.*

'Come on, dude,' said Grace, handing me my china cup. 'This'll sort you out.' Grace was trying. She really was. But she'd never known her dad. He'd left her mum before Grace was born, and Grace only ever referred to him as The Dickhead. I think it was impossible for Grace to imagine the sort of bond I had with my father. She and her mum had a functional relationship, largely based on independence. They would meet up on rare special occasions and speak with a jokey bravado that made them appear like sisters. Grace called her mum by her first name, Sophia, and when I asked Grace what Sophia did for a living, she replied: 'Something in America.'

I took my teacup, looked briefly at the delicate bluebells adorning its surface, then drained half the contents. My tongue was starting to go numb, and I knew I was getting drunk because I was beginning to open my eyes wider than normal. Always a sure-fire sign. I don't know why I did that. Flirting with life, I guess. Later, my eyelids would start to droop, but only when I was very, very drunk.

'Hey, look at that mutt,' Grace said, pointing to a small, brown dog asleep by the solid fuel burner at the other end of the room. 'Do you dare me to walk up to it and stroke it?'

I laughed. 'No.'

'Bet you it's a Brussels Griffon. You can tell from the grumpy mouth and the hipster beard.' Grace used to have a dog rescue app on her phone, and freaked out every time a new one was listed locally. She'd threatened to adopt several of them, despite being in a top-floor flat in Chinatown that didn't allow pets. She sent me their pictures, accompanied by first-person statements such as 'Let me in your bed' and 'I lick my own butthole'. In those days, I was temping around Manchester, doing copywriting jobs for various companies whose businesses I barely understood. I'd be trying to produce copy for the 'About Us' section of some pharmaceutical company, and then my phone would vibrate and I'd start sniggering, drawing dirty looks from my workmates.

'Look at this one,' she said, showing me a photo of a Cavalier King Charles Spaniel, with the name 'Mickey' under it. Mickey was sitting on the grass looking up at the camera with rheumy eyes. I'm a cat person, having had a black-and-white Domestic Shorthair called Cloud as a child, but I settled back in my seat nonetheless, and let Grace start to flick through endless pictures of small creatures looking for new homes. The more I looked, the more I started to relax. I took a few more gulps of my cocktail. Life was okay. Afternoon drinking with Grace was okay. My dad was going to be okay.

In fact, I felt so okay by six-thirty, that when Grace suggested we go and meet her awful mates from the orchestra, I said yes. Grace is seriously talented: she plays first violin in the Hallé

Orchestra, one of the most prestigious ensembles in the world. Unfortunately, you can play in an amazing orchestra and still be a jerk. And Grace's two musical pals proved it.

We were to meet up at Lee's house. Lee played the cello, and I'd never liked him, even though I'd slept with him once, which was entirely my own fault. The other guy, Kieran, played the contrabassoon, and Grace had a major crush on him. They'd hooked up a couple of times when they were drunk, but it had never progressed to anything more serious. Grace wouldn't give up hope though. She hardly ever dated anyone else, just in case Kieran decided to fall for her.

'It's that contrabassoon, man,' she once told me. 'Such a deep sound. Makes my fanny tingle.'

Lee lived in a house in Didsbury. His dad had bought it for him. We didn't know whether Lee paid his dad any rent, or if he got to live in a three-bedroom house in the most desirable part of Manchester for free. Lee's dad was once one of the UK's most famous conductors, and was friends with Sir Simon Rattle. Lee had a way of speaking that tried to let you know he was the sort of person whose dad was friends with Sir Simon Rattle.

By the time we got to Lee's, he and Kieran were already wasted. 'We took a load of speed last night at Gullivers,' Lee told us as he handed us a can of cider each. 'Didn't sleep last night.' He kissed us both on the left cheek. 'Nice to see you, ladies.'

'You maniacs,' Grace said, flashing Kieran a smile.

Kieran nodded, jaw clenched, teeth grinding.

'Kieran had a fuckload,' Lee explained. 'He's been like this all day. Thank god you tossers turned up.'

Grace opened her cider can, and it made that hissing sound I have always coveted. She slurped down several mouthfuls, and then jumped, stomach-first, onto the oversized beanbag in the corner of the living room. She was wearing a short skirt, and I could see the white of her knickers through the loose knit of her grey woollen tights. She and I had not yet had a threesome; that was to happen several months after my father's death, when my depression was at its lowest point. Before that encounter, I was vaguely interested in Grace sexually, though I never admitted that to her. The feelings normally emerged after I'd had a few drinks. She aroused and disgusted me in equal measure, which often seemed like the perfect mix. She'd never shown an interest in kissing me, though, and apart from that one night, where we'd only done it to try and score some free coke, she never would.

'Let's do something fun,' Grace sighed, rolling onto her back and smoothing down her skirt. 'I don't know . . . a drinking game or something.' She patted the beanbag beside her, and I, the faithful spaniel ('Let me in your bed'), went and sat beside her, my arse swallowed up by the beanbag, warm and safe. Straight away, Grace started playing with my hair. Back then it was long and coarse, full of knots, and Grace liked to arrange it into Medusa styles.

'Right you are, Missus. Something fun.' Lee stood to attention, saluting Grace, and then he left the room to go and find us some entertainment.

Kieran sat down on the leather sofa, and tapped his feet arrhythmically on the carpet. I knew Grace wished she was sitting on the sofa with him, instead of on the beanbag with me, and I tried to send her psychic signals to ask her to stay.

'How are you doing, Ottila?' Kieran asked, suddenly lucid. He and Lee both knew about my dad. Grace had told them. I knew Lee wouldn't mention it tonight – he wasn't like that – but it was nice of Kieran to say something.

I smiled. 'Actually, I'm okay. Having great friends helps.' I craned back my head and found Grace's fingers at the nape of my neck. She wriggled her fingers against my skin. I tilted my head back even further.

Lee rushed back into the room wearing an old army jacket. His lips were dry, with globs of white spittle at the corners. 'Cop a load of this,' he said, and he pulled a gun out from behind his back.

Grace screamed. 'What the fuck, Lee?'

'It's a point thirty-six calibre six-shot Percussion revolver. Like it?'

'Stop pointing it at us, dude,' Grace said.

'Fine,' Lee said, walking over and showing us the gun. 'It was my granddad's. Got it when he died.' Suddenly, he stopped and looked at me. 'Oh. Sorry, Ottila.'

I wasn't sure why he'd apologised, but I shrugged.

'Antique from the Civil War. No idea how my granddad got it, probably bought it on the black market or something. Anyway, it's mine now.' He turned the gun over in his hands a few times. It was long, with a silver barrel and a walnut handle. If it hadn't been a weapon the object would have had a certain beauty. 'So what do you think?' Lee waved the gun around, pointing it again absent-mindedly, first at me, then at the lampshade, then at the TV. 'Let's play Russian Roulette.'

'Okay, mate, you've had some fucking stupid ideas, but this one really is the most fucked up,' Grace said, jumping off the beanbag and snatching the revolver. She sat on the sofa beside Kieran. He was out of it, muttering something incomprehensible, looking over at the fireplace. Grace looked stupid, pressed up against him, a gun between her legs, the barrel between her thighs.

I honestly don't know what came over me in that moment. 'Come on, Grace,' I said, standing up. My words were slurring. 'Don't be a pussy.'

I took the gun before Grace had a chance to stop me. It felt so cold in my hand. Then I pointed it at my temple. My eyelids drooped heavily. 'I'll go first.'

Grace screamed again.

I pressed the trigger.

I continued to press it, as hard as I could, but it wasn't moving. I stood there in a suicidal freeze-frame.

'You maniac!' shouted Lee, grabbing the gun off me. 'It's not cocked or loaded. It was just a joke. You're a loose cannon, you are, Ottila!'

Grace's open mouth exploded into peals of laughter, and Lee put the gun in a drawer. We went back to drinking cider, grinding away our tooth enamel and talking crap. And as the night wore on, I started to feel normal again. But that's not the point.

Text Message to Grace

Fri 21 Mar 20:40

Sounds like fun, give Saz a hug from me. Better rain-
check tho. Gonna sort thru some boxes, throw away
some old photos, work out which relics to keep. You kids
play safe. 🐿 x

Death Certificate

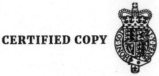

Application Number **SO23141TY**

CERTIFIED COPY OF AN ENTRY OF DEATH

Given at the General Register Office

Registration district North Ayrshire	
2011 DEATH in the Sub-district of Largs	
1. Place and date of death 27 August, 2011 Vikingar! Centre, Largs	
2. Name and Surname Bernhardt McGregor	**3. Sex** Male **4. Age** 52
5. Occupation Viking Re-enactor	
6. Cause of death Pericardial tamponade due to metastatic lung cancer	
7. Signature, description and residence of informant Ottila McGregor, daughter, Manchester	
8. When registered 30 August 2011	
9. Signature of registrar	

CERTIFIED to be a true copy of an entry in the certified copy of a
Register of Deaths in the District above mentioned.

Given at the GENERAL REGISTER OFFICE, under the Seal of the said
Office, the thirtieth day of August, 2011.

CAUTION: THERE ARE OFFENCES RELATING TO FALSIFYING OR
ALTERING A CERTIFICATE AND USING OR POSSESSING A FALSE
CERTIFICATE. 'CROWN COPYRIGHT'.

WARNING: A CERTIFICATE IS NOT EVIDENCE OF IDENTITY.

93

Snapchat from Mina

 Teenymeeny 〉

Today

TEENYMEENY

| Not in the mood for Bananagrams. I want to die.

Text Message from Grace

Fri 21 Mar 20:58

ok dude I just gave saz a big juicy snog and said it was from you. if you change your mind, rd, you know where to find us!

Blog Entry by TeamEdward247

Sunday, 28 August 2011

WTF WEIRDEST DATE EVER

Hullo, blog-fans! I've got something important to tell you, but before I say it I should prolly say this: *trigger warning*. Like srsly. If you get distressed when you hear about death or dying, you should look away now. Promise I'll write something upbeat and awesome tomoz and you can join me back here then. The rest of you: bear with me. This gets dark.

Yesterday I went to a festival. And I don't mean a kewl festival like T in the Park. I mean an oldie thing for history dorks. It's called the Largs Viking Festival. Ikr? Me. At a history festival. I'm (almost) fifteen. I'm into shapeshifters, Combat City and boys. So what was I doing there? Get this, blog-fans . . . I was on a date. With a totally, insanely hot guy. 5 Seconds of Summer hot. Those of you who've been following my blog closely (hi, Rachael) know I've been WhatsApping this guy for the past 12 weeks. Well, today was the day I was finally going to meet him. I'd seen pics of him (drool) but this was the first time I was going to see him irl.

And, *no*. I didn't choose the venue for our first date. But the guy I met (who shall remain nameless . . . I'm superstitious about these things) was working at the festival, so I was heading to meet him there! Not only that, but I was going to see him dressed up like a freakin' Viking. And if you think that's psycho, wait 'til you hear what's to come. Btw, I'm including more suspense in my blogs cuz this year's <u>Young Blogger of the Year Awards</u> shortlist is full of peeps who say stuff like *you'll never guess what happened next* . . . I'm looking at you, <u>LittleMissMysteryGal</u>. Love ya really, doll.

I arrived at the festival an hour early cuz I'm a numpty, so I ducked into Greggs for a cheese and bacon wrap (y'know what I'm like) then I headed to the promenade. The stalls looked vaguely interesting, so I checked my make-up in the mirror on the back of my phone (pays to be prepared, girlies), and had a look around. It was really busy, even though it was so wet and windy. I think it's pished it down pretty much every time I've been here. Mum and

Dad tried bringing me and my brothers to the beach a few times when we were wee, and every time the weather was so bad we just went to Nardini's for an ice-cream then drove home again. Never mind. Nardini's rules.

The selection of jewellery was actually fairly decent. I asked a woman at one of the stalls how much a rune necklace cost. It was a silver pendant with a wonky F on it. There was a label next to it saying the rune was for *gaining knowledge*, but I chose it cuz my real name (which I'll never reveal online to you cretins, mwahahaa) begins with an F. Not quite as eye-catching as some of the other pieces of jewellery, but I'm trying to work on this capsule wardrobe thing at the moment and make sure all my stuff goes together. I figured the necklace was the most versatile or whatevs. The woman serving me had a fake owl perched on her shoulder (I might have been into that when I was ten, fml). I bought the necklace for £3.50 (see pics of me wearing it <u>here</u> and <u>here</u>) and scooted off. I was beginning to get extremely nervous.

As I wandered around the festival, every time I looked at a guy vaguely my age, I was like, *that could be him*. Some of the guys working on the stalls were honestly rather hot, and it got me thinking: you can actually be a fit Viking. That's right, blog-fans, I've totally cracked! But srsly, a boy in a tunic isn't as bad as it sounds, and some folk can even rock a beard. Luckily I was fairly sure my guy, the cute sixteen-year-old from Cambuslang I was here to meet, was away preparing for his performance. Oh yes, you heard me right, beautiful people. I said performance! I was going to watch him doing a battle re-enactment before meeting him. Do you think I've gone batshit crazy? I think it's kinda romantic. (My pals at school think I'm a total loser. Ach, at least my dad didn't come with me like he threatened to do when I first told him about it. He just asked me to text him every hour instead: #yawnorama.)

Right. About this reconstruction. It was a re-enactment of the Battle of Largs. That's a fight that took place in the thirteenth century (Googled this beforehand, so I didn't look like an eejit). The King of Scotland was trying to kick out the Norwegians, which seems a bit racist, but fair play, it was the olden days. The King of Norway was narked, natch, so he started raiding and pillaging, or whatevs Vikings were into. But then his plans got messed up cuz of the weather (welcome to Scotland, pal) and his ships got stuck on the rocks, mega oops. When he and his men came on to the shore, the people of Largs chased them away. 'Mon the Scots! So, it was almost half three and I finally plucked up the courage to head over to the arena. The re-enactment started with some trumpeting, then this woman shouted something and a load of men in tunics ran out onto the grass. I was excited at this point, I don't mind admitting it to you, peeps! I mean, he was *out there somewhere*. The guy I'd been chatting to for the past three months. I knew his star sign was Capricorn, his top three movies were *Karate Kid*, *Gladiator* and *Lord of the Rings* (dunno which one tbf), and his pet hates were places with no 3G and Rangers fans, but I'd still never seen him in the flesh. Annoyingly, almost everyone was wearing helmets, and I couldn't remember if he'd said he was a Scot or a Norwegian, so I just stared at all the tunics thinking: one of you is being worn by the boy who might potentially turn out to be the love of my life. (Cringe.)

There was a lot of fighting, and I mean a *lot*. Swords were flying and making a racket, and occasionally people dropped down dead on the grass. I have to say, it was really hard to tell which side any of them were on. But I noticed a group of noisy English peeps booing every time one of the biggest guys stabbed and killed anyone. I'm not sure whether the English would be anti-Norwegian or anti-Scot. Maybe they just hated to see folk doing well. I hoped my guy was still standing. I weirdly wanted him to be the winner.

After a very long ten minutes (no offence, boy of my dreams), the fight looked as if it was coming to an end, although there were half a dozen people who seemed invincible and they just wouldn't go down. I was secretly hoping they'd hurry up and die already, cuz this was eating into my precious date time. Then one of the guys, who I think judging by the fancy-schmancy crown thing on his head mighta been the King of Norway, dropped his weapon and put his hands up. An old dude with a bright red beard next to him shouted something indecipherable but angry, prolly along the lines of, 'I'll never surrender!' then he beat his chest, and dropped to the floor. The English people beside me cheered. A few of the guys in tunics looked at each other and shrugged, threw their hands up to the sky and everyone clapped.

Most of the spectators started walking away at that point, but I stuck around, staring at the carnage, wondering which dead guy was my date. The old dude with the red beard who'd been the last to fall was still thrashing about, while a few corpses around him rose from the dead. You know me, blog-fans. I'm a nosy parker, so I moved a bit closer, and saw Beardy's eyes were rolled back. Someone in a cloak held his wrist. Someone else pushed him onto his side, and another lingered over his mouth, as if preparing to give him the *actual kiss of life*. The English folk stuck around beside me, pointing at the guy on the floor and giggling, but then an ambulance drove up, and at that point it turned into a real commotion. Dead guys were resurrecting themselves all over the place, crowding around the old dude and flailing about like panicky ghosts. The ambulance crew ran over, sweeping Vikings away left and right, and finally they got to old Redbeard. One of the paramedics got out one of those defibrillator thingies that you always see on *Casualty*, but the guy on the floor wasn't responding.

I dunno how long I was staring for but, after a bit, I felt a tap on the shoulder. It was a guy in a cape. I recognised him immediately from his photos, thank God. (I'm not even religious, so don't ask me why I'm thanking God. I'm a weirdo, I suppose.) I was still too traumatised to be ecstatic, so I just said a quiet hi, and then he said hi back to me, and I noticed what a lovely voice he has, and then he used his lovely voice to tell me that I'd just seen someone *die*. I mean, wtf? I almost greeted my eyes out there and then. Poor man. What a way to go. And what a way to start a first date. It was so bad it was almost brilliant. But in all seriousness, it was mainly epically bad.

My date said he didn't know the old dude, but they'd spoken earlier that day about the fact the soup smelt good. The guy had introduced himself as Bernard, which reminded my date of St Bernard dogs (I'm a cat person). Bernard said he came here every year, had a bit of a coughing fit, and then he'd gone out to fight to the death. Like, for realz! My date said he'd been on the side of the Scots, and the old dude was playing a Norwegian. I made some weird joke about the Scots *really* winning the battle today, and I tried hard not to start bawling, cuz srsly: seeing someone die is not good for first date nerves.

Trying to shake off the horror show we'd just seen, we went for an ice-cream at Nardini's. Could be worse! Over a shared Raspberry Snowball Delight (highly recommended, peeps), we chatted about normal stuff like school and hobbies, and it was actually really nice. Not love yet, of course (keep watchin' this space!), but it was nice. And oh yeah, blog-fans, he was hot. Like, superhot. Like, Edward Cullen *hot*. And hopefully he's not reading this.

He hasn't texted me since the date of course, and there's no freakin' way I'm texting him first, but whatever happens (fingers crossed for another rendezvous, *puh-lease*), I'll never forget that old dude kicking the bucket on our first date. Anyway, enough of this or I'll well up again.

In other news, it's four years today since I started this blog, hence the picture of the cake at the top of this entry. Thank you to everyone out there who reads this thing. Whether you've been with me from the start, or you're a newbie who joined last week, thanks so much for all your comments and support. I love you all, each and every one of you *with cherries on top*. Plenty more of my nutty chatter to come. But for now . . . over and out, blog-fans. Over and out.

~ Being his forever is a dream come true. Team Edward! ~

7 comments

Posted by TeamEdward247 at 3:51pm
Labels: largs, vikings, boyfriend, first date, romance, death, dead guy, dying, gaining knowledge

[*Apart from his death certificate, this is the last public record of Dad's life. I'm amazed the local paper didn't report it, but here they are, the last words said about my father on the Internet: 'that old dude kicking the bucket'.*]

Happiness is the art of never holding in your mind the memory of any unpleasant thing that has passed.

Anonymous

Email from Mum

From: Alice McGregor
To: Ottila McGregor
Date: Tue, 25 March, 2014 at 10:04
Subject: Nothing to Lose

Sweetheart,

I went to Mina's ward round yesterday. The doctor – he's really rather nice, young, Croatian, very handsome – wants to refer her for a course of electric shock therapy. He says her depression has been going on for so long, at such a profound level, that this is probably her best chance for recovery. And *don't worry*, electric shock treatment is apparently nothing major nowadays. It's not like in the movies. A perfectly safe procedure. Dr Lukić says he's referred hundreds of patients for it before. Well, maybe not hundreds, but you know. He says he gave it to twins and one of them had real success with it. I don't know about the other twin. It strikes me now that I never asked.

So, darling, I'm afraid it looks like Mina won't be getting out any time soon. Honestly, though, this ward's not as bad as the last one. There's a smoothie-making group on Wednesday mornings, and although Mina's not allowed near the equipment, someone made her a raspberry smoothie last week and she drank almost half of it.

How are you doing, by the way, love? How's work going? Haven't heard you talking about it for a while. I really admire you working at the Maggie's Centre, you know. I think you're awfully brave. Your father would be so proud. And bravo for taking a bit of time off the drink. Very sensible. You know I've been concerned about your drinking for quite some time now, and I'm so pleased you've managed to sort yourself out.

I've posted you a copy of the leaflet Dr Lukić gave us. Let me know what you think. Mina's indifferent, but I say we go for it.

We've nothing to lose. Except Mina's memory . . . Goodness. You'll have to excuse me. It's been a long day. And it's only ten in the morning!

Mum xox

P. S. Love you.
P. P. S. _Don't worry!_

Mantra of the Week

Aakhan jor, Chupai neh jor,

Jor na mangan dayn na jor,

Jor na jeevan maran neh jor,

Jor na raaj maal man sor,

Jor na surtee giaan vechaar,

Jor na jugatee chutai sansaar.

Rough translation: I've got no power to speak or keep silent, no power to beg or give, no power to live or die, no power to rule with wealth or mysticism, no power to understand intuition or spiritual wisdom, no power to find the way to escape the world.

ECT Information Sheet

Tinder Centre Information Leaflets, Series 3
Information Sheet on Electroconvulsive Therapy (ECT)

What is ECT?
The idea for Electroconvulsive Therapy (ECT) came about in the 1930s, after psychiatrists noted that some of their distressed patients with epilepsy seemed to experience an improvement in their mood after an epileptic fit. They realised that passing an electric current through the brain could trigger a seizure, and that this may help treat a variety of patients. By the 1950s and 60s, ECT – known originally as electroshock therapy – was used to treat a wide variety of psychiatric disorders. These days, it is still used, but for a smaller, more focused range of conditions, notably severe depression. In the UK, around 4,000 patients receive the treatment every year.

How does it work?
We do not know exactly why ECT is effective, although we have several theories. One theory proposes that depression is caused by too much brain activity, and ECT helps decrease brain connectivity in the dorsolateral prefrontal cortex, helping the brain's neural networks return to normal functioning. Another theory is that an induced seizure encourages the release of certain brain chemicals, particularly those regulating mood, energy, stress and appetite. Recent research also suggests that it may help stimulate the growth of new cells and nerve pathways in the brain.

Who is ECT for?
ECT can be used to treat patients with:
1. severe depression;
2. resistant mania;
3. catatonia.

It is generally used when other treatments (medicinal and psychological) have proved unsuccessful, or when the patient's illness is thought to be life-threatening.

What happens during ECT?

A course normally consists of between six and twelve treatments, administered two or three times a week. A change may be seen in the patient's symptoms after the first three to six treatments. If a patient does not seem to respond to treatment after six sessions, treatment may discontinue.

1. **Before** starting a course of ECT, you may be given blood tests, a chest X-ray, and an electrocardiogram (ECG). Food and drink must not be consumed for six hours prior to the treatment so that the general anaesthetic may be administered safely.
2. **During** treatment, you will be asked to lie on a trolley, where you will be connected to equipment that monitors heart rate, blood pressure and oxygen levels throughout the procedure. One arm will have a blood pressure cuff attached, which means it will not be flooded with muscle relaxant, and you will be given a rubber grip to hold in your hand, allowing medics to monitor your convulsive response. General anaesthetic will be administered via a cannula, while oxygen is provided to help you breathe. Once you are asleep, the muscle relaxant will be administered. A mouth guard will be put between your teeth, and electrodes will be applied to your temples. The shock will be administered for around four seconds. You will convulse for up to sixty seconds.
3. **After** treatment, you will be moved to a recovery room, where you will be monitored and given oxygen. After ten minutes or so you will wake up, and outpatients may be able to leave the hospital within two to three hours.

Bilateral vs. Unilateral ECT

Bilateral ECT involves a current being passed across both sides of the brain, whereas unilateral ECT targets just one side. In both scenarios, a seizure occurs in the whole of the brain.

1. **Bilateral ECT** is most widely used in the UK. It tends to be quicker and more effective than unilateral ECT, but may cause more side-effects.
2. **Unilateral ECT** is associated with less side-effects, but the patient may take longer to respond to treatment.

What are the side-effects?

There are possible short-term and long-term effects of ECT. Short-term side-effects may include:

1. headache
2. muscular aches
3. contraction of jaw muscles
4. nausea
5. confusion
6. distress
7. fear
8. temporary memory loss

Long-term side-effects may include:

1. permanent memory loss
2. changes in personality or habits
3. death – as with all anaesthetic treatments, there is a very small risk of death or serious injury (1 in 80,000 for each treatment, or 1 in 10,000 for a course of treatments)

What happens after ECT?

ECT is only one part of treatment for depressive illnesses. After a course of ECT, psychological or psychiatric treatment may still be given, and it is important to continue to support the patient in his or her recovery, however dedicated medical practitioners see fit.

ECT controversy

Many people do not agree with ECT as a course of treatment. The infamous scene in *One Flew Over the Cuckoo's Nest* reflects the opinion of many members of the public, that it is a brutal and dehumanising experience. The controversy is furthered by the fact that we still do not know exactly why it works, how effective it is, and what the side-effects are.

However, there is evidence that ECT helps many people. Given that it is only administered in severe circumstances, the patient is often in a life-threatening condition to begin with, and so ECT may be perceived as a risk worth taking. Many doctors believe that it saves lives, and some patients who have previously undergone a course of treatment request the treatment again if their symptoms worsen.

Alternative treatments

If a patient refuses ECT, the treatment will not be administered, even when that patient has been sectioned under the Mental Health Act. Alternative treatments include:

1. trying a different medication
2. intensive psychotherapy
3. giving the patient more time to recover naturally

It should be noted, however, that these alternatives will normally have already been tried before ECT is prescribed.

Email to André

From: Ottila McGregor
To: André Marsh
Date: Wed, 26 March, 2014 at 9:27
Subject: Re: new twitter campaign

Hi André,

I asked Claire Farwell if she'd be up for being a talking head for the new #*checkoutthosebreasts* campaign as you suggested – and yes, those *Daily Mail* shots were great – but I reckon we should think about asking a couple of *non*-supermodels too. Sally Webster off *Coronation Street* might be up for it, and what about Jennifer Saunders? She'd be fab. Tell me who you'd like me to get, anyway, and I'll make it happen. Probably best you leave the communication to me though; not everyone likes the word 'tits' as much as you.

Also, I need to leave work early today please. Got a doctor's appointment in Chorlton at half four.

Hope all's good with you.

Thanks,

Ottila

Referral

Barton House Psychological Services

Dear Ms Arkwright,

Re: Ottila McGregor, NHS number 0375909285

Further to your communication, I have started the patient on a course of Campral. I have also recommended she consider taking a low dose of Fluoxetine, as her mood has worsened since her sister's detainment in psychiatric hospital. So far, however, Ms McGregor has expressed a firm desire to avoid antidepressants, although in the past they appear to have helped. She mentioned in our last meeting that a CPN once suggested she may have Borderline Personality Disorder traits; this remains unconfirmed. If she does have a personality disorder, antidepressants may be unsuitable.

Please let me know the outcome of your assessment when possible. Any information you can give regarding a diagnosis or recommendations for follow-up treatment would be helpful.

Yours faithfully,

Dr Chakrabarti, GP

Email from Grace

From: Grace Shotts
To: Ottila McGregor
Date: Sun, 30 March, 2014 at 21:35
Subject: Re: Re: Re: dude where are you?

holy hell rd, how can it be nearly a month since you last emailed me, and why the eff haven't i got round to replying yet? i checked my phone to see if there were any messages i couldn't remember and sure enough we texted last weekend. what the frig, man, spring cleaning on a friday night? and it's not even spring yet. or is it? sounds like you're serious about this whole sobriety thang. i guess i didn't quite realise that last time you emailed. i'm sorry for saying it was another one of your phases. i lurve your phases, but that's beside the point. everyone in the orchestra was doing that dry january thing or whatever, and i basically thought you were just doing that, but in february. i mean, it's the shortest month, so that's when i'd do it. ha.

if you're serious, though, and it's what you want, then how about this . . .

we could do it together!

i mean, like, for every day that you don't drink, i don't drink either? i'll only crack when you will. i could use a bit of a break and it might be fun. i remember this one week where i was completely broke and i went with kieran (rip) to that drum & bass club in fallowfield, i forget its name, and i swear to god man, i became a better dancer that night. like, learning to dance sober really teaches you what's what.

time for me to 'fess up now, and i haven't mentioned this to saz, but i've been getting a bit of a pain in my side lately. your liver's on the right hand side, yeah? thinking about you not drinking has sort of inspired me. it'd do me good to have a bit of a detox, and honestly, if you can do it, so can i. so what do you reckon? the smirnoff sisters stop getting comfortably numb and spend a while getting filthy gorgeous sober instead? that's an attempt at some scissor sisters references, which i thought a lezzer like you might appreciate. i was trying to work in something about an indefinite hiatus but it sounded a bit forced.

i've had half a bottle of schnapps tonight, but i'm stopping soon cos i've got a rehearsal in the morning for this big deal vaughan williams thing we're doing at the weekend. katherine broderick doing soprano, blah blah. should be better than the 18 effin 12 overture which we had to play for like the millionth time at the russian 'spectacular' last week but anyways. tchaikovsky's not my thing, dude, you know that. shonky modulations, imho. but yeah, we're rehearsing strings at 9 a.m. tomorrow, and this viola player, rachel, she's new, you don't know her, she keeps playing sharp and doing my head in. not what you want to be hearing with a sore bonce, believe.

right i'd better dash – there's a new grey's anatomy on, and you just don't understand how badly i need to watch it. it's a medical emergency!

shotts x

Snapchat to Mina

 Teenymeeny 〉

Today

ME

| Hope you're ok, sis. I sent you a Tinkerbell toothbrush in the post (Mum hinted you might be stockpiling them). Sorry I can't do more. Sorry for everything. I will come and visit when you're ready.

Fault

Apparently, the following things do not cause your sister to develop autism: telling her that the rudest way to swear is with her pinkie. Giving her the smaller 'half' of a broken biscuit. Tiptoeing into her room in the middle of the night and chopping off every strand of her rag-doll's long, raspberry hair.

It's difficult to accept I am not the root of all her problems.

Mina has been given so many different diagnoses over the years. Each one is an instruction manual, which we are meant to use in order to be able to understand her better. Asperger's is the latest. When Mina was given the diagnosis, I spent several months seeking out portrayals of autism in popular culture. I watched *Rain Man* and considered giving Mina a phone book to memorise. I read *The Curious Incident of the Dog in the Night-Time* and wondered whether a bloody murder might occupy her troubled mind. I'd have killed for her, I swear. Then I saw *The Big Bang Theory* and *Sherlock Holmes*, swooning over what a saucy, eccentric genius my sister might yet become.

As time passes, though, Mina's condition deteriorates, and I just can't connect any of that fluffy Asperger's stuff with her. She's not the geeky best friend, the misunderstood teenager, or the comically inept lover. She is clever, but too anxious to make a career out of anything any time soon. Even reading books has become a struggle. And although she enjoys arts and crafts, she has developed carpal tunnel syndrome from embroidering too many kitten brooches in too short a space of time, and so she has taken to staring at the wall instead. She could never work as a detective solving complicated crimes, like Saga Norén in *The Bridge*, because anything involving one person hurting another causes Mina to curl up into a ball and bash her skull with her fists until her knuckles go from white to red. I guess she was always fine with hurting herself.

On bad days, she was fine with hurting *me* too.

It's odd: I'm speaking about her in the past tense now, as if she's gone. I do that sometimes. My sister isn't dead. She just wants to be. And it's difficult to accept that I'm not the reason she wants to disappear. If I had been a better older sister, letting her play the tiger in Wacky Wheels, instead of the moose or, worse still, the panda, then maybe she'd have been altogether happier with her lot in life.

O: *How about you take the top bunk tonight, sis?*
M: *Thanks, Ottila! The top bunk is reserved for the wisest, coolest and most respected sibling, and your symbolic gesture has just raised my self-esteem by one hundred per cent.*
O: *Want the last packet of pickled onion Monster Munch, Mina?*
M: *Really? You'd let me have it? I suppose you do love and value me, which leads me to think I ought to love and value myself.*

I've played these scenarios out in my mind so many times. But I know, deep down, Mina's mental health problems are not down to me. It's not my fault she's in psychiatric hospital. It's nobody's fault. Not even hers. It's just the way it is.

She's on twenty-four-hour watch at the moment, which means there's someone with her all the time. Last week they reduced it slightly and only checked on her every five minutes, keeping a log of her behaviour, but they caught her picking the plaster away from a window frame, trying to peel her way out, and they immediately started observing her round-the-clock.

It's so strange, this suicidal behaviour. Mina never *used to* want to kill herself. She used to want to be a vet. And a microbiologist. And a mother. She once started to write a poetry collection, each poem based on a painting by a famous artist. She wrote about Édouard Manet's 'A Bar at the Folies-Bergère' and, rather than focusing on the solemn-looking central figure of the barmaid, she wrote a sonnet about the trapeze artist, flying high in the rafters, full of dreams and ambitions.

When the nurses at the hospital watch Mina this week, this is what they see: a frowning, twenty-eight-year-old woman sitting on her bed, a book of crossword puzzles open and untouched in her lap. Sometimes she wraps up her belongings in a square of cloth and shuffles in lace-less shoes from her bedroom to the TV room. She sits, re-opens her crossword puzzles, and frowns at nothing in particular once more.

But the nurses are not fooled, and neither am I. Though her eyes remain still, her mind is busy, continually picturing new ways to end her life, and wondering if she'll ever build up the courage to do it.

And it's not my fault.

Email to Mum

From: Ottila McGregor
To: Alice McGregor
Date: Wed, 2 April, 2014 at 18:51
Subject: sorry times 1,000

Mum, I'm so, so sorry. I can't believe I forgot to post your card in time. I feel like such a terrible daughter. You're a brilliant mum, and I hope you get the belated gift I've sent soon. I'm glad you received the card this morning, anyway. The Custard Cream on the front reminded me of a Mother's Day when I was about seven or eight. Mina and I woke up super-early and crept downstairs to make you biscuits. We mixed up flour, eggs, butter and sultanas. I think we found the recipe in one of your Delias. I left Mina licking out the bowl, while I put the biscuits in the oven and got the kettle on. We weren't really allowed to use the kettle in case we scalded ourselves, but we decided you'd be so pleased with our surprise that you wouldn't mind.

While we waited for the biscuits to bake we made a card. I drew a sheep and Mina felt-tipped flowers around it. I Pritt-Sticked some toilet roll onto the sheep's body, and we shook glitter onto the background to make it look like a sunny day. Do you remember that card? Took ages to make.

So long, in fact, that by the time I got the tray out of the Aga, the biscuits were little black discs of charcoal. Mina was devastated and wouldn't stop crying, but I bravely took you your card and (cold) tea, and explained what had happened.

You've always been so organised, never seem to make any mistakes, and I remember feeling terribly ashamed as I explained my first attempt at baking to you. Do you know what you said to me after I told you, Mum? You put your tea on the bedside table, then jumped out of bed and brushed my hair out of my eyes. 'What a marvellous excuse to bake more biscuits!' you said, laughing. 'Let's go downstairs and make them again.'

Mina didn't join us that morning. Dad had probably been working at a fête the day before because I remember him being exhausted, and he went back to sleep. Now I come to think about it, maybe he was hungover? So it was just me and you that day, Mum, making that tray of biscuits. You spoke to me so softly, explaining why we needed to cream the butter and sugar together, how half a teaspoon of vanilla essence would improve the flavour, why we needed to line the baking tray with parchment, and check the clock after putting the biscuits in the oven.

It's one of the only memories I've got of the two of us. No Dad. No Mina. Only us.

I love you, Mum.

Ottila xxx

Little Book of Happy

Dear Absolute Derivative of the Little Book of Calm,

Last night I dreamt I was at my own funeral. There was no conductor, there were no speeches and, in fact, there were no guests. The only thing there, other than my coffined cadaver, was a pile of old letters I'd received throughout my lifetime. For some reason, I hadn't replied to any of them, and I'd lost touch with everyone. So I just lay there, dead and alone.

What a joyful book this is turning out to be. Here, have a picture of a baby taking its first steps.

[*Hand-drawn picture of baby walking here.*]

From Your Grave Friend

Email to Grace

From: Ottila McGregor
To: Grace Shotts
Date: Fri, 4 April, 2014 at 22:27
Subject: Re: Re: Re: Re: dude where are you?

Really sorry to hear about the pain in your side, mate. Have you seen the doctor about it? Maybe it *would* do you good not to drink for a while, at least until you get it checked out. And thanks for suggesting doing the sobriety thing together . . .

The problem is, though, I think this is something I need to do myself. I mean, it'd be great if you stopped drinking too, if that's what you want, but I don't want you to rely on me to be your gauge. If you don't drink one day that has to be because it's what *you* want, not because you're copying me. Because honestly, Shottsy, I don't know if I'm ever going to drink again.

I didn't tell you how bad it was before because I didn't want you to think I was blaming you, or criticising you, or anything like that. But I was drinking a lot, a hell of a lot, every single day, and it was getting dangerous. It's so hard to see just how bad it is when you're in the midst of it. I don't know, maybe it's like that for you too. Have you ever checked out the government guidelines on drink? They reckon it's fourteen units a week for women. Any more than that and you significantly increase your risk of mouth cancer and liver disease and all that horrible stuff. And do you know how much fourteen units is? One measly bottle of wine a week! Well, it's like one and a third or something, but who drinks a third of a bottle? That's ludicrous. But fourteen units a week is what they say. You and I were having that every *day*. And then some.

Look at us, eh? Pair of codgers now we've hit thirty. Let's do something wild. Ever heard of bouldering? It's rock climbing without a harness. Don't worry, if we go here there are crash mats: http://www.manchesterclimbingcentre.com

Rocket Dog

Recovery Meeting Transcript

PATIENT: What does it feel like to enjoy things?

THERAPIST: You don't enjoy anything?

PATIENT: I've made a list of 'Ten Things to Do That Might Be Fun'. I used fluorescent pens to make it look more exciting. I squirted the paper with Calvin Klein Obsession.

THERAPIST: What sort of things have you put on there?

PATIENT: Bake a lemon cake. Feed some ducks. Pet a cat.

THERAPIST: Have you tried doing any of them?

PATIENT: I made a cake. I don't think I put enough lemon in though, because it tasted of cardboard.

THERAPIST: Did you enjoy making it?

PATIENT: Breaking the eggs. Stirring in the sugar. They're all just processes, aren't they?

THERAPIST: Processes can be fun. They're often more satisfying than the final product, in fact. Have you managed to find any new friends yet?

PATIENT: Nobody's answered my advert. I can't think why. [*Pause.*] I'm being a dick.

THERAPIST: It's quite unusual to hear you swear.

PATIENT: Sorry. I just feel like a bad person today.

THERAPIST: Swearing doesn't make you a bad person.

PATIENT: *You* don't do it.

THERAPIST: I swear plenty when I'm not here.

PATIENT: Is 'dick' a swear word, strictly speaking?

THERAPIST: You've been taking the Campral for about four weeks now, haven't you?

PATIENT: Something like that.

THERAPIST: One of the potential side effects is a loss of interest in things. Difficulty experiencing pleasure.

PATIENT: I don't know if it's the Campral.

THERAPIST: What do you think might be causing it?

PATIENT: What does electric shock treatment feel like?

THERAPIST: I don't think you're quite at that point yet.

PATIENT: It's Mina. I'm scared she's going to stop being my sister.

THERAPIST: Your sister is starting a course of ECT?

PATIENT: [*Sniffing sound.*]

THERAPIST: She won't feel anything when it happens, you know. It's performed under general anaesthetic. And it's unlikely to cause her any lasting problems.

PATIENT: But it might. You know that game, where you look at a load of objects on a tray for, like, a minute or so, and then the tray is taken away and you have to remember what you saw?

THERAPIST: Kim's Game.

PATIENT: Is it? We used to play that at Brownies, Mina and I, back when I was a Seconder of the Imps and she was a Sprite. Mina used to remember everything on that tray, every time.

THERAPIST: She might not lose her memory after ECT.

PATIENT: I used to be so desperate to beat her.

THERAPIST: It's perfectly natural, you know.

PATIENT: Before we left Brownies, the last badge Mina got was Stargazer. Guess which one I got?

THERAPIST: I don't know.

PATIENT: Friendship.

THERAPIST: Why are you touching your liver again, Ottila? Are you feeling guilty about something?

PATIENT: [*Patient mumbles something incomprehensible. Sounds a bit like 'disgrace'.*]

Climbing

Grace makes the sign of the cross as we near our destination. 'Jesus, Rocket Dog, I've not been to one of these since I was a fricking kid.'

This place used to be a church, made out of the same red bricks as all the local cotton mills. Inside, it has been transformed. You can climb right up into the vaults, getting closer to heaven than anyone ever did from a mere church pew.

'You?' I say. 'You were never a kid.' I make crab claws and pinch her waist. My fingers close in on the space beneath her ribcage, and I feel her oblique muscles move. I'm not ready for this level of intimacy and my hands recoil.

I'll never know how Grace has managed to stay so skinny all these years. She's always had a perfect figure. And a perfect face. I'm the one with Danish heritage, but she's got the Nordic looks. Blonde hair and high cheekbones. I've been riddled with spots since I quit drinking. I counted three this morning. The way I see it, the toxicity is working its way out of me bit by bit. Maybe Grace is pus on the inside.

'I can't believe I've agreed to this,' she says, taking a crumpled cigarette out of her jeans pocket and lighting up. 'If I fall, you have to catch me, dude.'

I stand next to my best friend, looking the other way. There's so much of Manchester I don't know, even though I've lived here for the past seven years. Experiencing it sober has been like moving to a new city. I'm seeing parts of it I never bothered going to before, and the people feel different too. More families. More people reading newspapers. More people who don't drink, like me. I really thought everyone in Chorlton was out to get wasted on a Friday night. Turns out there are people who go for a chickpea burger and a glass of orange juice; or people who nurse half a pint until seven o'clock, then head to the city centre for a life drawing class. There are people who do circuit training and Muay Thai and all the things I should have been doing for the past decade but I've been too drunk or hungover to manage it.

'Oi, dreamer.' Grace flicks cigarette ash in my direction.

'Sorry. Just enjoying the sunshine.'

'You don't know how much this friendship means to me,

mate.' Grace yawns. 'I've had, like, four hours sleep.'

I've never been climbing before. I don't really know what I was thinking suggesting it. I'd heard one of the service users talking about it the other week. She's called Pru, and is recovering from Stage 2A cervical cancer. She puts me and the rest of humanity to shame with the amount of cool shit she does. This time she was talking about bouldering in Fontainebleau. *It's so humbling*, she was saying. *Me, clinging to a rock, and the rock, clinging to the surface of the world*. Truthfully, Pru is extremely irritating, but that doesn't change the fact she does cool shit. When I asked Grace to go bouldering with me, I think I wanted to be someone who does cool shit too.

'Come on.' I grab the cigarette stub out of Grace's mouth and throw it onto the pavement. 'It's time.'

'You've got to be smegging kidding me,' Grace says as we walk into the church. 'I'm not going up there. I'd rather go to frigging actual church.'

'Oh god.' I look up at the walls. They're studded with colourful lumps, which look too far apart to me, and yet there are people grabbing onto them, making impossible shapes with their bodies, many, many metres up in the air.

We pay for our session and the guy at the till asks our shoe sizes. 'Your climbing shoes will need to be at least half a size smaller than normal,' he says. 'You want them nice and snug.' I wonder how many times a day this guy says 'nice and snug'.

'Gotcha.' Grace winks.

He hands us some plimsolls and we remove our outdoor shoes, which takes Grace an age, given the complex way she's done up her Converse high-tops. I slip off my Reeboks, wondering why I always manage to look so unfashionable, no matter what the occasion. For some reason, I thought jazzy leggings would be appropriate today, along with a Lycra top that screams 'Jane Fonda video'. I'd hoped that Grace would be the odd one out in her Levis, but actually, a lot of the tattooed guys three-quarters of the way up the walls are wearing jeans, rolled up over the ankles, showing off their nice, snug feet.

Fortunately, the bouldering section is not as intimidating as the climbing area. 'It looks like the kids' section,' Grace scoffs, as we survey the crash mats and low walls. 'Nice one, dude.'

Not only does this *look* like the kids' section, but it is in fact *overrun* with small people. It must be the start of the Easter holidays. I'd forgotten things like that existed. Seeing the kids makes me realise that this kind of activity is only good for people who don't worry about getting hurt. Only the brave boulder well. I notice a strange fizzing in my abdomen.

A hot guy with blond dreads approaches us and offers Grace some chalk.

'Chalk? Street name for crack, right?'

'It's to improve your grip,' he explains, clearly used to dealing with children.

Grace holds out her hands, as if expecting this guy to bend down on one knee and chalk her palms for her. It doesn't happen. He hands us each a pouch of white powder. I dip my fingers in the pouch and cover myself in as much chalk as possible.

'Either of you ladies been bouldering before?' he asks. I think he's South African. Maybe Kiwi.

We shake our heads.

'The best bit of advice I can give you is to focus on what's going on above you. Don't look down!'

I feel sick.

The guy points out the different parts of the room with the tiniest of shrugs, so as to show how relaxed and casual it all is. 'That bit over there is for beginners; they're the easiest *problems*. This bit here is for the more advanced climbers. I'd suggest starting over there, see how far you get, and then take it at your own speed. Probably a good idea to *spot* each other too.' He points at a man standing on the crash mat nearby, holding out his arms below a small girl, presumably his daughter, who is clambering up the wall above him. 'Make sure if your partner falls, she doesn't fall head first.'

'Yeeshk.' Grace and I head to the crash mat then we stop and look at each other. Her eyes widen like she's about to burst out laughing. My eyes widen too. For a second it's almost like old times, like we're at that sweet spot on a night out, where there are still several hours left to go. Where we're feeling warm and good and like the world is a wonderful place that belongs to us and us alone.

But Grace doesn't laugh. Her focus shifts to one of the bumps on the wall. She charges towards it, grabs on, hoists her body up and places her toes neatly onto a couple of holds. 'Don't forget to spot me, mate,' she yells, as she begins scaling the wall, with so much dexterity and so little apprehension that I suddenly decide I actually hate her.

I can feel it now. I'm willing her to do badly. I'm willing her to fall. My arms hang limply at my sides.

'This is fun,' she calls down.

I look at her perfect little arse and wish she'd crap herself.

'I loved that,' Grace says, skipping along the pavement.

I can only bring myself to grunt in reply. Turns out bouldering is shit. Grace is shit, Pru is shit, and bouldering is definitely shit, shit, shit.

Suddenly Grace stops skipping and I notice with horror who's walking along the pavement towards us. 'Ben!' she calls, waving.

I think about all the great ways there are to die, and how I haven't got time to do any of them right now. Ben looks different. Thicker, firmer, more muscular. It's the first time I've seen him since last August, when we he told me I was high maintenance and I screamed at him to *maintain this* while throwing my laptop onto the street. It was meant to be a pile of his clothes, but I threw the wrong rucksack.

'Thought we might see you here,' says Grace, as Ben reaches us. 'I did tell you he'd been into climbing lately, didn't I?'

Oh fuck. Is that why I suggested climbing to Grace? I'd completely forgotten she'd mentioned this, but maybe it had lodged in my mind. My subconscious didn't want to bump into Ben here today, did it? I nod at Grace.

'Alright, our kid,' he says, nodding at me and then flicking his eyes down to Grace's trainers. Jesus, he really couldn't have sounded more Mancunian just then if he'd tried. He's even got himself one of those Liam Gallagher parkas, but it's tight, like his body's straining to get out of it.

'Hi,' I say quietly. I'd forgotten how awkward Ben was with eye contact. He's the most confident man I've ever known in the bedroom, but he can't look me in the eye when we're standing on the street.

'Band on the Wall tonight?' Grace asks, in a way that sounds like she sees him there all the time. I wonder if Grace and Ben have ever slept together. I hope not.

'Nah. Probably just Common with a few mates. Big one last night.'

'We're heading into town for some grub. Join us?'

Ben casts me a quick look. 'Maybe in a bit. Got a session first, haven't I?' He lifts his sports bag.

Grace sticks out her tongue and starts walking off, leaving Ben and I to share a moment.

'Yo,' he says. 'How's things?'

'Fine thanks.' I'm thinking about the time I went down on him in a bar while he was using the fruit machine.

'Nice one. Well, I'd better scoot.' He chucks his sports bag on his shoulder and walks off.

I wait until I've caught up with Grace before freaking out. 'That was really fucking awkward.'

'Was it?' Grace asks. 'Ben's alright. He doesn't give a fuck.'

I don't ask what Ben doesn't give a fuck about. Instead I stay silent, thinking about all the amazing sex Ben and I used to have. Always drunken and messy, but amazing.

We're zig-zagging through town, heading towards Piccadilly Gardens. Until Grace mentioned food I had been hoping to get the bus home, spend the afternoon watching old episodes of *Spaced* and *Black Books* and any other fuzzy British comedies where the characters bicker all the time, but ultimately, inevitably, are best friends, with bonds that never break, in spite of all their differences.

'This'll do,' Grace says dragging me into a doorway and leading me into Fab Café. I know this place well. It's TV and movie themed, with a definite sci-fi bias. I once heard a woman read a poem here in Klingon. That was before I fell asleep, nestled among the Dr Who memorabilia.

'Oh, Grace, I'd really rather not . . .' My voice trails off as I see her chest pressed up against the bar.

'They do Pot Noodles here now,' she says, and promptly orders a Bombay Bad Boy, a packet of Space Invaders, and two pints of Stella.

'I'm not drinking,' I say quickly, not giving myself a second to change my mind. 'What about your side?' I lower my voice. 'The pain.'

Grace bites her lip. 'Oh fuck, sorry, I completely forgot. I'll have yours. What do you want?'

'A Coke, I guess. Only one, then I'm leaving.'

That's what they all say,' she says, grinning.

Drunk people smell of the thing they're drinking, but like a more powerful, more rotten version of it. Grace smells of three pints of Stella, a double vodka Coke and a red wine. She's got a film of grease over her eyeballs, like the glint in someone's eyes before they decide to do evil things to you. She slurs and forgets her train of thought, and it feels horrible to think I was once like this too.

I've tried to leave three times. I've put away four pints of Coke; my teeth are sticky and my heart's racing. I can't explain what's been keeping me here. We've been sitting in the dark, surrounded by Daleks and retro arcade machines for over five hours. The evening drinkers are starting to appear, in their Topshop dresses and checked shirts, and here I am, in my leggings, stone cold sober.

'She's not even a good fucking dancer,' says Grace. She's talking about Saz, who tried to beat her at some kind of dance-off at Funkademia a couple of weeks ago.

I yawn. 'I'd really better be off now, Shotts. I've got stuff to do, and it's already gone six.'

'Gone six?' she says. 'I'd better bail too. Need to get changed before Band on the Wall. Reggae thing tonight. Sure you're not up for it?'

I yawn again.

She drains the rest of her pint and I decide to leave my Coke. We walk out, blinking, into the light.

The bus stops and I prod her repeatedly in the ribs. 'Wake up, Grace.'

'Oi, quit it.' She rubs her eyes and gets up, lurching towards the front of the bus. 'Cheers, mate,' she says to the driver, and starts walking down Wilbraham Road.

'Grace? Aren't you going home?'

She looks back at me, as if only just remembering I'm there. 'Yeah, just gonna get some stuff for dinner. Come with, if you like.'

I walk beside her, a bitter bodyguard, wishing nasty things upon her.

'So weird we ran into Ben earlier,' Grace says. 'Do you still fancy him?'

'No,' I say quickly.

We head into the Co-op. Grace picks up a pack of spinach and ricotta tortellini and I get one too. I want to spend all of ten minutes cooking and eating this, then I can curl up under the duvet feeling sorry for myself. Yep, I've got big plans.

Grace heads off to a section of the shop I was once so well acquainted with. As I pay for my tortellini, I watch her pick out a bottle of red wine. I start to feel a bit sorry for her. What if that pain in her side is serious? What if she's got cirrhosis? Would it be obvious if she had it? Would she be jaundiced?

She brings a bottle of Shiraz to the till. 'Gotta get it all in before I go out. Saving my pennies.'

'What you saving for?'

'My rent.' She laughs, embarrassingly loudly, but the only person flinching is me.

We head out of the Co-op and Grace swings her carrier bag in wild circles, almost knocking a homeless guy's dog. *Sorry*, I mouth to the guy. Grace hangs a right down Brundrett's Road. I went on a few dates with a woman who lived on this road when I first moved to Manchester. It was around the time I met Grace, and she found it hilarious. 'You are the most boring-looking lesbian I've ever seen,' she'd said. Bisexual people get the raw end of the deal. I don't look enough of one thing, or act enough of the other. Girls rarely take an interest in me because they don't trust the fact I also date men. Guys, including André, assume I'll always be up for a threesome.

The woman I dated, Louise, had a kid called Alfie. She told me Alfie was conceived using the secret spermatozoa of Princess Diana's second cousin, via a website called Man Not Included. A few years later, that website made front page news. It was a scam, delivering fresh sperm to people's doors in dirty coffee flasks. How Louise had managed to get pregnant that way, and (presumably) avoid STIs, I don't know. She was a nice enough woman. Ex-military and came on a bit strong. Wanted me to take a trip to Alton Towers with Alfie on our third date. I wasn't ready. When we broke up, she texted me saying: YOUR NOT MY TYPE ANYWAY BLOODY BI GIRLS.

'Where are you going, Grace?'

Grace pushes a rusty gate. 'They never lock this fucking thing.'

'What the hell are you doing?'

'Some guy took me up here last week to do poppers.'

I follow her into a loading bay at the back of the Co-op building. There are two giant dustbins and several crates of old bottles. I'm a fool for doing this, whatever it is we're doing.

Grace starts climbing a metal staircase on the side of the building. 'It's basically public property.'

'Grace, it's not safe. Come down. This is ridiculous.'

'I wanna show you something.' She loops her plastic bag around her wrist and grabs a flimsy-looking ladder attached to the wall.

'Oh my god. You're way too drunk to do this, Grace. Get down or I'm telling someone.' These words hang between us, pathetic and ugly.

Grace looks back at me. Her expression softens. 'You're genuinely worried about me, aren't you?'

And now here's my chance. My chance to tell her that I think she needs help, that it's not normal for people to carry on like this into their thirties, that she's going to end up hurt, really hurt, if she doesn't sort herself out. But I can't bring myself to say it.

'Just come down, mate,' I say gently.

'In a mo. Wanna show you something first.' Grace climbs the ladder and disappears onto the roof of the building.

Unable to do anything else, I climb the stairs and ladder too. The ladder wobbles and I cling onto it with sweaty palms. *Just don't look down, Ottila.*

As I haul myself onto the roof, I exhale with relief. I can't believe that several metres beneath me there are people picking up tins of tomatoes and packs of wholemeal rolls off the shelves. Can I find a way to enjoy this?

Grace is looking over the edge. She's shaking with laughter. I should probably leave her like this. Laughing her head off at her hilarious life of capers and calamities, while I go home to watch comedies without breaking a smile. It seems like a fitting end to our friendship. Except now that I'm closer, I realise Grace isn't laughing. She's crying.

'I've had enough, Ottila,' she says, then takes a long drag on a cigarette.

I stand beside her and look down onto the street. There's nobody there.

'You can stop, Grace,' I say. 'You can stop any time, like me. I can help you. You don't have to live like this.'

She turns to me and raises her eyebrows. 'What are you . . . ?' That greasy glint in her eyes returns. 'I'm not talking about *me*, dumbass. I'm talking about this. Us. Drifting apart. I can tell you've been judging me all day.'

I want to say: *No. No, I haven't.* But I have. I've been noticing all the ways alcohol is ruining my best friend and ignoring all the ways she's brilliant, and I can't help it. 'I don't like living like this any more, Shottsy,' I tell her. 'I don't like the chaos.'

Grace nods and wipes her nose with the back of her hand. 'And I do. There's nothing wrong with that.'

'I think I've been feeling angry with you today because you manage to maintain this crazy lifestyle, to embrace the chaos, and you're fine. I mean, where are your wrinkles, for god's sake?'

Grace drags on her cigarette again, then blows smoke into my face. 'I'm having too much fun to get wrinkles.'

'Look after yourself, Shottsy. Please.'

She puts her arms around me, wiping her tears onto my cheeks. This is it. Our break-up hug. I've never broken up with a friend before, and I didn't know it could be done. I let the hug last as long as possible.

I know this stale, boozy smell so well. I inhale deep lungfuls of it. 'Sorry,' I say, when I eventually pull away.

I go first down the ladder, and then I stand at the bottom, arms in the air, spotting Grace like I was meant to do earlier. This time I'm doing it properly, waiting to catch her if she needs me.

'I'm fine, I'm fine.' She jumps down onto the stairwell. There's a huge clatter and an eerie echo, but thankfully, the platform doesn't fall apart underneath us.

I walk down the stairs, onto the tarmac, and turn around to see Grace, tall and glamorous, her face barely even showing the fact that she's been crying. She walks down the stairs like Scarlett O'Hara in *Gone with the Wind*, until, finally, on the bottom step, she trips and falls down, face-first.

'Fuck,' she says, laughing. 'I think I chipped my smegging tooth.' She raises her head. There's blood on her mouth. She wipes it and looks at her finger, then fishes around in her mouth with her tongue. 'It's just the corner. I'll look like Taylor Swift or whatever.'

I look inside her open mouth. 'It's really not that bad; barely noticeable,' I lie. 'You okay?'

She gnashes her teeth.

'Good. Get home safe, all right?'

'You too, Rocket Dog.'

I open the gate and turn left on Brundrett's Road, knowing Grace will be turning right.

It's not even eight by the time I get home, but I take my tortellini straight to bed. I don't watch any programmes involving great friendships overcoming all odds. Instead I watch a nature documentary about puffer fish. The voiceover man tells me that ingesting puffer fish can cause tingling lips and light-headedness, followed by muscle paralysis and death. When the documentary finishes, I roll over and look up at the ceiling. It's good to look at the ceiling while firmly rooted on the ground.

Eventually, I get up and go into the living room in my pyjamas, where Laurie is sitting with his mates. 'Mind if I join you?'

Laurie looks up from his central position on the sofa, with his two friends, David and David, either side of him. They may as well be fanning him with palm leaves. 'We're having a *kanabō* club meeting at the moment, Ottila. So unless you know your Colada from your Tizona . . .' One of the Davids sniggers.

Kanabō club is Laurie's single most loserish activity. A *kanabō* is a spiked truncheon used by Japanese demons. Laurie and his friends get together once a week to discuss their favourite mythical weapons. There are swords, spears, bows, rods, staves, axes, hammers, clubs and projectiles out there that you wouldn't believe. Literally. They're mythical. But it's possible to discuss them for hours. Which would be the most effective for killing a burglar, for instance, out of a *sagitta* or an *uchide-no-kozuchi*? A *sagitta* was the projectile weapon used by Hercules to kill Aquila, the eagle gnawing at Prometheus' liver. An *uchide-no-kozuchi*, on the other hand, is a Japanese hammer that can 'tap out' anything you wish for. So the answer is clearly the *uchide-no-kozuchi*, because you could tap out something to kill the burglar – a gun, for instance – and then you could tap yourself out a whole new security system for your house, and maybe even a new house too if you fancied it. Laurie told me that once, while handing me a cloth to wipe my muddy shoe prints off the bathroom lino.

'You know what? I'll leave it thanks.' I walk out of the living room, and one of the Davids, the other David, says goodbye.

I go back to my room and lie on top of the duvet. I touch my mouth, my nose, my forehead. I imagine how it would feel to die from puffer fish poisoning. I touch my neck, my breasts, my stomach. I think about how incredible it is to be alive, even though life can get rough sometimes. I touch my knees, my shins, my feet. I'm in control of all these parts of myself.

I pick up my phone from my bedside table with great solemnity and write a text message. I nod as I re-read the words, then hit 'send'. As I put my phone back down, my knuckles smack ceramic. Shit: my WORLD'S BEST SISTER mug. I've lost countless cups this way, but in the past I've always been drunk. This time I'm sober; my reflexes work. I reach out and catch. The mug doesn't smash into a million little pieces, and neither do I.

Text Message to Thales

Sat 12 Apr 21:16

Let's make it work.

THREE

A Memory

Mina and I started menstruating one week apart. Her first, then me.

'Blood sisters,' Mina had said, mystified.

When I was an undergraduate, Mina visited me at university.

'Take good care of her,' Mum said on the phone. 'She's delicate.'

'Let's get drunk,' I said to Mina, switching off my phone. 'It's punk night at Rock City. We can gel our hair into spikes and write marker-pen swear words on our clothes. I'll buy you as many Snakebites as you like.'

'I don't know,' Mina said, nose tucked between her knees, fingers pinching the carpet. 'I don't like going out.'

'It'll do you good! Help you snap out of it.'

Mina growled.

All students drink at least a bottle of wine in their rooms before going clubbing. You only need three or four pints at the club that way. Drinking in my room also allowed me to wait for Mina to change her mind.

'Have this. Just a mouthful.'

I hated hearing her teeth grinding together.

'Come on. I'm meant to be looking after you. Drink up and let's go dancing.'

'I hate you, Ottila.'

'Fine. I'll finish your bottle.'

I shut the door, leaving Mina in my room, and I headed out for the club. The next thing I knew, I was waking up, back in my room with Mina again. Time had surely passed between the two events. Hadn't it?

'I've opened the window because you threw up on your pillow,' Mina said, wrapped in her sleeping bag on the floor, an angry worm. 'It stinks.'

I looked down and saw the Newcastle-Brown-Ale-coloured stain. 'What happened?'

'Some goths dropped you off here at four twenty-three in the morning. One of them was wearing a Cradle of Filth t-shirt.'

'So I went out last night?'

Mina bashed her temple with her fist. 'I want to go home.'

I got to my feet, hunched over, like I'd gone back several evolutionary stages. I staggered to the bathroom and looked at the oats splashed all over the wall. I'd had apple crumble for dinner last night.

Then I looked down at the lino. There was a trail of blood leading to the shower. I had a history of cutting myself when I came home drunk, but I wouldn't do something like that while Mina was here no matter how trashed I was . . . I hope. 'Oh god, Mina. What did I do?'

Mina smiled. The remarkable thing about her smile was that the corners of her lips pointed downwards. 'I did that,' she said.

That was over a decade ago.

These days, every moment that passes in which I don't have a drink, I feel less and less inclined to splash my blood all over the lino, to mix it with Mina's.

Who is in Your Life Now?

Here is an exercise that will help you see how the people you know fit into your life. Write the names of family, friends and acquaintances on the chart according to how often you see them.

Can you find a way to bring the supportive people further towards the centre of your chart, and push the names of those who are not supportive further out?

Email from Mum

From: Alice McGregor
To: Ottila McGregor
Date: Tue, 15 April, 2014 at 14:33
Subject: Re: (no subject)

There's something I want to tell you, Ottila, that I haven't got round to saying yet. I mentioned in one of my recent emails that I'm proud of you for laying off the alcohol, which I am, darling, I really am. But it's time I come clean myself.

I've *started* drinking. Just a little glass of wine in the evening, nothing outrageous. I know it probably sounds preposterous given that you've never seen me touch a drop of alcohol in all your life. You know I used to drink, before I got pregnant with you, but once I knew that something, someone, was growing inside me, well, admittedly I didn't stop immediately. In fact, it wasn't until the second trimester that I gave up entirely, but after that, I never looked back. More or less.

The day your father died, I bought myself a jar of Kalms and breathed through it. The grief, I mean. I'm still breathing through it. We all are. But sometimes, herbal remedies and relaxation exercises aren't enough. Do you know what I mean? Gosh, perhaps I shouldn't say that, when you've already . . . I'm sorry, sweetheart. I should be brave enough to tell you this over the phone, but, truth be told, I'm ashamed. Some days all this affects me more than I'd like to admit.

I want you to know that I love you and I think it's important we're honest with each other! Also, just FYI, I'm going to start getting out more. There's this thing called Death Café running in Trowbridge next Wednesday. Have you ever heard of it? It's what they call a 'social franchise'. The events are run internationally. People get together in a relaxed setting and chat about death. A bit like where *you* work, I imagine. I was thinking I might pop along and see if I can make some new friends. Plus, it's being held at Boswells, and their carrot cake is divine.

Anyway, love, toodle-pip and I'll speak to you soon. Oh, I almost forgot to say: Mina starts her ECT next week. I asked her how she was feeling about it this morning but she said she's so fed up she's barely thought about the procedure. I think *I'm* more nervous than she is.

Speak to you soon and thanks for listening,

Mum xoxo

Maggie's Centre

'Hi, Maude, I was thinking we could have a chat.'

Maude comes to the centre at least once a week. Lately she's been coming more than that.

I've been thinking about how you can end up becoming friends with anyone, regardless of gender, age, or background. All that counts is that they're a good egg. Maude might be fifty years older than me, but she's excellent friend material.

I'm trying harder to make friends with good eggs, and steer clear of bad ones. In my therapist's words, it's the difference between *healthy thinking* and *stinky thinking*. Maude is the first person I've seen today who isn't my boss or my flatmate. Both André and Laurie are of the rotten ovum variety. You can tell when a hen egg is bad by placing it in a glass of water. If the egg sinks to the bottom, it's fresh. If it floats like a dead koi carp, then steer clear. I suppose, in times gone by, we did the same thing with people, at witch trials. She sinks, she's innocent; she rises to the top, we kill her. These days, that sort of thing is frowned upon. Trying to work out whether people are good or bad is much more complicated than that.

Whenever Maude laughs, her eyes wrinkle up all the way, not just a bit. That shows she fully commits herself to a joke. Furthermore, she's tough. I won't say *tough as old boots*, because that's a patronising way of saying someone elderly is resilient. Besides, in my experience, boots either come unstuck at the soles or wear out after around six months of use, and you have to be really lucky, or spend an awful lot of money, to get a pair that last. No, Maude is tough as a *brand new* pair of boots. She once told me she used to be part of an underground women's boxing club in Poland and offered to teach me some moves. A friend who laughs and fights? Sounds perfect to me. Finally, and maybe this is the most important thing, Maude reminds me of my grandmother. The one on my mum's side. I never knew my dad's mother; she lived in Copenhagen and we visited her when I was too young to remember. But Granny Joyce, she was special. She made toasted teacakes for breakfast, and let us have two lumps of sugar in our tea. She taught me to paint with watercolours, and sang 'Don't Worry, Be Happy' whenever anything bad happened. She wasn't scared of anything, even spiders. I miss having someone like that in my life.

So as I sit in the relaxation area, flicking through interior design magazines on my morning break, and notice Maude pass me by, I call out to her. It's time to tell her the good news: I'm going to move her towards the centre of my support network. I probably won't word it exactly like that. 'Maude?'

Maude stops and turns to face me.

'Oh god. Maude, are you okay?'

She's sucking in her bottom lip as the tears roll down her cheeks. She looks both strong and vulnerable.

'Hi, Ottila,' she says, nodding. She walks on, past the kitchen. The door of Counselling Room 1 opens and André steps out. He's holding a box of tissues.

I mustn't stare, so I continue flicking through the pictures of renovated Victorian homes, with grey walls and white paint accentuating the original features. 'You can "spline" the gaps in your old floorboards or, if you need a quick fix, try a homemade remedy such as sawdust mixed with shellac,' says Sandy Cunningham in the *Good Homes Magazine*.

Is it just me, or is everyone around here crying lately? How am I meant to be happy when everyone is crying? Is that a selfish thought?

Mum's email has sent me into a bit of a spin. Normally she's all: *hey, don't worry, darling, I've got the whole thing covered*. But now I can feel it. She's losing control. This has only happened once before, after Dad died. She stopped telling everyone else not to worry, and started worrying herself. I've never found out where she went the week she disappeared.

Mum is meant to be the strong one. The only one in the family who's never been prescribed antidepressants. Dad took them for a while after leaving that Heritage Consultant job. Mina's been on them for fifteen years. I've taken them on and off for ages. But Mum. It's not right. I wish Granny Joyce was here. She could scratch Mum's back and make her a sugary tea. That's what's needed: tea, not booze. Or am I just jealous that she's drinking and I'm not?

'Many people carry out home "improvements" that turn out to be damaging,' says Sandy Cunningham.

I haven't seen Thales at work for days now, not since I sent that text asking him to get back together. I brought my lunch in yesterday, but I went to the cafeteria and bought an extra sandwich in case I saw him. I didn't see him. I just ended up eating two sandwiches, and I had to undo the top button on my trousers for the rest of the afternoon. Thales probably hates me. Oh well. Today I'm going to heat up some healthy soup in the staff kitchen and not worry about it. Don't worry, be happy!

'If you're thinking of extending, it's important to know where your boundaries are,' Sandy explains.

I hear a roar of laughter. The door to Counselling Room 1 opens again and André and Maude walk out. Maude pats André's hand and tells him he's a *dobry chłopak*. Then they walk off in separate directions, Maude wrinkling up her eyes all the way, and André straightening his tie, heading for his office, looking totally professional, and truthfully, not the least bit in love with himself. I don't know, maybe some eggs can be bad and good simultaneously. Maybe people are nothing like eggs and it's a pointless comparison. Or maybe that's just stinky thinking.

Letter to Mina

20 April 2014
2.16 p.m.

Mina, it's Mina here.

The hospital staff have made me write this in case you forget what's going on when you wake up after your first session of ECT tomorrow. Apparently you might not remember consenting to the treatment, so I've got to put it down in writing, and they'll deliver the letter to you when you wake up from the general anaesthetic.

Um. Surprise. It's me . . . you . . . Mina from the past here. I've just signed a load of consent forms letting the doctors know it's okay to electrocute my brain twice a week for the next goodness-knows-how-long. I promise you I'm fine with it.

But why should you trust a letter more than your own memory? What if the doctors have forged this to trick you into thinking you've consented to a barbaric procedure? I know that's what you're thinking, Mina, because I'm you!!! I expect I need to say something to convince you that it's really *you* who wrote this letter. To write something that only you (we) know.

The problem is, this electric shock could potentially eradicate any one of your memories, and it might even change your personality. So I've got no idea what you'll remember and what you won't. Dr Lukić tells me that it's most likely it will be short-term memory loss, but he won't explain whether we're talking hours, weeks or years. To be on the safe side I should talk about something from when I was really little. A really Teeny Meeny.

Do you remember the summer we stayed with Granny for a whole month? And she set up that sweet shop in the spare room? All your favourite types of Pick 'n' Mix. There were strawberry laces, foam bananas, gummy bears, mice, fizzy cola bottles, discos, rhubarb and custards . . . Even horrible liquorice allsorts and pink shrimps looked delicious on Granny's homemade sweetie stall. She had the perfect ratio of colour and quantity, i.e. plenty of both. The best bit, though, the bit you'd been fantasising about since the first afternoon that Granny had shown you the spare room, was the dish of flying saucers. Flying saucers! The very best, most splendiferous sweets of all time. Brightly coloured pockets of melty rice paper, filled with delicious sherbet. Miam-miam!! A handful of them was more precious to you than a handful of pound coins. But Granny had told you that you weren't allowed any until you'd had your dinner. *All* your dinner. And she was making corned beef hash.

Ottila remembers the clandestine meetings the four of you had – you, her, and your cousins, Harry and Lily. Discussing ways to sneak into the spare room without Granny's beady eyes catching you. Ways to get more than one sweet per person per day. But what none of them remember – not Ottila, and not your cousins – is the secret trip you took at half-past eleven at night. Way past everyone's bedtimes. The rush of adrenaline as you pushed open the spare room door, painfully slowly, so that the creak was barely audible. And the feeling as you dipped your fingers into the bowl!!!!!!!!

You took four flying saucers. Not too many, not too few. Just the right amount to assuage that salivating tongue. You tiptoed into the hall and sat on the carpeted stairs, the light from the streetlamp coming in through the window above the front door, casting an orange, UFO glow on the landing. And you popped the first one in your mouth. The sherbet felt so much fizzier when eaten in secret.

Then you ate the rest.

Nobody ever found out what you'd done. For the rest of that summer, you stuck to one sweet per day, after dinner, just like Granny Joyce ordered. But all summer long you felt happy, like life tasted that little bit sweeter now.

So there you go, Mina. Hopefully that's one memory you haven't forgotten. It's a funny one for me to pick, I suppose, because it makes it seem like you enjoy criminal activity, which couldn't be further from the truth. You hate breaking the rules. As long as your personality doesn't change too much after treatment, you'll always be that way. But there is something about that memory that has always felt pure. Like, somehow, those sweets were the one good thing you ever deserved.

Well, all that remains to be said now is that I hope you are okay. I hope it wasn't too awful getting your head electrocuted. I'd tell you I'm scared, but I don't think I am. I feel nothing. Nothing and hopeless. I hate being alive. I hate just about everything to do with it. I hate being such a cliché too: a depressed person who wants to die. There's so much more to mental health than the old 'death wish' trope. But there you go. That's me. Boring.

Getting my brain fried is a chance, however small, of something magic happening. I might never write poetry again, or get a job, or a husband, but at the very least, I might get a mind full of flying saucers.

Be brave, okay? And don't trust everything Dr Lukić tells you. I'm sure he's a con artist.

Mina.

Snapchat to Mina

≡ Teenymeeny 〉

Today

ME

| Good luck with your ECT, Meen. Here's a picture of a pineapple with sunglasses on.

Email from Thales

From: Thales Sanna
To: Ottila McGregor
Date: Mon, 21 April, 2014 at 13:42
Subject: Easter wishes

O,

It was quite a surprise to receive that text message from you.

I hope your sister is doing all right, and that you're all right too. I'm fine. I'm in Greece. Easter is a big deal over here, more so than Christmas, so I took ten days off work, which is basically my holiday entitlement for the entire year, but never mind.

Are you still managing to avoid the drink? I've been doing sort of okay-ish at not over-eating. I managed to lose four kilograms, but I'm sure I've eaten more in the last four days than I have done in the last four weeks. Putting food into someone else's stomach is about the most loving thing you can do for someone in my family, and my family show me *plenty* of affection.

You know how lambs are a symbol of Easter time? The lamb of God, etc.? And you know how cute lambs look, gambolling around in the countryside? Greek people love them too. They like to stick them on a skewer, mouth to anus, and spit-roast them. Yesterday we skewered two lambs and ate about three deli-counters' worth of meat in one sitting. More stylish than a chocolate egg, no?

There's another Easter tradition here where you bash eggs together, a bit like conkers. It's called τσούγκρισμα. Last night we hard-boiled a load of eggs and then dyed them. They're meant to be red to represent Jesus's blood, but we do them in all sorts of colours. My sister, Reatha, dyed her eggs baby pink and I made fun of her. Can't help regressing to a childlike state when I'm around family. The rules of the game are that you touch eggs with someone else, pointy ends together, then you crack them against one another. If your egg doesn't break, you win. The 'prize' is that you get to eat the other person's broken egg. Which is a form of torture after all that lamb. Plus, the eggs take on some of the colour of the dye too, so you're eating RED EGGS.

It's nice to see my grandparents here though. I only get to see them once a year, so they really spoil me. I mean, Yiayia doesn't recognise me most of the time, but Papou is well. He keeps himself healthy working on his garden, growing aubergines and vines. He says his heart is powered by olive oil and he'll go on forever. I once mentioned to him that our English equivalent, rapeseed oil, has less fat and just as many nutrients as his precious ελαιόλαδο, and his expression was so sharp it nearly killed me.

It's funny actually, when I come here I feel more Greek, somehow. Even though I was born in Coventry and my Greek gets rustier with each passing year, I still feel quite at home in my parents' country. I have to remember to pronounce my name the other way though, the Greek way. I feel like I've got two identities. The Ancient Greek philosopher Thales was supposedly asked what the most difficult thing in the world was, and he replied: 'to know thyself'. The main thing that I know is that the Greek me is more abrupt, eats a lot, and says everything is εντάξει (meaning okay). Mainly he eats a lot. I bet you've never heard me go on about food so much. When we were together, I was trying to hide that side of myself from you. I told you about the painkillers, but I think I'm even more embarrassed about the food. It'll probably come as no surprise to you to hear that I struggled with an eating disorder when I was younger. I don't make myself sick, not any more, but I do still binge. If I was a character on The Sims I suppose one of my three defining lifestyle traits would be 'glutton'.

What I'm coming around to saying, in the most repulsive way possible, is: if all this stuff hasn't caused you to puke up all over your laptop screen, then yes, in answer to your text, let's *think about* trying to make things work. I don't know if we can manage it just now, or if we're both too fragile, but let's keep the doors of communication open. I haven't been with anyone else since we broke up. I don't really care if you have; I don't get jealous about that sort of thing. Like I said, relationships aren't about owning someone. That said - if you *have* been with someone else, DON'T TELL ME ABOUT IT.

It has been good for me, having a bit of space to clear my head. I hadn't really had a chance to do that after I broke up with my ex-girlfriend in January, just before you and I got together, and this time apart has enabled me to process the end of that relationship. I think being in Greece has helped me with that to some extent. She and I were meant to be coming here together, on this trip, and it feels like closure being here. I'm sorry. I'll stop talking about my ex now. I ended things with *her* if that counts for anything. Something my parents won't let me forget. Look at me, telling you not to tell me about your past lovers, while I tell you about mine. Forget exes. This is about you and me.

I might go for a walk later. There's a little church along the seafront in Αυλάκι. It's full of icons of Mary and Jesus, which, over the years, people have worn away with kisses. I might go and get in on the action. I want some time to myself, really badly. First though, Dad wants to play Yahtzee. Last time we played it he threw a chair at the wall. Greek people are cool. They'll be starting on the beer soon. My grandfather likes to drink Amstel because he says it's a 'good, Greek beer'. I don't have the heart to correct him. I had some beer yesterday, as it happens. When I started going out with you, I decided I was going to quit drinking forever. And you know what? I found it really easy to stop. I've never been much of a drinker. Until things got a bit heated last night and I had half a can. The first mouthful was okay, but then almost immediately, I felt sick. You and I aren't together any more, so I didn't feel like I'd betrayed you exactly, but I felt like I'd betrayed myself. I'm probably just a big drip.

Well, if you're into hanging out with drips, I'll text you when I'm back. We can time our breaks to coincide and I'll sneak us coffees to drink while we walk around the block. Or, if you regret sending your text and want to go back to being 'friends' but not actually talking, we can do that too. Either way, it's εντάξει (okay). That's what the Greek Θαλής thinks about it anyway.

T

Pleasure only starts once the worm has got into the fruit; to become delightful, happiness must be tainted with poison.

Georges Bataille

Old Letter from Mina

[*This letter has been written on A4 lined paper, narrow rule. At the top of the first page is a puffy sticker of a bear in an aeroplane with googly eyes and Mina has drawn a speech bubble coming out of its mouth saying 'Hello!!!'*]

2 October 2006

Dear Dolphin-face,

Remember the old puffy stickers we used to have? The ones we stuck onto the sides of the Sylvanian boxes, which smelt of bananas when you scratched them? Even the unscented puffy stickers have a childhood smell, which I like.

How doth thou do? It must be exciting living in Scotland now. It's where Dad's ancestors were from, before they sailed off to Scandinavia. Do you feel weirdly at home? I hope you are enjoying yourself. It's funny we're both doing Creative Writing Masters at the same time. How about that? Twinny-twin-twins. Brontë sisters!!!

I just got some photos back and I look like a fat lump in them. I'm sending one of the better ones. [*This photo is missing from the envelope.*] You know what the others were like if I mention Miss Stairway Face. Double-chin ahoy! I hardly fit into any of my jeans because of this damned tablet business. I feel horrid. But I don't look as big as I feel, nor as big as my clothes tell me I am. At least I'm not producing breast milk any more and the blood blisters in my mouth have almost cleared up.

I'm finding my way around here OK. There's a café in Coventry called The Tin Angel. It has an open mic night for poets on the first Monday of every month. I might go along sometime, but not today because I am too anxious. I haven't been to the union yet either because of the queues. Too many people for little, wizened old me! Have you found the postgraduate bar yet?

I hope you settle down OK on your course. I am worried about you. You are so far away from us all. Have a rainbow. [*Rainbow sticker.*] But I'm glad to hear you've started seeing someone you like. Didn't take you long! And a girl as well! Snark snark!!! What would Mum and Dad say? They probably wouldn't bat an eyelid in all honesty. But anyway, she sounds nice. Reatha is a lovely name. Very swish. And she goes to art school. Exciting! I hope you are happy together.

Time to go and work on my poetry essay. Take care, cheeky-face. Remember that I love you. ALWAYS. Lots of slurpy snogs!!

Mina. x x

Google Search History

7:31 PM

Searched for: Is it okay to date siblings?
Top Answer: Having sex with your half-brother is illegal in most states.

Searched for: How common is the name Reatha?
Top Answer: The name Reatha peaked in popularity in 1937. It was given to five baby girls in 1960. Nowadays it is the 7,574th most popular name in the US (where 5,163 names are in current common usage). South Carolina has the most people named Reatha per capita. There are no men with the name Reatha. 94% of people named Reatha are over fifty-five. Six people in every ten million in New Mexico are called Reatha. According to our algorithm, this is a **highly atypical female name**.

Searched for: How common is the name Reatha among Greek people?
Top Answer: This name does not appear in the Top 100 Greek names. Less than 0.16% of Greek females have this name.

Searched for: "Reatha Sanna"
Answer: There are approximately 12 persons in the US with this name.

Search 5: "Reatha Sanna" UK
Answer: No results found for **"reatha sanna" uk**.

The Kiss

Thales is standing outside the Outpatients entrance, holding a paper cup in each hand. He looks tanned from his week and a half in Greece. I have to stop myself smiling too widely when I see him, so I raise a palm and nod solemnly, biting the insides of my cheeks.

I've decided not to mention Reatha. Not yet. I know it's a rare name, but it seems so unlikely that my Reatha really is the same Reatha as his Reatha. Besides, I'm *sure* she said her surname was Mavros, not Sanna. And there's no worse time to bring up something like this than when you're trying to get back together with someone. I'm giving it a month. Ten months. A lifetime. The old Reatha, my Reatha, never liked family stuff anyway. Chances are she'd never want to meet me.

'Ayup, cool dude,' Thales says, handing me a coffee. 'I thought we could walk to Burton Road and get ourselves a couple of vanilla slices each. Great plan, no?'

We make our way out of one of the lesser-known exits of the hospital, walking around the side way, trying to avoid both our bosses, for different reasons. 'How is it to be back in rainy old Manchester?' I ask. Weather chat: he's right about me being a cool dude.

'I stepped in a puddle and my trousers managed to suck up water all the way to my knees this morning. I'm going to start wearing shorts to work, I think. Or get those trousers you can unzip around the thighs.'

'Good to be back, then?'

'Idyllic.'

We head onto Palatine Road and I take a sip of my coffee as I negotiate the wet pavements. 'This tastes strong.'

'I had to make it black; Kerrie would have seen me adding milk.'

'So you stole these for us?' My voice comes out a little high-pitched.

'Technically, yes. In practice, no. Kerrie does it all the time for herself. She just doesn't tell anyone else they can do it.'

'Well, it's very nice,' I say, wiping the corners of my lips, where tarlike dots are no doubt collecting. 'Thank you.' We walk down the street in silence for a while. I listen to the sound of Thales's coat brushing against his trousers. I once read something about how heartbeats can synchronise among loved ones. There was a test carried out in this Spanish village, where participants and spectators at an annual fire-walking ritual were hooked up to heart-rate monitors. When a loved one walked over hot coals, their close friends' and family's heartbeats all synchronised with the fire-walker. Maybe my heart is beating in time with Thales's as we walk over these puddles.

'I was listening to a piece on Klimt in the staff room this morning,' says Thales, 'on the radio.'

'It wasn't on the Steve Wright show, was it?' I choose not to beat myself up for bringing up Steve Wright instead of focusing on Gustav Klimt. It's okay to do that sort of thing around Thales. He doesn't judge. Not like Ben. Why am I thinking about Ben?

'No, thank god,' Thales replies. 'Jim was off so I got to choose the station. Radio Four all the way.'

'So what did you learn?'

'Klimt didn't make his most famous painting, "The Kiss", until he was in his forties. He was inspired by the Byzantine mosaics of Italy. All that gold leaf sparked something within him.'

'I always think of his name as Gustav Glimt, because his paintings glimmer so much,' I contribute. At least I'm not still going on about Steve Wright.

'I was thinking that means I've still got time.'

'Time for what?'

'My films.'

'*Tractor Boy* and *Inanimate Objects*?'

Thales blushes. We reach the Burton Road Bakery. He turns to face me in a ridiculously serious way and I laugh.

'I mean it, Ottila. I'm going to really try with my films from now on.'

'And I'm going to do some sort of outstanding, disturbing, one-woman show about my life's struggles,' I say, catching Thales's enthusiasm like it's a disease. 'Let's not just settle for being happy. Let's get bloody famous. Fuck what anyone else thinks.'

Thales whoops and throws his arms around me and we embrace in the street. He holds me so close I can smell him, a sort of clove and nutmeg scent that tells me I'll never get into any trouble while it's nearby. It's probably just deodorant, but I like to think it's pheromones. It feels exactly right to hold my body close to Thales's again, and I know that being together like this is nothing short of art. I can feel the brick walls and pavements around us turn to solid gold, this glittering embrace surely worth thousands of crowns to any curator. Thales and I *will* make it work. Our future is written in the stars.

'Eep, it's raining again,' he says, untangling his arms from me and giving me a quick, shy peck on the cheek. 'Let's go inside and get those vanilla slices, friend.'

One joy scatters a hundred griefs.

Chinese Proverb

Recovery Meeting Transcript

PATIENT: I kept Listerine in my mouth for half an hour before spitting it out this morning.

THERAPIST: You could feel the alcohol content?

PATIENT: It's almost 27 per cent proof. The same as Blue Curaçao or a crème de cacao. It's stronger than Kahlúa. Half a pint of Listerine would send me under the table. Probably a quarter of a pint.

THERAPIST: You can buy mouthwash without alcohol in. There's a Total Care one, which doesn't have any–

PATIENT: I like the sting. It makes me feel clean.

THERAPIST: You can still absorb some of the alcohol sublingually, through your mucous membranes.

PATIENT: You can put it on a tampon too. Insert it into you.

THERAPIST: Have you done that?

PATIENT: No. [*Pause.*] Once. Not since I quit drinking. I did it about a year and a half ago. I worked in a bookshop back then. Put one in first thing in the morning. Thought it might make selling endless copies of *Fifty Shades of Grey* more bearable. A nice, wet, vodka-soaked 'sex', as E.L. James would say. It had nothing to do with the tampon scene in *Fifty Shades*. It was just a way of trying to hide the stench of vodka from my breath.

THERAPIST: Did it work?

PATIENT: I put the tampon in a glass of vodka and it swelled up so big that I could barely squeeze it in. Then it hurt. A lot.

THERAPIST: I take it you only did it the once.

PATIENT: Yeah, it killed all the bacteria and gave me thrush.

THERAPIST: Well, it certainly sounds unsafe.

PATIENT: So I added some garlic.

THERAPIST: You put garlic in your vagina?

PATIENT: To kill the yeast. It's really weird: a few seconds after you put it up there, you can taste it. I think that's when it enters your bloodstream. It doesn't work, though. Well, it didn't for me. Just gave me bad breath.

THERAPIST: So what happened with the Listerine?

PATIENT: Tea-tree oil didn't work either. [*Pause.*] Well, in the end, I spat the Listerine out.

THERAPIST: Does that mean you still haven't had any alcohol?

PATIENT: No. I mean yes. I'll spit it out sooner next time.

THERAPIST: Do you think you'd like to give a support group a go?

PATIENT: I don't know. I don't think it's for me.

THERAPIST: There are some very good ones around here. At the Brian Hore Unit, for example. We can refer you–

PATIENT: I tried going to a group last week, the day Mina started her ECT. It was in the Methodist Church. I didn't tell you about it because I was embarrassed.

THERAPIST: Why were you embarrassed to tell me about it? Going to a support group is something to be proud of.

PATIENT: I'm embarrassed because I walked out after twenty minutes.

THERAPIST: How come? Did it make you uncomfortable?

PATIENT: There are so many people out there who are more deserving than I am. Some of the people there, they've had the hardest times. There was this one man whose wife used to beat him with a broom; a woman whose stepfather sexually abused her kids; a girl who was a heroin addict from the age of fourteen, who was on a methadone programme and had never even learnt to read and write. And then there was me, Ottila, an ex-grammar school girl with a university education, and a penchant for too much wine and whisky.

THERAPIST: So you think that in order to be an addict, you need to have gone through some hard times? Even if that was true, which it isn't, you've had to deal with some challenges. Your father died a few years ago. Your sister has a disability.

PATIENT: Everyone has something. There are people far worse off than me, who are into smoothies and reiki, creating JustGiving pages for all the marathons they're running and heads they're shaving to raise thousands of pounds for charity.

THERAPIST: But you're *you*, Ottila. Part of the process of recovery is about accepting that and learning to love yourself.

PATIENT: I worry that I turned out like this because I didn't try hard enough.

THERAPIST: You were drinking over a hundred units of alcohol a week this time last year. You haven't had a drink in over three months. That sounds like trying to me.

PATIENT: Sometimes I feel like I just invented you to say nice things to me.

THERAPIST: Is that a joke or a delusion?

PATIENT: I'm not delusional. I think Grace is. She confided to me that her side hurts, where her liver is, you know, the place you say I always touch when I'm feeling guilty, and then she keeps on drinking, like nothing is the matter.

THERAPIST: She needs to find her own path to recovery. All you can do is advise and support her.

PATIENT: You know what? I don't want to. I came so close to having a drink while I was in the pub with her. That's one of the reasons I went to the group, to get my head straight. And that's why I felt guilty. Because it wasn't my violent wife or sexually-abusive stepfather who was threatening to derail me. It was my daft best friend.

THERAPIST: I promise you, Ottila, you are by no means alone on that one.

PATIENT: Friends, eh? Never mind. I won't be seeing her again. It's healthy relationships from here on in. Starting with a healthy relationship with myself.

THERAPIST: That's excellent news. And you can always try another group if–

PATIENT: I think Thales and I are getting back together.

THERAPIST: Oh, okay. Well, great. As long as you're looking after yourself. That's the main thing.

PATIENT: I think we're soulmates. He sent me an email telling me this thing about eggs in Greece, and I've been thinking about eggs lately too – good ones and bad ones.

THERAPIST: What?

PATIENT: Oh, nothing. It's going well, anyway. Except that I've been having these daydreams, like sudden visions of the future, and I keep seeing the same thing: Thales leaving me. I've been pushing nice men away from me since my dad died, in case I lose them like I lost him. I don't know. [*Guttural noise.*] I'm trying not to think about it.

THERAPIST: As long as you're not avoiding facing up to anything.

PATIENT: Of course not.

Little Book of Happy

Dear oh dear,

Normally the Tuesday morning 'Locust to Lotus' yoga class is the highlight of my working week. Delyth (she's from Swansea, has purple hair, edits a women's fishing magazine) runs the sessions and lets me join in. Doing yoga isn't within my job remit, strictly speaking, but I'm sure part of my role at Maggie's includes contributing to morale within the centre, and my chaotic postures usually raise a few smiles.

Today I was firming my buttocks, lengthening my back legs and preparing to strike the Sea Monster pose, when who should walk in but André. I mean, sure, he's the boss, so it's not *that* unusual that he should be striding into a room within his own workplace – it's just that he's never normally in before ten, so this is the first time he's ever caught me skiving.

I tried to act nonchalant, like maybe I was doing some secret, undercover Marketing and Communications research, but it's difficult to achieve nonchalance while doing a backbend. I kept my eyes on Delyth as I heard André's footsteps walking up behind me. He was so close I could smell his cologne: a smell that transported me right back to our first 'date', outside the Endocrine Unit in Department 63, and I remembered that first time he'd bent down to kiss me. How bad it felt, and how good that made it seem.

But this morning, while I was lying on my belly with my boss standing over me, everything just felt plain bad.

Delyth, professional as ever, made nothing of the fact André was lurking. Besides, even though we've had some great chats in the kitchen about tungsten putty and the fickle feeding habits of carp, Delyth has no idea about André and me, so it's not like she was bothered that the boss was present. She just told us to get in to partners, to feel how well the muscles in the backs of our arms were working.

'Partner A needs to straddle Partner B,' she said, in that lovely, lilting accent of hers.

I continued to lie on the floor, my cheeks reddening, while André's feet came closer. I didn't dare look up, but I could tell his brogues were either side of me.

'Partner A: lean forwards, pressing your hands firmly against your partner's triceps,' Delyth continued. 'That's it. Let them know how good their locust is.'

André's bony hands began to press down on the backs of my arms, and then I felt his breath on my cheek. 'I know what you've been doing, little locust,' he whispered into my ear. 'I know that your *girl*friend is actually that spotty blubber-guts from the canteen. I saw you with your vanilla slices.' His arms gripped me harder, too hard, and then he let go.

Actually, Thales isn't spotty at all – I'm the one with the acne problem. Obviously, I didn't argue this point. I lay on my stomach, and listened to André's shoes striding towards his office. Then I hooked my fingers under the base of my skull, transforming into a Sea Monster.

Speaking of monsters, even though Thales and I have started hanging out again, I keep thinking about Ben. I don't wish I was with Ben instead of Thales or anything, it's just . . . mental pictures. Running into him at the climbing centre like that brought back a lot of memories. How he'd lift me up with his strong arms the moment he came into my flat. How I'd wrap my legs around him. How we'd put on that Spotify playlist, 'Hip Hop Songs that Make You Wanna Break Stuff', and we'd drink beer and stick things into each other until we collapsed. He was so disgusting. I wish I could stop thinking about him.

I wish I could stop worrying about Reatha too. Worrying about Reatha is also making me remember *her* sexually. How much my body used to yearn for hers. How we'd spend hours drawing each other sprawled on the bed naked and I'd lick squirty cream out of her softest parts. I loved her so much.

I need to get a grip. Thales and I are about to commit to each other again and, this time, I don't want it to fail. We're going to the Cornerhouse to see a film about artificial intelligence tonight. If he kisses me on the lips, I think I'll cry.

Please don't hate me, LBOH.

From the little locust

Email to Delyth

From: Ottila McGregor
To: Delyth Hughes
Date: Wed, 30 April, 2014 at 23:12
Subject: probably the most awkward email you've ever had

Hi Delyth,

I just wondered if you fancy hanging out and going for a coffee or herbal tea together sometime, outside of work? I don't mean as a date if that's what you're thinking, although I'm sure you would be very lovely to date (shut up, Ottila). Actually I'm kind of dating the hot Greek guy from the cafeteria. Well, we're in the process of getting back together after a brief break-up. That said, we went to the cinema to see *Transcendence* last night and we didn't so much as taste each other's popcorn. Is this TMI???

If you fancy having that cuppa, I can fill you in on all my gossip. I hate the word gossip. But maybe you like it. If you do, that's obviously okay by me. My gossip is really boring but, on the plus side, I'm a chronic over-sharer, so chances are you'll find out some terrible secret about me that will make up for all the stories about popcorn-touching that you'll inevitably have to sit through.

Oh god, why is trying to make friends so awkward when you're a grown-up?

Please excuse the weird formality of me contacting you via work email like this, rather than just talking to you in person, but I figured this way you'd get the chance to think of an excuse to get out of it, whereas if I ask you face-to-face you might feel trapped.

Hope your candlelit yoga session goes well this afternoon,

Ottila

Email from Mum

From: Alice McGregor
To: Ottila McGregor
Date: Thurs, 1 May, 2014 at 16:36
Subject: Mayday! Mayday!

Sweetheart,

Mina had her fourth session of ECT today. So far it doesn't seem to be making a jot of difference. Except by slowly turning her brain into a fried egg. You should see her when she first wakes up after it's done. It's terrifying. I'm starting to feel like I only agreed to the whole bloody thing because Dr Lukić charmed me with his good looks. I'd say more on the subject but I'm trying to put my negative thoughts on a 'shelf' whenever I'm at home, to try and keep the house a positive space. So I'm having a glass of wine and putting my feet up.

Very intrigued to hear about this Greek chap you mentioned in your last email. However: proceed with caution! Hellenic men are extremely passionate and likely to want to move the relationship along very quickly. Be careful and don't do anything I wouldn't do!

Who am I kidding? I was engaged to a Greek guy before your father. That's how I know these things. Come to think of it, he wasn't Greek at all. He was Turkish. Ah well, close enough. I'm sure the Greek and Turkish people would be the first to admit that they are very similar when it comes to love. Liable to whisk you off to a beach in Santorini, ply you with ouzo, and then propose to you beside the active crater of a volcano. You'll be so swept away that you'll jump into a yellow lake, and you'll do things in there that tourists really shouldn't do during a self-catering fortnight with a complete stranger. I don't think I ever told you about Berk (that was his name!) but we only stayed engaged for the second week of the holiday. He was a snorkelling instructor, and I bumped into at least three goggled women on that trip who told me they were recently engaged. I don't know for sure that Berk was the culprit, but I saw sense before I got on the plane home and gave him back his great-grandmother's nickel-plated, diamanté ring. Haha! See, your old mama hasn't always been the Sensible Sarah you thought. Anyway, what I'm saying, love, is: take it slowly. It's for the best IN THE LONG RUN.

GOSH, I'VE JUST SPILT RED WINE ONTO MY LAPTOP AND DON'T SEEM TO BE ABLE TO GET CAPS LOCK OFF. SORRY IF IT LOOKS LIKE I'M SHOUTING. PROMISE I'M NOT!

RIGHTY-HO, I'M OFF FOR A HAIRCUT NOW. THINKING ABOUT GOING FOR A RESTYLE. I WANT TO BE COMPLETELY UNRECOGNISABLE WHEN THEY'RE DONE.

OH, AND I'M GOING TO PO NA NA TONIGHT WITH A GROUP OF GIRLS I MET AT THE DEATH CAFÉ. THEY'RE UNDERGRADUATE STUDENTS, WOULD YOU BELIEVE, STUDYING PHILOSOPHY AND SOMETHING OR OTHER, AT BATH SPA UNIVERSITY. DON'T KNOW WHY THEY WANT TO HANG AROUND WITH A FOGEY LIKE ME, BUT HEY HO. I HAVEN'T BEEN CLUBBING FOR OVER A QUARTER OF A CENTURY. BEEN LISTENING TO RADIO ONE ALL AFTERNOON TO GET IN THE GROOVE.

HAPPY MAYDAY!

LOVE MUM XOXOXO

Snapchat from Mina

Today

TEENYMEENY

| My brain feels weird, like it's wet. Could you ask Mum to ask the doctor if there's any way some water could have got into it? Also, what's your middle name? I'm forgetting everything and I don't like it. :<

Email to Mum

From: Ottila McGregor
To: Alice McGregor
Date: Sun, 4 May, 2014 at 16:22
Subject: Re: Mayday! Mayday!

Hi Mum,

I'm sure Dr Lukić knows what he is doing. Maybe four sessions is too early to tell. There might be something magical that happens after four sessions and Mina's brain will gush out a load of happy chemicals all of a sudden, and we'll be so relieved she had the treatment. Let's wait a little longer.

I'm worried about you, Mum. I know you're always telling me *not* to worry, and I can hear Granny Joyce's voice singing the old Bobby McFerrin tune, but in this instance I can't help it. When you went missing after Dad died, I never asked you where you'd gone because I didn't want to upset you. I *was* worried though. Worried sick. I nearly called the police several times, but I knew you were alive because you left your inbox open on your laptop and I could see you answering work emails, polite and bubbly as ever. It didn't make sense. I was so confused. I'd hate to have to miss you like that again. I couldn't bear it.

Are you sure hanging around with those undergraduates is a good idea? They're very young. They haven't even had their first smear test yet! Imagine that while you're on the dance floor, busting shapes to 'Shiny Disco Balls' by Scotty Boy featuring Sue Cho. They've never even felt the icy twinge of a speculum.

It's nice to hear about your past before Dad. Berk sounds like an exciting guy, albeit an absolute rogue. It's reassuring to know that I'm not the only one attracted to the dark side, now and then.

But don't go too far into the darkness, Mum. Please. I need you.

Love Ottila xxx

P. S. I've sent you some seeds. The days are starting to get brighter now, which made me think of you.

Page 32 of my Notebook

30 Things from the Day You Turned 30

1. swan with one leg
2. exhibition on the history of Alexandra Park
3. homemade lemonade
4. calypso drums (yippee!!!)
5. man with his face painted like a painting of a face
6. ostrich burgers
7. your thumbnail painted red with my nail varnish
8. bicycle-powered cinema among the trees
9. the first seven minutes of *Mr Peabody and Sherman*
10. sulphur tuft mushrooms (your diagnosis) on a fallen tree
11. a winning scratch card (£2 prize)
12. three non-winning scratch cards (£1 each)
13. 'the world's worst cappuccino'
14. three identical china dogs in one charity shop
15. your winkled nose, when we smelt that perfume
16. a group of toddlers in fluorescent jackets with 'pedestrian training' on their backs
17. the house with the tomato plant in the garden (a.k.a. 'dream house')
18. two whole blocks when we managed to walk in time with each other's footsteps
19. woman with three buttocks (?)
20. the inspired purchase of some gherkin seeds
21. the shop where everything for sale is French
22. raw chocolate at the Unicorn deli
23. Cornish Yaaaaaaarg
24. fish and chips on the grass
25. a Google document entitled 'plans for the future'
26. 'become a member of a political party'
27. 'family'
28. our first kiss in nearly two months (finally! look at us making it work, for realz)
29. three episodes of Arrested Development
30. saliva trail on your left sleeve, discovered upon my waking

Email from Delyth

From: Delyth Hughes
To: Ottila McGregor
Date: Sun, 11 May, 2014 at 15:06
Subject: Re: probably the most awkward email you've ever had

Matey, sorry it's taken a couple of weeks to get back to you. Been rushing to get the latest issue of *Reel Women* ready for print. I'll leave a copy in your pigeon hole when it's back from the printers. There's a double-page spread on in-line carp rig safety. It's lush, you'll love it. Sorry too I had to rush off after yoga the other morning and didn't get a chance to chat. Your Lotus is really coming on for what it's worth.

Going for a coffee sounds fabby dabby. Let's go to the Spoon Inn in Chorlton. I made the mistake of trying out the new Costa the other day and it was *erchyll*! That's Welsh for bogging.

I've stopped doing those candlelit yoga sessions. Gene had a mild seizure (she's fine) and we almost set the place on fire. André's pissed off because there's nothing running at the centre on Wednesday afternoons now, but I've got shit to do, and I'm only a part-timer, though you wouldn't believe it with my hours. You see, lady, we're both brimming with exciting gossip.

Throw me a text on 07881445640 and we'll meet for coffee asap. In fact, you're not around this afternoon, are you?

Chi blessings, Delyth x

Portrait of Delyth

[We went out for a cup of coffee and I'm feeling exhilarated. Delyth is my new best friend.]

sometimes actually says some of the stuff people say on Gavin and Stacey

Likes Victorian style shirts with high collars

surprisingly muscly

goes on fishing retreats with her mum once a year; caught an 80 pound blue catfish in Virginia, which is apparently not even close to a world record

drinks five cups of coffee a day and says caffeine is an antidepressant for her

Wears velvet like a boss

believes that women should harness the special power in their yonis

Email from Mum

From: Alice McGregor
To: Ottila McGregor
Date: Mon, 12 May, 2014 at 12:36
Subject: Dangerous to Continue

Sweetie-pie,

The gherkin seeds are really thoughtful. I've put them in a propagator in the kitchen, and hope to move them outside in a couple of weeks once they've germinated. We've actually been really lucky with the weather lately. My astrantias are flowering early this year. They're the Hadspen Blood variety, and the garden is lit up with bright spatters of deep red. It's most beautiful.

I'm afraid I've got some bad news. Dr Lukić says Mina won't be receiving any more ECT. The doc and I had a meeting about it today. She's had six sessions, and unfortunately she doesn't seem to be responding. If anything, it's making her worse. I asked the doctor if there's any way we could try one more, for the road, and he told me there wasn't. 'It would be dangerous to continue with the treatment,' he said. 'It's time for you to find a source of hope elsewhere, Mrs McGregor.'

I've been making mental lists of all the things I'm grateful for. Mina is alive. You're doing well. My keyboard fixed itself once the wine evaporated, so I don't have to shout-type any more. Gosh, I'd love to shout. Just drive out to a corn field in the middle of nowhere, and really let go. Know what I mean?

I've attached a picture of my new hair. I went for something bold and asked for a mullet. What do you think? Jean Paul Gaultier sent his models down the catwalk wearing mullet wigs at Paris Fashion Week. My hairdresser says they're all the rage. Do I look like a young Suzi Quatro to you, or merely an old Ron Wood?

Tonight I'm going out on the town with the girls again. I must have done something right the last time! And darling, I completely understand what you mean about how very young they are, but honestly, they're a real laugh. It's liberating to be around people with no responsibilities once in a while. I'll behave myself, I promise. I won't even drink that much. I'll just dance till I drop. Do you remember how your father used to refuse to dance with me? Never mind two left feet, he was just stubborn! I swear I saw him wiggling his hips to the 'Just a Minute' theme tune one day in the kitchen when he thought I wasn't looking. Anyway, no need to worry about me. I'm just trying to keep myself busy. Keep that positivity flowing forth. Maybe I should retire from my retirement. Go back to work.

Thanks for the call on Thales's birthday. It was strange to speak to him! I hope he doesn't think I sound too silly. I'm not very good on the phone. Sounds like you had a wonderful day together. You know, tomato plants are remarkably easy to cultivate. You can grow them on your windowsill. You could have that dream house of yours before you know it.

Love from your grizzled old Mama xoxoxo

Email to Mum

From: Ottila McGregor
To: Alice McGregor
Date: Tues, 13 May, 2014 at 7:50
Subject: Re: Dangerous to Continue

Mum,

I don't think it would help if you got a job. You're retired, for goodness' sake! You've planned enough Bar Mitzvahs and corporate Christmas parties to last a lifetime. Why don't you take up an adult education class in something you're interested in? This whittling class looks good: http://www.adultlearningwiltshire. org.uk/index.php/arts-and-crafts/knife-carving-techniques. Do you like whittling? How about yoga: http://www.yoga4u.com/ stressbustingpostures?

Sorry to hear about Mina. I wish there was more we could do.

Love the new hair. You look like yourself: vibrant and brave.

Ottila x

Text Message from Delyth

Tue 13 May 12:44
P'nawn da! Here's a link to that thing I was rabbiting on about the other day: http://www.artsgrantsinc.co.uk. My friend Tami got £4,000+ for her photo exhibition. Better than a slap in the face. Your matey boy might want to apply too? x

Ottila's Proposal, First Draft

Name of Activity
~~Closing Time~~ / ~~A Dummy's Guide to Drink~~ / ~~How to Be an Alcoholic Writer~~ /Cheers / ~~The Devil's Drink~~ / ~~Bottoms Up~~ / ~~Drink: An Idiot's Guide~~

Start Date
TBC

Amount Requested
£6,023 [Be exact. Helps them think you have a budget.]

Proposal
~~My name's Ottila McGregor, and I'm an ale~~
~~Every year, thousands of people die from~~
~~I'm desperate for a~~
I have a problem with drink. My uncle has a problem with drink. The woman who works in the key cutters on Wilbraham Road *clearly* has a problem with drink. [Is this libellous?] ~~We all, in some way, have a problem with drink.~~

My name's Ottila, and I've been alcohol-free for a quarter of a year. I've achieved this through counselling sessions with the community alcohol team, a psychologist and two small white tablets, taken three times a day. I've also been focusing on things other than alcohol: spending time with my partner [make sure we're officially together before sending this off]; finding new friends; walking home from work the long way; thinking about starting an exercise class [go to a class, lard-arse].

Despite focusing my attention elsewhere, however, I would now like to devote all my time to thinking about nothing *but* drinking. [Is this dangerous?] I want to plumb the depths of this terrible affliction and figure out what drove me to drink in the first place. I will present my findings in the form of a one-hour, one-woman show, using spreadsheets, pie charts, a Powerpoint presentation and plenty of dark humour. Throughout the show, I will top up audience members' glasses with wine, encouraging them to drink freely.

At the end of the show, I will invite the audience to pour any of their remaining drinks into a bucket, which will have been sitting centre-stage throughout the performance. I will then, in one final act of defiance, ~~pour the bucket over my head~~ drink the entire contents of the bucket.

[What brand of wine shall I give out during the show? Choose sth. cheap but tasty.]

[Should I give people whisky instead?]

Your Experience
Although I have never performed a one-woman show before, I *have* abused alcohol, which I feel has prepared me to undertake this work. I have a Masters degree in Creative Writing, which has also proved incredibly useful in fuelling my drink habit, so I feel further prepared for the role.

Management and Finance
I will require a six-month Research and Development phase for this theatrical piece, and will use the money from Arts Grants Inc. to pay myself a wage throughout this period.

Given that I am not a professional, I would like to perform the show for free.

[Something about how I came up with my budget. Could the £6,000 be for me and the £23 be for a bucket? Check Argos for expensive buckets.]

Partnerships
I have not yet approached any venues, but I did see a girl at The Lowry Theatre doing a show about her struggles with cocaine last year, and quite a lot of people went to see it, so I feel that there is an audience for this sort of thing. In many ways, it has already been done before.

Mantra of the Week

Om Eim Saraswatyei Swaha

Rough translation: Greetings to the feminine energy associated with artistic and academic endeavour, which is connected to the seed sound *Eim*.

Email from Thales

From:	Thales Sanna
To:	Ottila McGregor
Date:	Thurs, 15 May, 2014 at 16:13
Subject:	T minus far too many minutes

Work is going very, very slowly today. I am writing this to you while hiding in a toilet cubicle, avoiding having to engage in the mephitic art of conversation with my line manager. Just because Jim smokes he's allowed to take extra breaks, so I figure an extra pretend poo here and there is the least I should be allowed. Kerrie has asked me if I need some Imodium though, so I probably shouldn't keep this up forever.

Thanks for sending the information about grant applications. Unfortunately, it looks like they don't fund films, but you inspired me to look online and find out who does. I feel like such a fool for brimming with élan after listening to that Klimt documentary on the radio a couple of weeks ago. Every time I've sat down to work on my script since then, I've felt sick. I've lost a lot of confidence in my work lately and maybe something like this would help rekindle my self-belief.

Wish I was doing something with you right now! It'd be cool to go back to Manchester Museum sometime. I'd love to hold your hand while looking at mineralogical material. I know we still haven't properly defined what we are to each other yet, you and me, but really, I'm feeling so strongly that being with you is the best thing that has ever happened to me. Even better than *Tractor Boy* getting shown at the Keswick Film Festival. Even better than the mushroom-picking course I did. Seriously. I would trade knowing that the *Amanita muscaria* is a poisonous psychoactive basidiomycete fungus for a date with you any day. Even if I had to go and live in the wilderness and this lack of knowledge would kill me.

I've been telling myself to hold back, to take things slowly, but what say you and I take things to the next level? Ottila: would you like to be my girlfriend? I will ask you this again in person when I'm not sitting on the loo.

I hope Mina's all right by the way. Giving up on the ECT must be tough. I found this interesting-looking book on Amazon called *Aspergirls*, which is about how to empower women with Asperger's. I was thinking we could read it together, or even send Mina a copy if she's able to read it? Maybe that's a doltish idea. You're probably tired of reading that kind of thing.

Hey, I know you're interested in festivals, like Burns Night and Lupercalia, which we so successfully celebrated this year, and I heard about a new festival today which I reckon you might be into. Drum roll . . . the World Marbles Championship! It's held in a pub car park in West Sussex every year. We've just missed this year's unfortunately, but why don't we get ourselves a bag of shooters from The Entertainer and start practising for next year's competition? When we get really good at it, we can start buying artisanal marbles. These ones have ACTUAL SCARABS AND STINK BUGS encased inside them: http://www.specialistmarbles. com/bugsinlucite. I could even pop to the Arndale Centre after work and get us a cheap bag o' taws tonight. What do you reckon? Fancy rolling glass orbs with me?

Right, time to go and talk to Kerrie about her favourite pair of curtains in the new Argos catalogue for the remaining 78 minutes of my working day.

Your friend / belching basilisk, T x

Text Message to Thales

Thu 15 May 16:52

Lovely email. You are lovely. I was thinking, though, that I'd like to do some work on my one-woman show tonight. I'm trying to harness the creative power deep within my yoni. See you in a few days?

Little Book of Happy

Dear Little Book of Hear-me-out-before-you-judge-me-please,

I didn't manage to say no to a date with Thales for long. Half an hour after I sent that text, I buckled. We didn't get round to playing marbles, but I said yes to becoming his girlfriend and then I sort of (completely) moved in with him.

I know what you're thinking, LBOH! But suck it up. I'm in love. And Thales Alessandro Sanna loves me too. I've mentioned it before: oxytocin. It makes me do the craziest things. Amazingly, *he* suggested it. I'd offered to cook a lasagne and take it to his, and he replied saying, 'Why don't I cook it while you bring all your stuff over?' Moments later there was a second text: 'I don't mean anything weird or sexual by that. I mean: do you want to move in with me?' I can't believe I've met someone as mad and impulsive as I am.

Obviously I know you'll be hearing alarm bells, LBOH. And I'm not completely deaf to them. This is all moving very quickly. I have a history of jumping in head-first, then getting my fingers burnt. Think I mixed some metaphors there. But I *will* be careful. I need to make sure I don't reel him in too eagerly, only to realise I never wanted him all along. I have a history of people proposing to me, don't ask me why, and then I say no and turn them into gibbering wrecks. It happened with André just before Christmas. That was an odd proposal. 'Ottila, I'm a married man, but once I'm divorced, why don't we tie the knot?' He said that to me at the staff dinner, while handing me my Secret Santa present of a glow-in-the-dark bottle opener. Then there was Ben. He asked me about thirty seconds before having an orgasm. I said no, of course, but only after he'd come. Didn't want to spoil the moment.

But Thales is a nice guy. What if he asks more of me than I'm ready to give? Commitment is terrifying. Even if I know that the present me likes someone enough to commit, how do I know what the tomorrow me will want, and the me after that?

I mentioned to you that I'd been thinking about past lovers. Truthfully, I've been thinking about everyone I've ever had sex with. Is that normal? I'm thinking about Dreadlock Dorian's absinthe 'n' anal night, and then the curry and crotchless knickers disaster with Gerald, and I'm thinking about the sheer girth of Ben's . . . No. I'm not going there. I've moved in with Thales, and I'm taking a punt on happiness. Things are going well between us, so why wait? This is the best time to do it, before the rot sets in.

Plus, Laurie has really been getting on my nerves lately. Even more than usual. I mean, *kanabō* club indeed. Can you believe such a thing exists? He helped me load up the taxi with my belongings. Couldn't get me out fast enough. He also told me he'd 'guesstimated' that I'd taken 20 per cent more showers than him and somehow that means I owe 76 per cent of the last electricity bill. I know I've got almost a month's rent left on that place, but I really couldn't take another day of it.

I won't tell work about my change of address yet. I'll leave it six months. Or twelve. I'm avoiding anything that involves having to go within a five-metre radius of André's office. I told Delyth about the fact André and I used to have a thing, and she just shrugged. 'Sometimes we do things to hurt ourselves, matey,' she said, eating a salted caramel cookie. I think that probably applies to both me *and* André. It's so good to have Delyth as a friend. Until I quit drinking, I didn't think I was worthy of being close to someone like her. The happy people, I always thought – they don't need people like me dragging them down. Turns out even Delyth isn't perfectly content. She texted me earlier to say she got a parking ticket and punched a lamppost. That made me grin, ear to ear.

Thales has suggested we plant a daffodil in the alleyway between the two flats, so we remember the route we used to walk to meet each other. I'm not sure why he felt a daffodil was particularly significant, but he was emphatic about it. I think daffodil season is over, though, because they stopped selling them at Morrison's ages ago. Maybe I'll ring Mum and ask her; she'll know. It's her wedding anniversary today. Normally she spends it watching *Indecent Proposal*. I'll wait until tomorrow.

Bottom line is, I'm with Thales and without Laurie. Sweet relief. Although when I told Thales about *kanabō* club, he sounded surprisingly enthusiastic. Hope there aren't any demons in my new flat.

O.

Rota

Amazing New Flatmates'
Super Special Household Chores Rota (ANFSSHCR)

☺   ☺   ☺

Monday night	Laughter therapy i.e. watch comedy boxsets
Tuesday night	Dominoes Two for Tuesday and a foreign film
Wednesday night	Pick a random street 45 mins away and walk to it together
Thursday night	Playstation games
Friday night	Meditate with incense, then work on our separate creative projects
Saturday	Cook a different world cuisine (see world food map)
Sunday	Go swimming/jogging/do 50 star jumps

☺   ☺   ☺

Email from André

From: André Marsh
To: Ottila McGregor
Date: Wed, 21 May, 2014 at 11:12
Subject: apols

Ottila,

Please find attached an e-flyer for Mubeen's new sleep workshop.
Can you chuck the info up on the website, find a stock photo of
someone smiling with their eyes shut or whatever to go with it?

Soz about my pathetic attempts at power play lately. lame bids to
win you back. shame on me. Should have contacted you sooner.
been busy licking wounds, yada yada yada. I hope you and the g(r)
eek boy are very happy together. you seem it. Never thought you'd
last long as a lesbian anyway.

Best wishes,
André

ps back with the wife

Jambalaya Ingredients

<u>Serves 4</u>

2 chicken thighs

2 chicken drumsticks

150g ~~chorizo~~ *Wall's sausages*

10 ~~king prawns~~ *frozen prawns*

1 small onion

1 red pepper

1 ~~stick celery~~

3 cloves garlic

~~2 tins tomatoes~~ *ketchup*

600 ml ~~chicken stock~~ *veggie stock*

300g white rice

~~2 bay leaves~~

1 tsp ~~cayenne pepper~~ *cumin*

seasoning

This took ages to make and tasted bland and slightly offensive. Plus, I've noticed Thales gets really tetchy when he's hungry. Think we'll stop doing the world cuisine night and have a cheese-on-toast night next week.

Email from Mum

From: Alice McGregor
To: Ottila McGregor
Date: Mon, 26 May, 2014 at 12:36
Subject: Attempt

Just a quickie, love, I'm in a rush.

Mina had a funny turn this morning. She punched the common room window with her fist and cut her knuckles, then managed to run out of the staff exit and climb up a drainpipe while wearing her pyjamas. She was standing on top of the hospital building for half an hour before they got her down.

The police were involved but it's sorted now. She's been moved to a high security ward, and they've put her on Section 3 – I think that means she could be inside for another six months.

I really felt like ECT was our last hope. What are we hoping for now?

Mum xox

Text Message to Thales

Mon 26 May 17:06

I'm going to walk home from work alone today. Planned a route that doesn't go past any pubs as I'm feeling a bit 'triggery'. I know it's a Monday but I'll skip the Seinfeld boxset if you don't mind, and start work on my one-woman show. I mean it this time. Why don't you work on your grant application?

Thales's Proposal, First Draft

Application for Film Development Fund, BFUK

1. Project Details

Film title: Inanimate Objects

Name of producer: Thales Sanna

Name of writer: Thales Sanna

Name of director: Thales Sanna

2. Proposal

i. Idea

Imagine if your kettle could speak. But what if, each time you used it to make a cup of tea, it had forgotten who you were and you had to introduce yourself to it all over again?

Inanimate Objects is a short film starring a range of sentient household objects. I have been thinking about this idea for the past three years, and have written five very rough pages of script for it. The idea came about when my grandmother, Yiayia Enora, developed Alzheimer's, a progressive disease affecting over forty million people worldwide. What if inanimate objects could experience Alzheimer's too, I wondered? How would our relationship to those objects change?

ii. Strategy

With this grant, I would be able to take one afternoon a week off my day job, which involves working as a barista in a hospital cafeteria. This would enable me to focus on the project for three and a half hours a week, for the next two years.

~~On a practical level, I have moved my desk into the hall, in order to create a workspace free of plug sockets. This means I~~

~~won't be able to play games on my laptop, so there's no danger~~
~~of getting sucked into a five-hour session of *Divinity: Original Sin*.~~

3. Finance

Amount requested: £5,000

Details of any current financial partners for this project: n/a

4. Supporting Information

We may contact you to ask for further material, such as:

· a treatment and sample scenes
· a showreel
· a detailed budget

I confirm that the details I have given here are, to the best of my knowledge, true and correct. I am happy to provide further evidence for any area of this application.

Signed: [*Thales Sanna*]

Letter to Mina

Hello, lovely-head,

I was reading through some of our old correspondences recently and thought about how nice it was that we used to send each other letters. So much more exciting to receive an envelope than an email, isn't it? So here you go. Your first letter from me in about six years. I'm meant to be working on my idea for a theatre piece tonight, but I'll get to that later.

I hope you are feeling a bit better now the ECT is over. It must have been horrible for you having general anaesthetic twice a week, feeling so disoriented. I'm sorry to hear the ECT didn't work for you. I've been thinking of you lots, and am sending positive vibrations to you through the air.

What a shame you weren't allowed two of the books I sent to you via Mum. I knew you were having trouble concentrating on reading, even with the blue cellophane they gave you, but I didn't think about the fact you wouldn't be allowed picture books with staples in. What do they think you'll do with them? Stick them in your eyes? Swallow them? I guess that's exactly what they think you'll do with them. Ignore me.

At least you got *The Owl Who Was Afraid of the Dark*, though. Plop, Plop! Thought you might enjoy re-reading it. Learning about Orion's Belt and the constellations. What are the lessons the little owl learns again? That the dark is exciting, dark is kind, dark is fun, dark is necessary, dark is fascinating, dark is wonderful and dark is beautiful. I remember Dad reading it to us because I had that phobia of going to the loo in the night. I seem to recall we had chickenpox at the time, and our faces were smeared pink with calamine lotion. We had to rub our fingers in the centre of our palms to stop ourselves scratching, to avoid making scars.

Do you remember the time I got a poo stuck halfway out of my bum? You stood at the top of the stairs and screeched: 'Daaaaaad! Tilly's got a poo stuck!' The postman was delivering our mail, and got quite a shock. Dad had to press a hot flannel against my bottom. I quite literally ripped myself a new arsehole that day.

Sorry. Just trying to make you laugh.

Well, I don't have too much to say right now except that I'm rooting for you. And I'm doing really well. You don't need to worry about me. I haven't drunk alcohol for over four months. It feels great to be so healthy. I'm making Jerusalem artichokes for dinner. Never had them before. Apparently people call them Jerusalem *fartychokes* because of the effect they have on you. Oh dear. I'm obsessed with bums.

I hope you feel better soon and that your mind starts to feel less foggy. It must be horrible to feel like you can barely remember the last ten years. And just to clarify in reference to that Snapchat you sent me last week: yes, my middle name has always been Frandsine. Don't feel bad for forgetting it, though! It's not like we use our middle names very often, is it? I think if I have children I won't bother giving them a middle name. It's not fair on the middle name, feeling all secondary like that.

It's okay if you're not up to writing back to me. Just thought you might appreciate the post. Snapchat me when you're allowed your phone, but only if you feel like it.

Exciting, kind, fun, necessary, fascinating, wonderful, beautiful love to you.

Ottila X

Stuff I Never Knew

Here's some stuff I never knew about Thales until we moved in together:

- He weighs himself on the bathroom scales three times a day: after he gets up, after work, before bed.

- He likes his peanut butter crunchy, not smooth.

- He lets me read his texts and emails.

- He leaves the room to fart, and when he does, he mutters 'oopsy' very quietly under his breath.

- He doesn't mind at all when I fart, loud and sonorous, on the sofa beside him.

- He doesn't like it if I leave suds on the washing up.

- He speaks to his parents on the phone in Greek. You can make out the odd English phrase like 'BBC One'.

- Sometimes, when he's talking to his parents, I hear the name Eleni.

Email from Ilias

From: Ilias Sanna
To: Thales Sanna
Date: Thurs, 29 May, 2014 at 16:41
Subject: Eleni

Γιε μου, Elenaki visited us for a cup of coffee this morning. Such a lovely, sweet κούκλα. I think she's forgiven you for your silliness at the start of the year and would like to give things another go. Why don't you give her a call?

Με αγαπη, ο μπαμπας σου x

Drink App

YOU HAVE BEEN

SOBER

FOR

141
days

That's:
12,182,400 seconds
203,040 minutes
3384 hours
141 days
20 weeks and **1** day
4 months, **18** days
38.63% of 2014

Rewards!

4 chips earned
$1817.24 saved
707.1 hours of drinking saved
122,660 calories saved (**416** burgers)

Letter from BFUK

BFUK
Delivering support for filmmakers at every step of their career

5 June 2014

Dear Mr Sanna,

Thank you for your recent application for a Film Development Fund. I am sorry to tell you that on this occasion your application was unsuccessful. There was insufficient evidence of quality in the following sections:

- 2.   Proposal
- 2. i.   Idea
- 2. ii. Strategy
- 3.   Finance

Section 1 (your personal details) and Section 4 (your signature) were deemed eligible. If you would like to address the above areas of your application, please take a look at the guidance notes on our website, and you are welcome to reapply.

Yours sincerely,

Alan Briggs
Grants Officer

Email from Thales's Agent

From: Sue France
To: Thales Sanna
Date: Mon, 9 June, 2014 at 15:26
Subject: *FUNDING*

Dear Thales,

Sorry to hear about your application. Afraid I've still had no luck placing *Tractor Boy* with a distributor. I've spoken to a few potential investors about your next film, the one with the talking kettle, but the consensus seems to be that the tractor one was a success despite any funding and it would be risky to ruin a formula that obviously works for you.

So, my advice to you would be FORGET FUNDING. Get that script sorted, take your phone out of your pocket and get on with it!

Sue France
Primrose Film Agency

Little Book of Happy

Dear Increasingly Big Book of Still Not Perfectly Happy,

I just ripped out one of your pages and posted it under the bathroom door. It was a quotation attributed to Buddha about the beauty of suffering.

The problem is, Thales has been locked in the bathroom for the past twenty-five minutes, and he's not coming out. Another thing I didn't know about Thales until we moved in together is that he doesn't take rejection very well. He got an email from his agent today that sent him over the edge. He didn't say a word on our walk home from work. I mean, the fact he even has an agent makes me green with envy, but I think everyone's struggles are scaled differently, aren't they? When Thales's agent tells him to go and make another movie on his iPhone, I hear: *I believe in you.* He hears: *You're a failure.*

I've never seen Thales angry with anyone, let alone with himself. It's quite exciting not to be the emotional wreck for once, but I'm worried about him. In addition to the wise words from your old pal Siddhārtha Gautama, I've also posted a picture of a pretzel saying I LOVE YOU under the door, and I've played the song 'Don't Worry, Be Happy' on repeat three times. It's not as good as having Granny Joyce here to sing it, but it perked *me* up. Didn't bring Thales out of the bathroom, though. Nor did my Pollyanna-like comment that at least the grant application was rejected quickly, which is surely better than being rejected slowly . . . His response was a snort.

I've decided to sit in the bedroom and wait it out. Last time I sat waiting for someone to come out of the bathroom like this I was twenty, home from university for Christmas, and Mina was in the bathroom slashing her shins with a razor and taking all the Ibuprofen in the medicine cabinet.

I just called out to ask Thales if he's okay. He actually sounded surprisingly perky. Told me he's on his phone, engaging in a bit of retail therapy. Think I'll go and look for more two-dimensional objects to post under the door, all the same.

Ottila

Email to Ilias

From: Thales Sanna
To: Ilias Sanna
Bcc: Ottila McGregor
Date: Thurs, 29 May, 2014 at 16:41
Subject: Re: Eleni

Dad,

I know you are finding it hard to process me breaking things off with Eleni, and I know Yiayia and Papou are still upset about it, but I promise you, I've done the right thing.

I have a new girlfriend. Her name is Ottila, and she's incredible. She really looks after me, you know. I've attached a photo of the two of us at Manchester Museum taken earlier this year. We're posing in front of a cabinet of Ibeji figures. Have you heard of them? Allegedly, the West African Yoruba people give birth to a higher number of twins than anyone else in the world. The infant mortality rate is high, and whenever a twin dies, the grieving mother is given a carved figurine, to represent the dead offspring. She cares for it, just like the living twin. Eventually, given time, I suppose the parents are able to come to terms with their child's death and perhaps even have more babies to love and cherish, even though their bond to the old ones will never be broken.

Φιλάκια,

T x

Fridge Magnets Arranged by Thales

WOuLd u 1ik3 tO M33t mY P3r3ntS th15 We3X3Nd?

[Also attached to the fridge, beneath the 'w' and 'e' magnets at the start of 'weekend', is a leaflet called 'A Forager's Guide to Fungi', with a picture of a toadstool on the front, and the symbol of a skull and crossbones beside it.]

Written on a Train Ticket to Stockport

What you listening to?

'Sussudio' by Phil Collins. U?

World War I podcast.

Nervous. Hope they like me . . . x

[*A return ticket from Stockport is included, but there is no handwriting on it.*]

Email to Thales

From: Ottila McGregor
To: Thales Sanna
Date: Sat, 14 June, 2014 at 23:26
Subject: Argh

Oh god. Please. Let me explain.

Before today, I really, truly didn't know for sure whether I'd dated your sister. It was eight years ago, for the grand total of three months, and it was in Scotland! She wasn't one to talk much about family, and I *swear* she said her surname was Mavros. Honestly, I had a minor freak-out when you first told me your sister was called Reatha, but I just hoped and prayed it was a common Greek name and a massive coincidence. I've been known to self-sabotage in past relationships, and ours has been so good that I didn't want to ruin it by saying something weird like, *Oh hey, Thales, it's been really great French-kissing you this morning. By the way, did I date your sister?* Ugh. I mean, *I'm* shuddering, so I've no idea how this must be affecting you.

I'll come back to this mess in a second, but the next thing I need to say is even more important: I truly had *no idea* that Reatha hadn't told your parents yet. She was always so assured back when we . . . you know. I assumed she'd have shouted it from the rooftops. I mean, she attended marches and spoke on the local radio station. Her hair was rainbow-coloured! How was I to know she'd been keeping it from your mum and dad? I never in a million years meant to *out* her.

Do you have any idea how nerve-wracking it is to realise you've dated both siblings in one family? You have to find a way to make it okay with everyone. I thought a joke, something about working my way around the family, telling your mum she's next . . . I thought that might seem endearing. I'm such a buffoon. Worse than a buffoon. A complete jackass. How much was the teapot worth? I know, technically, it was your sister who smashed it, but

I can't help feeling responsible. Let me pay for it, at the very least. I'll buy a whole new tea set if it'll help.

I was definitely planning on telling you about Reatha, my Reatha – Reatha Mavros – at some point. I thought we'd just sort of agreed not to bother talking about our exes. We were bound to get round to it eventually, but I just wanted to spend some time not worrying about the past. Being *happy*. You've been happy too, haven't you? I haven't been this happy since before Dad died.

I haven't really talked to you about my dad yet. He died of lung cancer almost three years ago. We knew he didn't have long left, but when it happened, it floored me. I know you've been trying to be tactful, not wanting to bring it up in case you upset me, but I'd like to talk to you about it sometime. My dad was the best. And you'd be amazed how much of me has come from him. I've lost one of my closest friends.

If I lose you, I'll lose another.

I still can't believe Reatha was there. It was so bizarre, seeing her again after all these years, seeing how much she's changed, realising how similar the two of you look. Now her hair's not rainbow-coloured and it's dark brown like yours the resemblance is *uncanny*. I've been such a fool.

Okay, Thales. This is the part of the email where I say that if you don't want to hear any more about me and your sister, then look away now. But if you want to know, here's the truth.

I dated your sister for three and a half months. Back in 2006, when I was doing my Masters in Glasgow. But I guess (deep breath, Ottila) it was a bit more serious than I might have made out during our hissed conversation on your parents' patio, when I realised it was definitely her. I should have been more honest at that point, but really, I felt under quite a lot of pressure having to have that conversation at your family home, while your mum was serving up three different types of cheese pie. Look. Me and Reatha. It was one of those relationships you have when you're young and naïve, and you've got so much time to put into it. It was short-lived, but it felt important.

The reason I'm telling you this is because there are things you might find out. The main one is this: the reason I broke up with Reatha was because I found out she was going to ask me to marry her. Well, it would have been a civil partnership back then but, nonetheless, it was a big deal. And I panicked. I have a weird history of people asking me to marry them. I don't know why exactly, and I certainly don't deserve it, but I have a feeling it's because I come on too strong, before I'm ready . . . I had no idea how much I'd upset Reatha. Putting two and two together, from the brief words she uttered today, she went teaching in Japan because of me.

I can't believe I'm writing this. I'm not even drunk. (I didn't go and buy any whisky like I said I would. I'm sitting on your sofa, *our* sofa, with my laptop and a pint of shame.) But I want to be open with you. If we ever stand a chance of making this work, I feel like you have to know everything. It's like ripping off a plaster. Your sister is the second woman I've been out with. The first was a goth called Laura who ate hash browns for breakfast every day. Two years ago, I slept with a married woman while her children's guinea pigs ran around, squeaking, on the carpet. In total, I've slept with fifty-seven people. Forty-two men and fifteen women. I've been keeping a tally. There. It's all coming out now. Is it helping you? It might be helping me.

I keep remembering your dad's expression when he found out. I don't know what all that stuff he said in Greek meant. But I did recognise the word κακός. It's in that song you played me, the one about the guy who's been sailing around the world for seven years and has just run out of butter. It means bad, doesn't it? I'm not a bad person. I'm really not. I've been telling myself that on repeat for the last two hours. It feels like it's become about half a per cent truer since I started saying it.

I've got cramp in my left foot. Wish you were here to flex it out for me. I can't believe we've only lived together for a month. Our flat just feels like *your* flat when you're not in it. I wish you'd come back with me tonight, so we could talk in person. I also wish I hadn't spat out your mum's *tiropita* onto the tablecloth. It was delicious, incidentally. Well, I think I'll go to bed soon. Maybe you'll have replied to this by the time I wake up. Maybe it'll all work out okay. I'm sorry again about the teapot. Wedgwood is an expensive make, isn't it? (I guess it's true that Greeks really do like throwing crockery . . . I'm sorry. That joke has been trying to erupt out of me all evening. It's totally inappropriate and I hate myself.) Does this teapot look like a good replacement? There are three hours left to bid on it: www.ebay.co.uk/itm/VINTAGE-WEDGWOOD-BLUE-FLOWERS-DESIGN-90S-TEAPOT-ONLY-TWO-SMALL-CRACKS/.

I'm sorry I dated your sister and that you only found out about it today. I really feel like a different person now, if that helps.

Let's make it work, my philosopher.

O x

P. S. I hope your migraine is a bit better this evening. Take paracetamol if you need it.

Old Letter from Reatha

15 January 2007

For fuck's sake, Til.

You don't expect me to just sit here and take it, do you?

You haven't answered your phone for three days, and I'm just supposed to be okay with it, am I?

As if.

I'm gonna teach you a thing or two about break-ups, because it seems there's a lot you need to learn. NUMBER ONE: doing it face-to-face doesn't involve meeting up for a pub-jazz date, then handing someone a letter and sitting there in silence while the dumped recipient reads it beside you. You and your obsession with letters! This isn't *Les Liaisons Fucking Dangereuses*, you know, it's real life. The only reason I'm writing you this now is because you've left me no choice.

Fuck! It's just not appropriate, Til. I'll never be able to listen to old-man jazz again, without remembering phrases like 'although I have strong feelings for you' and 'I think there's a difference between *love* and *being in love*' and 'maybe it was just the *idea of you* and not *you*'. Horseshit! It turns my stomach, just thinking about it. And now I've got this piece of paper, detailing your reasons for not wanting to be with me, which I can't bring myself to throw away because, I don't know, I'm weirdly sentimental about it, and it's just sitting there, on my desk, next to a permanently replenishing pack of Marlborough Reds and an old copy of *The End of the Affair*. I'm so corny, no wonder you don't love me any more ... Oh, *sorry*, you do love me, you're just not *in* love with me. Balls!

Where was I? Oh yes. NUMBER TWO. After you've broken up with said person, you're not supposed to just sit there and get drunk with them, watching them cry and making them laugh, buying them half a dozen pints of Guinness and then going back to their place and shagging them senseless. Especially if it's the best sex of their life. Drunk, painful, emotional, perfect sex. You bastard.

And NUMBER THREE, if you *do* do that, you don't break up

with them again the next morning, in the form of *yet another* letter, hastily scribbled and left on the kitchen table for them to find upon waking, and then refuse to answer their sodding calls for the next three days.

I'm well within my rights to loathe you, Ottila. You don't get to treat people like this and get away with it. You've destroyed me. I've been smoking, reading about doomed romances, moping on the living room floor and trailing around Glasgow Green in a headscarf and sunglasses like I'm bloody Grace Kelly. It's better than having people see my Rainbow Brite hair and assuming I'm *fine*. I haven't painted so much as a brushstroke. I'm scared that I'm just gonna paint the whole canvas black. I am a walking, wailing, heartbreak cliché.

Except for this: I've started doing something I've never done before. I've become a thief, Til! I don't know why I'm doing it, but I've been walking into pubs and stealing salt shakers. It started the night you broke up with me. When you went to the loo I snuck the salt shaker I'd been fiddling with into my handbag. I completely forgot about it until the next day, when I found white grains on my phone and in my wallet. I pressed some of the grains onto my finger and licked them, hoping they might be drugs. Alas: plain old sodium chloride . . . Then I remembered that salt is supposed to kill witches, and I had this fantasy that if I shook my bag out over my body, letting the granules coat my skin, it would stop me from ever getting hurt again. (Feel free to read into this the implication that I'm viewing you as a witch, Til. Hopefully that came across.)

So, since the night you dumped me, I've been stealing salt shakers. I've been going from bar to bar, in the evenings, when I'd normally be watching *Coronation Street* and smutty arthouse movies with you, and I've been adding to my collection. I've got thirteen of the little pricks now, lined up on my windowsill. I'm thinking about painting them, but I'll wait until I feel like I've gone *truly* berserk before I start that venture. Maybe once I start cackling to myself I'll know it's time. By then, *I'll* have become the witch.

The point that I'm trying to make is not that I'm mentally unstable. And I swear I'm not trying to make myself appear more 'dangerous' and 'exciting' to you, to make you want me again or summat stoopid like that. My point is this: in spite of it all, in spite of all this anguish (three days, T! three days!) I'm missing you like shitting shit. I'm not even concentrating on the bad times. I know it might seem that way, from this letter. I've just had two big swigs of that cinnamon–flavoured Aftershock you left behind last weekend. Fuck that. Honestly, my mind keeps racing through all the good times. The night we slept on the back lawn, and woke up at 3 a.m. absolutely freezing because it was the start of October. Do you remember how blue the tips of my fingers were? And how you put them into your mouth to keep them warm and told me, mouth full of my fingers, that you were falling for me? The time we painted your bathroom tiles crimson and the gloss dried in drips, making it look like a murder scene. The hot chocolate at the top of the Necropolis, when you told me to pretend we were in Paris. I didn't really know what you meant, but I spoke French to you for the rest of the night. It's a shame you don't speak it too, because I told you some *choses très merveilleuses*.

Fuck's sake. I'm speaking like we were together for years, like I'm ploughing over the last decade and revealing the choice bits. Three and a half months. That's all it's been. But I know how I feel. If you could just let me come over to your place and talk to you. Or if you'd give me ten minutes on the phone. Maybe we can sort this out. I have a feeling you're just scared. I know you've never had a serious relationship before. That you've always felt young for your age. That you get distracted by the problems with your sister, and that you feel guilty in case the relationship between us makes her jealous. I really, really didn't mean to say those nasty things about Mina on New Year's Eve. I know she can't help being the way she is. And I'm sorry I called you an 'enabler'. I was trashed. We both were. Forgive me, Til. I promise you: it'll be worth it. Our lives are destined to be connected forever.

Right. I'll leave you now. I hope you'll at least keep this letter for your great epistolary novel someday. I'm no Dostoyevsky, but I do love you.

Ree

P. S. Holy fuck. There's a museum of salt and pepper shakers in Tennessee. Come with me?
P. P. S. Consider this my last attempt to win you back. I think I've debased myself enough for one lifetime.

Happiness is a myth we seek.

Kahlil Gibran

Text Message from Thales

Sun 15 June 17:06

I'm going to stay at my parents' house another night.
Maybe longer. I'll grab some stuff from the flat once
you've left for work.

Letter from Arts Grants Inc.

17 June 2014

Dear Ottila,

Thank you for your application. We love your proposal!

However, I am sorry to tell you that we are unable to provide you with a grant, given that we have just funded an almost identical project and it is our policy to only fund the same activity once.

Please feel free to apply again in the future if you have a unique idea.

Warm wishes,

Fawiza Massoud
Grants Administrator

Letter from Thales

Ottila,

I'm writing this on paper, because I don't trust myself to write an email. I'll get too angry and write too fast, and say things I'm not sure I truly mean. Sitting in the conservatory, writing on my mum's floral notepaper, with my dad's *paleá dhimotiká* CD playing in the background, it's impossible to pen anything too savage. Plus, I've still got a massive headache, so I'm saving my energy to look after my own needs, rather than giving it all to you.

I wish you'd told me about dating my sister. Even if it was just a hunch. You can't just sweep something like that under the carpet and expect it to deal with itself. That's childish, Ottila, and you know it.

I'm trying to think this all through sensibly. Like, deal with each little piece of information bit by bit. So, finding out you've dated women is no problem at all. Why would it be? Plus, I totally get that myself. Like, I'm not so much attracted to a gender or identity as I am to particular people. I suppose I'm pansexual, but extremely fussy. I fancy hardly anyone. Seriously. And I also make very bad decisions about who I do fancy. Maybe I'm idiotsexual.

So, if I'm fine with you having dated women, then supposedly the problem is that you dated my sister. However, *in theory*, I should be fine with that too. In the same way that I don't believe relationships involve possession, I also believe in the freedom to love whoever you want to, regardless of race, sex or background. All right, so I have some strong doubts about the viability of incest and I'm naturally vehemently anti-paedophilia (why does stating that make you sound like a paedophile?), but apart from that, really, I can't say that I *should* have any more of a problem with you having dated my sister than anyone else. But that's just it. As much as I hate to admit it to myself, I *do* have a problem with it. A very big problem.

I can't bear thinking about you with Reatha. I've got your exes lined up in my head as these nondescript, shadowy blobs, and when I do give them features I try and make them really unattractive. I've placed you with some GROTESQUE miscreants. Look for a picture of the kuo-toa in my Dungeons & Dragons

Monster Manual, and you're halfway there. Think: scaly men with fish heads. Unfortunately, I can't blur out my sister's face and replace it with a bulette or a rust monster, because I know *exactly* what she looks like. I can imagine the two of you together, crystal clear. And as filthy and foul-mouthed as Reatha can be, she's also my big sis', the girl who picked me up when I fell in the mud, who gave me the biggest hugs when I cried after having my brace put in, who once punched a teacher in the leg for giving me dinner duty. She's fiery and she's fun and she's sweet and she's full of love.

Love which used to be aimed at you.

You broke her heart, Ottila. You smashed it to pieces.

And not only am I scared that you could break mine, but it already breaks at the thought of you and her together. Did you have a nickname for her? I'm your philosopher; what was she? Did you stroke the back of her head when she couldn't sleep? Did you slip notes into her coat pocket? If I think about it for too long, I want to stick pins in my eyes.

It shocks me to discover I'm not the free-loving hippie I thought I was. Turns out I'm just a jealous guy. Makes me wonder what else I don't know about myself. Maybe it's just this damn headache, but I feel like I'm splitting in two. There's the me I always hoped I was, the me who makes award-winning iPhone films and has long-term relationships and makes a perfect cup of coffee. And then there's this other me. The me who can't write for shit, and who only goes out with sociopaths. I do still make good coffee, although I haven't felt like eating or drinking for the last few days. Saying that, I *did* think about having a beer last night as some sort of twisted revenge act, but when I opened the can, I didn't feel like it.

Now that I've called you a sociopath I feel a bit better. I realise it's not medically accurate, though, so please don't go Googling sociopath and adding that to your already long list of problems to feel sorry for yourself about. What you *can* add to the list, if you want, is outing my sister. I've managed to keep that secret from my parents for the last decade, but somehow you let the cat out of the bag within ten minutes of meeting them. After you left, Mum cried, trying to work out why her little girl couldn't be honest with her. She keeps asking if she's been a terrible mother. Dad's just been staring off into space, shaking his head and saying 'It makes sense, it makes sense'. You've really had a big impact on this family, Ottila, and we all need some time away from you now. Maybe for good.

Thales

P. S. Don't bother about the teapot.

Sometimes it Helps to Have a Good Cry

Had a bad day? Suffering from stress? Feeling the burden of modern life? If this describes you, chances are you'll be fighting a powerful urge to drink right now. But instead of reaching for the bottle, how about this? Have a good cry.

Go on. Try it. Let all that tension just fall away. You'll feel cleansed and ready to face the world anew. And, if you're lucky, your desire to drink might fade too.

Email from Mum

From: Alice McGregor
To: Ottila McGregor
Date: Tue, 24 June, 2014 at 14:34
Subject: Emergency

I wouldn't normally say this, darling, but I think this time <u>we ought to worry.</u>

Mina has written a will. I think she might have posted you a copy. **Warning! Don't open it!** It'll only upset you; I know what you're like. She hasn't had anything to eat or drink in three days, and she's very weak. I think she's given up.

They found her this morning with some thread around her neck. I don't know where she got it. She's bruised, but no permanent damage.

There's a train that gets into Oxford at 12.59 tomorrow. Is there any way you can get some time off work? I wouldn't ask unless it was a red alert.

Mum xoxox

P. S. I've had minor facial surgery. It's not fully healed yet. Don't be shocked.

Will

THIS IS THE LAST WILL AND TESTAMENT

of MINA ALEXANDRINE McGREGOR
of 12a Maple Road, Oxford, OX3 6HN

Dated 26 May 2014

1. I HEREBY REVOKE all former Wills and testamentary dispositions made by me under the law of England and Wales and declare that the proper law of this my Will shall be the law of England and Wales.

2. I APPOINT my mother, **ALICE McGREGOR**, to be the Executor and Trustee of this my Will (hereafter called 'My Trustees' which expression shall include the Trustee or Trustees for the time being hereof) AND in case the aforesaid should die in my lifetime or shall refuse or be unable to act in the office of Executor and Trustee then **I APPOINT** my sister, **OTTILA FRANDSINE McGREGOR**, to fill the vacancy in the office of Executor and Trustee hereof.

3. I GIVE the following legacies:

(I) I give to my mother, **ALICE McGREGOR**, my laptop, my books on craft and cookery, and the succulent on my kitchen windowsill, if it hasn't died already. She will already know this, I'm sure, but the sap is poisonous, so please remind her to wash her hands thoroughly after touching it.

(II) I give to my sister, **OTTILA FRANDSINE McGREGOR**, all my remaining books, my upcycled coffee table, which is scruffy but she tells me she's jealous of it whenever she visits, and any of my clothes that fit her / she likes.

(III) Please give the woman who works in Boots on the high street who has a name badge saying **DAVINIA** on it the lilac kitten brooch attached to my leopard print coat. She has complimented it on two occasions, and I think she'd be touched.

(IV) I give the Autism Alliance (Registered Charity

Number 1112897) absolutely the sum of all money in my bank account, which currently stands at £86.42. If they want to sell some of the cushions and blankets I have made, or give them to people in care homes, they can have them. Otherwise, throw everything else away.

4. I DECLARE THAT if any share of any legacy in the above paragraph 3 of this my Will shall fail then from the date of such failure such share or shares shall accrue and be added to the share or shares in that legacy (if more than one in the proportion which such other shares bear to one another) which shall not have failed at the date of my death and be held subject to the same provisions and conditions as those affecting such other share or shares **AND I FURTHER DECLARE THAT** if any legacy in the above paragraph 3 of this my Will shall fail entirely or be declared void then it shall fall into and form a part of my Residuary Estate.

5. I GIVE, DEVISE AND BEQUEATH all my real and personal estate of whatsoever nature and wheresoever situate (including any property over which I may have a general power of appointment or disposition by Will) to my Trustees upon Trust to sell, call in and convert the same into money with full power.

6. I FOUND THIS template on the Internet, and do not fully understand it, so if anything is wrong with it **PLEASE FORGIVE ME** and **TAKE IT SERIOUSLY** despite any errors. I make so many mistakes these days, and **I INTEND TO STOP**.

Text Message to Mum

> **Wed 25 June 10:08**
> Just waiting on platform. No delays showing so far. See you soon. Hope your face is okay. x

Text Message to André

> **Wed 25 June 10:17**
> Having a family crisis. Afraid I'll need a couple of days off work. I'll call the office later - on train at the mo.

Text Message to Thales

> **Wed 25 June 11:36**
> Just letting you know the flat will be empty until tomorrow night. If you want to pack up the rest of your things and move out while I'm gone, now would be a good time to do it.

FOUR

Email from Mum

From: Alice McGregor
To: Ottila McGregor
Date: Wed, 25 June, 2014 at 11:55
Subject: Fwd: Appeal for Help

---------- Forwarded message ----------
From: Alice McGregor <alice.mcgregor54@mcgregormail.com>
To: aart@aartjonckers.nl
Date: Wed, 11 June 2014 at 11:54
Subject: Appeal for Help

Dear Mr Jonckers,

I wouldn't normally do this. I only really use the Internet to speak to my eldest daughter and to order seeds, but I looked up 'best Asperger's doctor in the world' on Bing and your name appeared at the top. Apparently you're a consultant rather than a doctor, so I think I'm meant to refer to you as Mr rather than Dr, but please accept my sincerest apologies if I'm being grossly offensive in my assumption.

Mr Jonckers: I'm writing to you because my youngest daughter, Mina, was diagnosed with Asperger Syndrome two years ago. She will be twenty-eight next month. She also has OCD, Persistent Depressive Disorder and an underactive thyroid, which makes her skin dry. While it would be entirely possible for my daughter to have permanent residence with me, it has been her decision to live in Oxfordshire, some eighty miles away. Three years ago, shortly after the death of her father, Mina announced that she could no longer stay in our family home and wanted to escape the memories, so we found her a nice little place in a pretty part of Oxfordshire, an area which Mina used to love visiting as a child. At first I saw the move as a positive thing. Not only did Mina gain more independence, but the Mental Health services in Oxfordshire are very good. Plus, she's entitled to receive far more help if she lives alone than if she was here, relying on me. Unfortunately, though, things have gone from bad to worse.

I'm not going to beat about the bush any longer, Herr Jonckers. Despite varying forms of medication and several courses of CBT, my daughter is extremely unwell. She has been in hospital for three months and has even had a course of Electroconvulsive treatment, which was discontinued because it was thought to be making her worse. I mean, who would have thought that forcing her to have bi-weekly epileptic fits would have made her worse!

I'm writing to you because you are my last chance saloon. My daughter is tormented by thoughts of self-harm and suicide (particularly hanging) and is finding life a daily battle. At the moment she is in a psychiatric hospital in England, under Section 3 of the Mental Health Act. The hospital environment includes many violent patients and this makes her anxiety ten times worse. Staff consider her to have a personality disorder and she has also been diagnosed with schizophrenia in past years. We know this to be incorrect, but every time a new member of staff meets her, we have to explain this all over again. She was even forced to have the Asperger's test twice, because the new doctor didn't believe us! There is just no way that my youngest daughter has Borderline Personality Disorder. I know that, Mr Jonckers, because I'm fairly sure my eldest daughter has it. But that is another story.

Dear me, let me get to the point. What I'm asking you, kind stranger, is do you know of any medication or form of treatment which could help her? Or could you recommend any specialist in this country where we could seek help? Better still, do you own a magic wand?

I am so frightened that she will never be happy again.

And if I lose hope I wonder how I can keep on living.

Alrighty then, deep breath. The key is to keep yourself occupied. Tonight I'm off to try out my first burlesque class. Fifty-six years old and donning the nipple tassels, Mr Jonckers! Can you Adam and Eve it? For now, though, I'm going to go and purchase some seeds. The winter jewel cabbage is just crying out to be planted at this time of year. Apparently, if I sow some mint seeds nearby, it will help deter flea beetles.

Please respond at your earliest convenience. I know you are a busy man, and you probably have a great many friends and family members, all vying for your attention, but I look forward to your reply when it comes.

Yours sincerely,

Alice McGregor

Emergency?

I'm on the train, somewhere near Stoke-on-Trent. The train is delayed, not because someone has jumped in front of it, but because a Kwik-Fit sign has blown onto the tracks. I've got a copy of *All My Puny Sorrows* on the table in front of me. It's a novel about two sisters, one of whom wants to kill herself. I read the first chapter but then put it down because I felt like I was identifying with the wrong sister.

I read an email my mum forwarded me too, and it made me want to buy an overpriced can of Stella from the man who's just walked by with a trolley. Instead, I've got an acrid, and now stone-cold, cup of coffee from the Pumpkin Café on the station platform and I'm listening to Weezer. Rivers Cuomo is singing about destroying my sweater. Before today, I'd always assumed this song was about friendship, but now I'm beginning to wonder if it isn't about depression. Either that or it's about me and Thales. Maybe the sweater that Rivers is singing about represents our relationship, and Rivers is me, begging Thales not to throw the sweater away just because it's become unravelled. Maybe the train delay is giving me too much time to think.

The other thing I've been thinking about is Mina. I'm trying to come up with a system to work out how bad this time is, compared to the others. In my head, I've created a table. The table contains six columns, and looks something like this:

Suicide attempt?	Did it result in hospitalisation?	For how long?	How much did I cry?	Did I visit?	Long-term damage?

Inventing the table is the easy part. Filling it in is harder. From what I can work out, Mina hasn't actually tried to kill herself this time. She's just stopped doing the things that make you live. The nurses have been bringing her water, tea, sandwiches and biscuits, and she's been leaving them untouched. Tying the thread around her neck: I don't think that's a genuine attempt. You can't kill yourself, as far as I know, with a piece of six-ply Tropical Sunset embroidery cotton. I don't know. Maybe you can. That's about the extent of the attempt, anyway: she's refusing orange squash, and she's embroidered herself. In the first column of the table, under 'Suicide attempt?', I opt for a non-committal 'perhaps'.

As for the second and third columns, she's already hospitalised, so I can't really judge those questions. Nobody's put her on a drip for dehydration, or moved her into an intensive care ward. I feel like these facts are important.

Have I cried? No, not yet, but then it seems like every time something new happens, I cry less and less. One day, it will get to the point where Mum will tell me Mina's committed seppuku, and I'll just nod placidly, maybe even give a knowing smile. But I'll be a mess on the inside. It's starting to feel like the less I cry, the more upset I become.

With regards to the final column, I don't know about long-term damage. How long can you live without water? I read online that it's somewhere between three and ten days. I hate the Internet.

Looking at the evidence, I'm going to grade the current scenario a five out of ten. It's not the best situation Mina has ever been in, but it's by no means the worst. Even though this is the first time Mina has written a will, this probably isn't one of her last few days on the planet. I just don't have that feeling in my bones. But then she's never killed herself before, so I won't know what that feeling is until I've felt it. Maybe it feels like the quiet hum of a delayed train.

What I *do* know is that it's vital that I gauge how bad the situation is, because I need to know how much significance to place on things. If this is the last journey I make before I see my sister's dead body, then I need to take in the details. Where was I sitting? (Coach B, 43A.) What were the distinguishing features of the passenger beside me? (Seat empty.) Did I keep the receipt from the Pumpkin Café? (In my pocket, folded over a glob of chewing gum.)

This has been going on for fifteen years. Cataloguing the last song I hear before Mina dies, the last time I cross the road before Mina dies, the last bit of corn on the cob I get stuck between my teeth before Mina dies. Placing so much importance on everything, having to retain so many memories, so often, makes little room for anything else. I feel like I'm constantly preparing to make a Crimewatch reconstruction scene.

What colour jumper were you wearing?
How many times did you hear her scream?

Now, to keep enough room inside me for normal thoughts and emotions (I might go for a walk later / it's time for bed / I hope Thales doesn't hate me, etc.) I'm trying to save my cataloguing for when I *really* need it. This is an emergency: yes. My sister has written a will and said she wants to die: yes. But it's probably not going to happen this week, or next week, or the week after. Probably.

This is what I'd class as one of our regular Type B Emergencies. A yellow alert.

Probably.

I wriggle back in my seat, close my eyes, and try to enjoy the feeling of my living, breathing, human body, living and breathing. And as I do that, the panic begins to take hold.

Family Reunion

'No, Mum – seriously, you look great,' I say as I rush through the turnstile to meet her. I've never seen her like this: out of the house without make-up, her hair unstraightened and messy. Actually, there is a strange new beauty to her. I feel like somehow I know her better like this.

'What about the eyebrows, though?' She moves her face up close to mine. 'Do you think it's too much?'

I study her, while at the same time ensuring that my expression gives nothing away. I can see faint yellow bruising beneath her eyes. Apart from that, I honestly can't tell the difference, and I'm relieved. 'It's very subtle.'

Mum grins, taking my rucksack as we head out of the station and across the car park. I've been visualising this moment, meeting Mum off the train, for the last hour or so of the journey. I've been wanting her to wrap her arms around me, to hold me tight and make everything feel okay again. But she has other plans.

'There's not much visiting time left now,' she says, throwing my rucksack into the car boot. 'We'd better hurry.' She pats me on the back, and I briefly enjoy the feeling of her warm hand between my shoulder blades.

The inside of the car smells like it always has done: Magic Tree air freshener, in Black Ice, a scent my dad used to buy. I think it was to hide his cigar-in-the-car habit, even though we all knew about it. Mum continues buying the freshener in homage to Dad. Cheap shower gel is how I'd describe the smell.

'Just prepare yourself,' Mum says, driving out of the car park entrance by mistake. 'She's very fragile. Hasn't eaten since Sunday night. Did I just go out of the wrong–? Never mind. She had a sip of squash this morning, but refused the rest.'

I try to conjure up a mental image of Mina, with sunken eyes and dry, flaky lips. I'm not sure how *preparing myself* helps.

'By the way, there's something in the glove box for you. I've been at Mina's, cleaning out the fridge and opening windows, making sure the place doesn't fall apart while she's gone. She's got so much clutter, that girl. Boxes and boxes of letters, leaflets, tickets. I've started sorting through some of it. All sorts of junk.

I'm sure it's been contributing to her depression. Anyway, I found an envelope addressed to you in one of the boxes and I thought you might want it. It's unopened. Seems she never posted it to you.' We swerve around a bus while it's indicating to come out. 'Could be something awful, but you can look if you want.'

In the glove box I find a yellowing envelope, crumpled at the corners. It has my old address in Glasgow on the front, but there's no stamp on it. 'I'll read it later.' I put it in my pocket.

'Now listen,' Mum says. 'I'm going to wait in the car while you go in. You'll only get half an hour, and it goes very quickly. She'll appreciate the chance to spend some time with you on your own.'

I notice Mum's hands are shaking on the steering wheel. 'Are you okay, Mum?'

'Fine, darling, fine,' she says robotically. 'We'll catch up when you've seen Mina. We can go to Prezzo for some marinated olives and a Vesuvio pizza.' We wait at a red light, which is only just turning amber when Mum revs the engine and drives over the white line. I've never seen her do anything like that before. All of a sudden, a terrible thought hits me. I wonder whether I can smell booze on her breath. *Oh, Mum.*

'How much further is the hospital?' I look for a side street where we might be able to pull in.

'Five minutes,' she says, swerving to overtake a lorry. 'Hold on to your hat.'

Text Messages from Thales

Wed 25 June 13:03

Was that text meant to be you dumping me? You could at least have the decency to talk in person. Also: I was renting the flat first, so shouldn't you be the one to leave it?

Wed 25 June 19:24

Started packing then found your mood ring next to the microwave. Apparently my mood is orange. I'll be back to finish packing another day. T

Recovery Meeting Transcript

PATIENT: Of course it's not that easy.

THERAPIST: What's not that easy?

PATIENT: Deciding not to let it get to me. It gets to me. I'm starting to think it'd be better if I just succumbed to it. Maybe all I'm doing – by learning how to resist falling apart on the outside – is breaking down internally.

THERAPIST: Can you explain that to me?

PATIENT: The fact that I can't cry any more is a real problem. I was going through my Recovery Workbook last week, and that was its advice: sit down and weep. Supposedly it's cleansing. I dropped to my knees on the bedroom carpet, trying to feel sorry for myself, but I just couldn't do it. I screwed up my face and thought about Mina, and Thales, but still no luck. I thought about dying puppies. Civil war in Syria. Nothing. So I did the next best thing. I Googled pictures of other people crying. Then, one thing led to another and I ended up on Wikipedia. Bad habit of mine.

THERAPIST: There are definitely worse things–

PATIENT: There are three types of tear, apparently. The first two are just for normal stuff, like keeping your eyes clean and moist, but the third type is interesting. They're called *psychic tears*, and they contain a natural painkiller. Isn't that amazing? A medicine cabinet in your own mind. That's why you get that tired, dreamy feeling after a good cry.

THERAPIST: Do you think crying would help you process your feelings better?

PATIENT: Maybe. Yes. At the moment I feel like I'm on autopilot: check Mum's okay; keep my phone on at night in case there's any news; check Mina's okay; repeat.

THERAPIST: And how is Mina? Can you tell me about the visit?

PATIENT: I keep thinking about how she looked behind the glass, as I signed in at reception. She had a blanket draped around her shoulders, and a security guard was bending over her. He looked like he was telling her off. I tried waving but she turned to me with this big, terrified stare, then ran off down a corridor.

THERAPIST: Did you get to talk to her?

PATIENT: Yes. I was told to go to the visiting room. The foam seats looked like they'd been bolted to the ground, and they were really uncomfortable. Opposite me was a poster of a blonde teenager with her head in her hands. Etched into the wall around her hunched figure were the words ALONE, FAT, STUPID, UGLY, SLUT, UNORIGINAL, BITCH and WHORE. I tried to memorise the helpline number, but my brain was darting about too much to focus.

Mina was eventually escorted in to see me. She was still wearing the blanket, and she was carrying a bundle of stuff wrapped in a hospital bed sheet. The security guard left the room and sat outside the door, watching us through toughened glass. I asked Mina what was in the bundle, and she opened the sheet out on the floor, revealing felt tips, a notebook and Tuffy, the teddy bear she's had since she was one. I picked up Tuffy and made him kiss her on the cheek, but she didn't react. She looked so thin, and kept lurching forwards, like she was going to faint.

THERAPIST: What did you talk to her about?

PATIENT: Well, I'd brought her an early birthday present, so I gave her that. I wasn't sure what she'd be allowed in the high security ward, and I didn't have long to choose something, so I got her a toothbrush-holder shaped like a ladybird. Ladybirds are one of her favourite animals. Plus, I think she has some sort of OCD thing about not using her toothbrushes for longer than a week. I was hoping having a holder to put them in might make the toothbrushes feel more hygienic, somehow.

Mina didn't say anything when I gave her the present. Just nodded. In fact, for the first ten minutes, she wouldn't say a word. Wouldn't even look at me. I finally got her to speak by asking what was in the notebook, and she showed me some of her pictures. The most recent one was of a screaming skull attached to the body of a cow, which was dripping blood out of its udders, in a field of red grass. In the sky she'd written: 'Hate Crime'. I said I liked the shading on the udders.

THERAPIST: Art can be therapeutic, in all forms–

PATIENT: I asked her what she wanted, if she could have anything, and you know what she told me?

THERAPIST: [*Silence.*]

PATIENT: She said she'd like her head scratched.

THERAPIST: Her head?

PATIENT: I spent the next fifteen minutes massaging her scalp. We didn't talk after that.

THERAPIST: It's nice that she asked you for physical contact.

PATIENT: When the guard took her away, I wanted to scream. *She's not a prisoner! You can't tell me when I'm allowed to visit my own sister! I'm rescuing her from this hellhole right now!* Of course, that's not what Mina wanted.

THERAPIST: I'm sure she really appreciated your visit, Ottila.

PATIENT: It was so sad seeing her shuffling away, the blanket falling off her shoulders. [*Long silence.*] Is it possible to die from an infection?

THERAPIST: Why do you ask?

PATIENT: I saw something on her hand, the length of maybe half a pencil. I didn't know skin could look like that. Kind of grey, like it had died.

THERAPIST: Are you sure it was an infection?

PATIENT: I asked Mum about it. Mina stole a needle from the craft room, and left it under the surface of her skin for almost a fortnight. The hospital eventually found it and pulled it out, but it's left a bit of a mess.

THERAPIST: I'm sure they've checked it, and will treat it with antibiotics if she needs them.

PATIENT: I think she might be trying to end things bit by bit. Like, she doesn't have the strength to do it all at once, so maybe if she just kills off a piece at a time, she'll get there in the end. Death by a thousand cuts.

THERAPIST: She has a history of self-damaging behaviour. It may not be that well thought through.

PATIENT: Is that what it says in my notes, too? *History of self-damaging behaviour?* Don't answer that. [*Pause.*] Mum gave me an envelope while she was driving me to the hospital. Something Mina meant to send me years ago, but then never posted. I haven't had the nerve to open it.

THERAPIST: What are you scared of?

PATIENT: If she didn't want to post it, maybe there's a reason for that. I don't know if I'm brave enough to face that reason head on.

THERAPIST: Why not put it somewhere safe for now? See how you feel in the future.

PATIENT: Okay. Good idea.

THERAPIST: Have you found the Campral is starting to help?

PATIENT: I still think about alcohol. I walk past Fuel and the Red Lion on the way home from work, and watch people drinking beer in the sunshine . . . And I just can't get the part of my brain that normally sparks up with desire to react.

THERAPIST: That's promising.

PATIENT: Most of the time.

THERAPIST: What about at the other times?

PATIENT: Thales hasn't been home for over a fortnight.

THERAPIST: Have you heard from him? Is he okay?

PATIENT: He's fine. Staying with his parents.

THERAPIST: Have you had an argument?

PATIENT: Do you mind if we don't talk about it? I thought I was in the mood to talk about it, but I'm not.

THERAPIST: What are you in the mood to talk about?

PATIENT: [*Scratching sound while the patient retrieves something from her rucksack.*] I bought these today.

THERAPIST: Boxing gloves?

PATIENT: Yeah. I'm going to become a champion kickboxer.

Text Message from Mum

Tue 01 July 06:50
Pinch punch first of the month, no returns!

More Stuff I Never Knew

Here's some stuff I never knew until Thales stopped coming home:

- The flat is actually not that nice. The hot water doesn't work properly and the lino has bubbles in it. The hall cupboard is damp for some reason and if you don't burn incense for a few days, the whole place smells of mould.
- There's a knack to making the oven work but I haven't figured it out yet.
- Thales is rubbish at packing. I've had to put extra parcel tape around them so they don't fall apart when he takes them away.
- He has a half-drawn picture of a bird in his sock drawer. Looks like a kestrel.
- He collects ketchup sachets.
- He doesn't keep any painkillers in the flat.
- His ex-girlfriend, Eleni, was beautiful.
- He was in love with her.

Letter from Thales

[*This letter was in Thales's bedside-table drawer, tucked inside a copy of John Lanchester's* Whoops!. *I've read it five times.*]

Tuesday 7 January 2014

Eleni,

We need to arrange for you to collect your things. I'm staying at my parents' house this weekend, so why don't you come and pick up your stuff then? You can post your key through the letterbox once you've finished.

I'm so sorry about the way things have worked out. It's hard to believe, having spent a whole decade together, that we're really doing this. But I think it's important that we try. I haven't been myself for the last eight years of our relationship. You must have noticed that I've gained four and a half stone since we met, even if you've never mentioned it. You do call me disgusting from time to time though, and I'm fairly sure that's why.

I shouldn't have let things spiral out of control the way they did. I'm an imbecile for not talking to you about my feelings sooner, for trying to suppress my concerns with painkillers. Somehow, at some point, I just gave in. You told me you didn't like my friends, so I stopped spending time with them. You mentioned you were jealous of my creativity, so I stopped making stuff. Except of course *Tractor Boy*, which I put together during the three months you went Interrailing with 'the gals'. They were the best three months of our relationship.

Actually, that's not fair. To begin with, being with you felt incredible. You are gorgeous, Eleni. Way out of my league if I'm being honest. You love comic books, you're funny, and you're kind to animals. I couldn't believe that first conversation we had in Forbidden Planet, when I asked you if the last issue of *Cerebus* had come in yet, and you not only pointed it out and told me you'd just finished reading it, but you told me in a Greek accent! Those early trips to Greece, meeting each other's families and eating σουβλάκι together – they felt like fate. Being with you felt like true love.

I know something switched in you that third summer, when you got the job at the animal shelter. You were starting to live your dream and I wasn't. I don't entirely blame Markus, but he certainly didn't help. When you confessed to kissing him, I should have broken up with you immediately. Instead, I forced you to a place of guilt and frustration. You began telling me what I could and couldn't do, and threatening terrible things if I didn't obey the rules. It wasn't just you. Your whole family got in on the act. I'm sorry I quit my job at such short notice, but working in an office selling sewage valves for your dad's company was never my choice. You know I've always wanted to work outdoors.

I suppose in some way I felt like I deserved it. I hadn't been a good enough boyfriend, and I had to suffer. Asking you to marry me though – that was my biggest mistake. The thing is, it wasn't just me asking. It was your dad, telling me at the water cooler that it was time I made an honest woman of his daughter. Γιαγιά was Skyping every week begging us to fix a date. My mum was already talking to you about dresses. I hoped that maybe if I asked you and you said yes then we'd find our way back to love. It would have been good, wouldn't it, if my plan had worked? If we'd managed to get back to where we once were? The halcyon days.

I will of course pay the cancellation charges for the reception, and I've phoned Beaverbrooks and they're refunding the rings. Γιαγιά and Παππούς are going to sort out the Greek wedding. We're stuck with the aeroplane tickets; I'm probably going to use mine anyway to go for Easter. Obviously you can use yours too if you want. Seats aren't allocated, so we could try and sit at opposite ends of the plane.

I'm sorry that I proposed to you out of fear. I know that you will find someone smarter, healthier, slimmer and better than me in no time. I hope your new job at the RSPCA goes well – you'll be running the place in another ten years. And I hope that you continue to find the love in those Leporidae that, ultimately, you were unable to find in me.

Thales

Text Message to Ben

> **Tue 8 July 22:12**
>
> Just watched an old episode of *The Mighty Boosh*. Made me think of the Halloween you dressed as Naboo and I was Bollo. Remember how hot we got in the Tundra?

Little Book of Happy

LBOH,

I'm technically in my thirties now. I need to be ready for all kinds of baggage. Children. Divorcees. Sagging testicles. But I wasn't remotely prepared for Thales nearly marrying someone else.

Did he really have to use that word? *Gorgeous*? I mean, what does it even mean? That he wanted to gorge on her? And as for saying she's 'out of his league' . . . I'd be lying if I said that phrase hadn't been swilling around my head all evening. Which league do I belong in then? *Thales's* league? Do I want to be in the same one as him?

I should probably be glad he *didn't* marry her. I think processing this would be easier if I had seen him in the last two and a half weeks. Instead, it just makes me want to do bad things. But I've got to stay strong. Sobriety. Happiness. They work in the same way: one day at a time. I might try and talk to Delyth about my feelings. Or I might just switch on the shower, the vacuum cleaner, the TV, the radio and the food blender, and shout as loud as I can.

Ottila

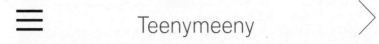

Today

ME

| This is a video of me drawing a picture of you.

Memory of Ben

Wilbraham Road in the height of summer. Ben would come over to my bedsit after work. He'd throw his Nike bag down on the sticky brown carpet, and then he'd stand there – like a big, sexy phallus – in the doorway. I'd look into his eyes for a moment, before leaping into the air and starfishing him. *Starfishing* is what we called it when I wrapped my arms and legs around him. (I've only since found out that it can mean . . . other things.)

That first summer we were together was so sweltering that I'd invariably be wearing a thin T-shirt dress and nothing else. I went to work braless and knickerless for a grand total of three weeks. Thinking back, I used to get very sweaty, and wonder whether a sturdy pair of cotton pants might have soaked up some of the moisture between my thighs.

One afternoon when he came by after work, I was wearing an ankle-length dress. In order to successfully pull off the starfish, I had to hike up the material above my knees. My vulva pressed against his shirt, leaving a damp patch on his poplin weave. But, for the first time since we got together, he said no.

'It's a nice day,' he said. 'Let's go out for a bit first.'

'Where?' I jumped down, lead-footed.

'I don't know, out.'

'I've no money.' Those were the reckless days of pubbing, clubbing and overspending with Grace. When I said I had no money, I did in fact have my overdraft. I was frequently going over the limit, but always seemed to scrape together enough for *something*. I'd already had two cans of cider that evening.

I put on my flip-flops and we headed down Wilbraham Road. There were children riding tricycles in driveways, hair curling with sweat at the temples. Women wore strappy tops that revealed ghosts of other strappy tops haunting their skin. Men walked bare-chested, pecs puffed out and tummies sucked in. Everyone was moving 50 per cent slower.

We ducked into the Co-op for some snacks. Then we went to Chorlton Park and sat on the grass, beside a tree stump with an eagle carved into it.

'I'm sick of that place,' Ben said, shaking his head. He was talking about work. It wasn't so much the job itself he hated, although that did sound incredibly tedious. He worked in insurance, but none of the interesting insurances like life, travel, or pet. He insured vans. I'd asked him what the job entailed several times, and never got much further than *processing legal documentation* and *updating the client database*. For Ben, the problem wasn't boredom though – it was people.

'Keith still doing your head in?' I asked.

'He's nicking my lunches.' Ben bit into a Scotch egg. 'Seriously, man, I don't know what his problem is.'

'Just your lunches, or everyone's?'

'Dunno. But what's the point of bringing in a couscous salad if that dickhead's just gonna have it? Anyway.' He handed me a sausage. 'Eat this. You didn't have any tea yesterday.'

I bit into the tiny, wrinkled piece of meat. 'Neither did you. Or lunch, by the sound of it.'

'You've been looking pale lately.'

'I have?'

Ben stopped chewing and wiped away a hair that was stuck to my mouth. He liked me with long hair, but it was wavy and rebellious, always getting in the way.

'Look,' he said. 'Tell me to *do one* if you like. I don't mean to mither you. You've just been on the coke *a lot* lately.'

I ripped a handful of grass out of the soil and let the blades rain down onto my lap. 'So?'

'It's not that I don't like it. Last night was fun. You know that. But you're not eating properly, kid. I've seen people go down these routes before, and . . .' Ben's older brother had been homeless for a while, and his mum had only just accepted him back into the family. It was a complicated story that I didn't like to pry into, but drugs were at the heart of it.

'I'll be fine, honestly. Grace is the one who –'

Ben popped a grape between my lips. 'Just making sure you look after yourself, babe.'

I spat the grape onto the grass and grinned. My sexy boyfriend was looking after me.

'Right, you little shit,' he said, putting a grape in his mouth, then spat it at me. Before long, we were spitting grapes all over the public lawn, as parents watched aghast, kids giggling.

'Fuck this,' Ben said after a while. He grabbed my hand and yanked me to my feet. We ran out of the park, leaving our picnic strewn across the grass behind us. 'Race you to the nearest bar.'

God, I loved that summer.

Joy is a net of love by which you can catch souls.

Mother Teresa

Snapchat from Mina

Today

TEENYMEENY

| Can we stop doing these now? They only appear for a few seconds then I immediately forget them. Makes me feel strange. Sorry.

Note from Ben

[*This was waiting on my desk at the Maggie's Centre when I arrived on Thursday morning. It was wrapped in newspaper — the horoscopes section — and, circled in red pen was my star sign, Leo, which said: 'Now's the time to take a huge leap of faith. No more Cautious Carol.'*]

Oh-la-la,

Alright, our kid. Long time no see. Thought I'd reply to your text with a letter; I know how pen and paper gives you thrills. Hope you don't mind me sending this to your work. Grace told me where to find you a while back. Cancer centre, huh? Seems intense. You always were fierce, mind you. Maybe you're just a mentalist. Either way, sounds like you haven't changed.

Saw this hardcover copy of Cindy Sherman's *Centerfolds* in Oxfam: the pictures turn you on, but make you feel guilty for being turned on. Made me think of you.

It's been about a year since we went to see that performance at the Cornerhouse. The one where that guy was writing poetry on his girlfriend's skin with a tattoo gun, but no ink. What's that called again? Bloodlining. I remember listening to Björk and looking at the girl's hoohas. It was mint.

How the hell are you, anyway? Got any new tattoos? Gimme a shout if you fancy a drink.

LongPig

Mantra of the Week

Neti neti.

Rough translation: Not this. Oh no, not this.

Text Message to Ben

Fri 18 July 20:59

How about tomorrow night?

Email from Mum

From: Alice McGregor
To: Ottila McGregor
Date: Sat, 19 July, 2014 at 5:20
Subject: Fwd: 5am morning brain

---------- Forwarded message ----------
From: Alice McGregor <alice.mcgregor54@mcgregormail.com>
To: aart@aartjonckers.nl
Date: Sat, 19 July 2014 at 5:18
Subject: 5am morning brain

Mr Jonckers, have you ever tried growing chard? Yesterday I sowed the Bright Lights variety. Its stalks are coloured like flames. By the end of summer, I should be able to harvest this little monster every two weeks. What a mild taste for such a fiery dragon of a vegetable. I could braise it with some lentils, or wilt it with a red wine reduction. We'll have a real treat on our hands!

I say 'we', Mr Jonckers. Really, it's just me. My husband died almost three years ago – I believe I mentioned that in my last email – and since then it has been me, and me alone, ruling my green empire. I do have my two daughters, of course, though they both fled the nest quite some time ago. Speaking of daughters, sorry to pester you, I know you must be a very busy man, but I don't suppose you've had a chance to think about Mina's case yet, have you? She's not getting any better, you see. In fact, she's getting worse. She won't even speak to me during some of my visits. I feel as though I'm losing her. I don't remember being this full of grief since Bernhardt left us.

Hey ho. Onwards and upwards. At least I can talk to you. It's nice to have someone to chat with around the 5 a.m. mark, when my 'early morning brain' is at its worst. Apparently, most suicides occur between 4 and 7 a.m. You probably know that already. It makes sense, doesn't it? The world feels deadest at this time.

Don't worry, Ottila! I'm not suicidal! (I'm forwarding these emails to my daughter – my eldest daughter, Ottila. She says we've got to keep a 'paper trail', even though this is an email. Between you and me, I think she's just keeping tabs. You know, Ottila is one of life's grafters. She tries very hard to succeed, but always seems to end up in some scrape or other. She takes after her father in that respect.)

Well, I have to admit, I've had a tipple or two, and I think the Nytol is kicking in, so I'm off to do my sun salutations, before I no longer know my up dog from my down. Ottila tells me Vinyasa works wonders, but the jury's still out. Currently, I much prefer chard.

Right then, Jonckers, my old chap, adieu for now! And if that reply ever feels like winging its way towards me . . . I'm always here.

AM

Text Message to Mum

Sat 19 July 10:28

If the yoga doesn't work out for you, how about meditation? I tried some this morning and feel great. I'll email some YouTube links. Works much better when you're sober by the way. x

Text Message to Thales

Sat 19 July 12:41

Your disappearing act is getting ridiculous, and I'm sick of tripping over your boxes. Let me know when you're moving out properly and we'll sort out rent, etc.

Ben

Ben once told me, in the dead of night, that he knew that he had it in him to commit a crime. Not something little – like cycling on the pavement or stealing a Post-it note – but something big. Something huge.

'What do you mean?' I asked. 'Like, rob a bank?'

'Maybe that.'

'Or kill someone?'

'That sort of thing, yeah.'

'What do you mean, that sort of thing? You'd commit homicide?'

'I don't know, something like that. Yes.'

We were having sex at the time. We'd put on 2Pac's 'Hit 'Em Up' on full volume, and we'd been shouting dangerous things to each other: *I want to peel off your eyelids with my teeth. If you do that, I'll snap your cock in two. Let's knock down the walls and fuck all our neighbours.* We were drunk, filled with passion. We didn't mean it.

At least, I didn't.

But we'd stopped shouting a long time ago. When Ben told me, while looking into my eyes as he made love to me, that he could kill somebody, I knew that he wasn't joking. My boyfriend was a potential murderer.

'Ben, would you kill me?' My voice came out small and fragile.

'Dunno, our kid,' he said, staring down at me thoughtfully, 'depends.'

Ben was never able to come unless we were in a very specific position. That meant he could do anything, rough or slow, and unless we did one special pose, he could go on forever. This was our anniversary, so before manipulating my limbs into their inevitable contortion act, Ben had chosen to adopt an hour-long missionary position as a treat. It was my favourite. But that night, as Ben and I made ventral contact, and he stared into my eyes, thinking about what it might take for him to end my life, he came inside me. Hard.

As I get ready to go out now, daubing ivory foundation under my tired eyes and spritzing my pulse points with Jo Malone's Pomegranate Noir – a present from Mum – I remember that night with Ben, and begin to feel excited. Anything could happen tonight. I don't need a drink inside me. I just need Ben.

I've opted to wear a short black dress with sheer panels down the sides, showing the pale glow of my torso underneath. Ben once fucked me while I was wearing this dress, before we went out to dinner. We got so drunk that night we lost our house keys and he punched a hole in the front door. I punched *him* after that, and spent the night at Grace's, hooking my leg over her as we slept.

There's water dripping down the back of the hall cupboard. I look at the sorry selection of damp shoes and pick out a dry pair. I'm going for a black kitten heel, which I believe says: *I might be feeling sexy, but I'm still exceedingly classy.* I remember buying this pair with Grace in Affleck's Palace. We went to the café opposite afterwards, pouring sugar into our tea, spilling it all over the tabletops decorated with collages of superheroes. Grace had bought a Victorian chamber pot in Affleck's, and wore it home on the bus on her head. We argued about something or other that night over three bottles of wine, and ended up arm wrestling beside a piss-filled pot.

Me. Grace. Ben. All these memories.

As I pull the shoes out of the cupboard, one of Thales's trainers tumbles out too. The trainer is big and impossibly clean. *I'm joining a gym*, I hear Thales say, choosing a pair of white ASICS in Sports Direct. *I'm running off this extra weight. I'm going to become handsome for you.*

You're already handsome, I hear myself replying. I throw the trainer back into the cupboard and shut the door.

Ben has suggested we meet at Common, his favourite bar in the Northern Quarter. It's full of people with shaggy beards and manicured moustaches. Not quite Ben's aesthetic, with his shaved head and Carhartt hoodies, but they play good music and serve decent beer. Plus, I once gave Ben a handjob in the disabled toilet, so maybe he's picked the venue for sentimental reasons.

On the tram on the way into town, a baby cries. 'She wants her methadone,' the baby's mum jokes to an old woman in a flowery headscarf. At least, I think it's a joke. The old woman looks at me and smiles. She senses I'm a good person. I hope she's right.

I look out of the window at the huge glass buildings of Salford Quays, gleaming in the evening sun. Then we pass the small red-brick terraces of Ordsall. A couple of years ago I saw an exhibition of old street signs, rescued from demolished Salford neighbourhoods. Havelock Drive. Countess Grove. Isaac Street. I read them aloud like names on gravestones. Manchester is thriving, and that makes it an appealing place to live, but regeneration always comes at a price.

Have I changed too much lately? Have I betrayed something that I once was? I study my reflection in the glass. When Ben and I broke up, I got my hair cut really short. Recently, I've been letting it grow into a messy bob. This in-between stage feels less like me than any other style I've had. I sometimes fantasise about shaving my head. Starting from scratch. I think if I ever went through with it I'd feel more lost than ever.

As the tram pulls in to St Peter's Square, the old woman widens her eyes at me. Her expression seems to ask: 'Are you really about to do this?' We both stand up and step out onto the street. She lights a cigarette and walks towards the library.

I head the other way, towards the city centre. Outside Primark a guy in a silver waistcoat sings R.E.M.'s 'It's the End of the World as We Know It'. It doesn't quite drown out the accusatory clack of my kitten heels on the pavement as I head down Tib Street. *We were having such a nice time in the cupboard with those trainers*, they tell me.

'Save yourself,' the guy in the silver waistcoat sings on the street corner behind me. 'Serve yourself.' I'm metres away now. Metres away from getting my old life back – at least for one night. For all I know, Thales has been on numerous dates since he stopped coming home. And that's what this is all about, isn't it? Thales.

Text Message to Ben

Sat 19 July 19:25
Sorry, mate. Won't be coming tonight. Change of heart.

Be Good for Me

Dad's final words are swirling around my head.
Be good for me.
Be good for me.
Be good for me.
What exactly did he mean? He was always saying it. *I'd best be off, darling. Be good for me.* Was he trying to prepare me for a time he'd no longer be around? *I'm dying of cancer, darling. Be good for me.* Did he really think I needed frequent reminders to behave? And to do it, not for myself, but for him? I don't remember him saying it once to Mina. To Mina it was always: *Big hugs.*

I haven't gone in yet. I'm standing on the opposite side of the street, looking up at the sign. Twenty Twenty Two. It's a place I've never been to before. Probably new. A quick search online has informed me that it's a 'bar, events, art, and ping pong space, located in the heart of Manchester's creative Northern Quarter'. It's possible that Grace would go to a place like this. Scratch that. It's *probable* that Grace would go to a place like this. But it's very unlikely that Ben would. And right now, that's what counts.

There's such a stigma around the word alcoholic. I'm an ALCOHOLIC. Even if you whisper it, it comes out at full volume. But people can change. I've been sober for six months. Half a year. Surely that counts for something. My liver must have repaired itself by now. And brains rewire themselves. What's that thing called? Neuroplasticity. My brain's probably moulded itself into a brand new shape, the shape of a normal drinker's. I can do this.

And it doesn't make me a bad person.

Does it?

Types of Happiness

QUIET HAPPINESS
e.g. lying on the floor, looking at the lampshade

LOUD HAPPINESS
e.g. drinking cappuccino + discussing your promotion

MAD HAPPINESS
e.g. running around the house quacking

BAD HAPPINESS
e.g. googling 'stab wounds'

TWEE HAPPINESS

e.g. meadows .... VISA DEBIT from customer

SERIOUS HAPPINESS

e.g. alphabetising books

REAL HAPPINESS

e.g. forgiveness ???

Voicemail to Mum

[*Recorded 20 July 2016 at 1.12 a.m.*]

Hi Mum. Only me. Nothing to worry about. I, um, I'm really sorry. I dropped something. I didn't mean to. [*Sobbing.*] I dropped it down the drain, on the road, you know. And now it's gone. I was only standing here for a minute, trying to find the money for a taxi, but I heard voices and it distracted me – I dropped it down the drain, Mum. I'm so sorry. Dad gave it to me and I love it. I don't know how it fell off but it was my favourite watch and I'm just so, so – It's not good. [*Pained cry.*] I'm not good at all.

Drink App

SOBER

————— FOR —————

0
days

That's:
7,020 seconds
117 minutes
1 hours
0 days
0 weeks
0 months
0% of 2014

Rewards!

No rewards yet. Check back later.

Voicemail from Mum

[Recorded 20 July 2016 at 10.50 a.m.]

Sorry I missed your call, and now you've missed mine. I'm just back from a women's paintballing group near Bradford-on-Avon. My back's covered in bruises; looks like I've got the measles. I'm really sorry to hear you're struggling, Ottila. And please don't worry about losing the watch. Your dad wouldn't mind one bit. We've been through worse than that! I couldn't hear very well through the tears: did you say you were hearing voices? Dad's voices used to tell him to do all sorts of nasty things. Maybe you should see a doctor? Anyway, send me an email sometime. I'm rubbish with my phone. Love you.

Little Book of Happy

Dear Little Book of Lies,

My eyes, my forehead, my stomach. They're all broken. I'm so hungover. Haven't felt this bad for years. I've been watching feel-good TV on iPlayer: *Snog Marry Avoid?, Jonathan Creek, Have I Got News for You*. It's not working. The worst thing, worse than the hangover, is knowing how stupid I've been. I put myself in so much danger last night. Maybe it sounds melodramatic, but I honestly think I'm lucky to be here, safe and sound in my own bedroom.

I only meant to have a couple of drinks. That sounds so predictable, doesn't it? But I did. I couldn't believe how strong the first glass of wine tasted. I could feel the alcohol vapours travelling up my nose as I drank. Almost put me off having any more. After half a glass, I felt tipsy. I started to get a numbness, a pleasant softening in my lips and tongue. So I kept going. Then I ordered a whole bottle. I scribbled my thoughts down feverishly on scraps of paper while I drank. It was like waking up after a long sleep.

That's when I got talking to Keith, an audiologist from Walthamstow. Keith shared the rest of my bottle, then bought another. I ran to the loo to be sick during our conversation, but Keith didn't care. He was in Manchester on business (a hearing aid convention, I think?), and after a couple of games of ping pong and a lot of flirting, he asked me to go back to his hotel. I remember telling him I was a lesbian – my default knockback – and I also remember wanting to phone Grace, to ask her to come and rescue me. But I forced myself not to. Because I'm not sure that's what I want. And even the drunk me knew that much.

First thing I did when I woke up was grab my phone. There was a pissed-off text from Ben, which I deleted before I read it in full. Something about me being 'up to my old tricks'. I shouldn't have stood him up at the last minute, but I know I did the right thing by not going.

I looked at my dialled numbers too, and saw that I phoned Mum at one, the Samaritans at two and a pizza delivery company at quarter to three. I've no idea what I said to the Samaritans. It's not the first time they've been there for me after a heavy night out. I vaguely remember the call to Mum, and I'm mortified. I must have sounded wasted. I'm gutted about losing the watch. Dad gave it to me for my birthday, shortly after we found out about the cancer. He said the 'gift of time' was the best present of all. He was right.

Mum's just tried calling again. I'll phone her later, when I feel up to it. The voicemail she left this morning has thrown me a bit. What she said about Dad hearing voices: how did I not know about it until now? I know Mina hears voices, but why didn't Dad ever tell us that he did? Plus: if Mina hears voices, and Dad heard voices, then does that mean I hear voices too? Maybe I do, and I just don't realise. Maybe the voices told me to drink last night.

I wish, at times like this, I could phone Mina. I'm so jealous of people who can talk to their siblings about what's on their mind. Who don't have to walk on eggshells, afraid they might say 'hello' in the wrong tone of voice. The envelope from Mina, the one Mum gave me, is in my sock drawer. Is this the right time to open it? It'd be nice to see one of Mina's funny little doodles, or read one of her zany jokes. But what if there's something horrible in there? What if it's a list of everything I've ever done wrong? All the ways I've hurt her? I think I'll lie back in bed and watch another episode of *Snog Marry Avoid?* No, hang on. I'm going to go and throw up. And then I'll get back to trying to laugh at people on TV who are not me.

Signed,

The Idiot

Picking up the Pieces

If you're filling in this page of the workbook, it means you've had a relapse. Chances are, you're feeling a lot of negative emotions right now.

'I'm worthless because I drink. I drink because I'm worthless.'

If that sounds like you, stop and take a deep breath. Being hard on yourself is not going to help. Think back to one of the early exercises we did in this workbook, 'Forgive Yourself and Move Forward', where we learnt that feeling bad can stop you feeling good. It applies here more than ever.

Below are some examples of *stinky thinking* surrounding your relapse. Fill in the *healthy thinking* column on the right hand side with a more positive way of rephrasing the beliefs. If you find yourself slipping into dangerous thought patterns, refer to this table, and find that positive energy deep inside you.

Stinky Thinking	Healthy Thinking
I'm no good	
I'll never get sober	
I deserve to be punished	
I've let everyone down	
There's no point trying	
I hate myself	
I want to die	*Actually I don't want to die. That's something.*

Mina's Unsent Letter

[*This is written on several loose leaves of writing paper tucked inside a card with a Quentin Blake illustration of 'Square Sweets that Look Round'.*]

Dear Otterpillar,

I'm sorry I quit my Masters, so we're not twinny-twin-twins any more. I just wasn't cut out for uni like you. Going to events and meeting other people and handing in essays all became too much for me. I tried doing breathing exercises and being mindful, but there's this screaming in my brain, and when I'm in a stressful situation it gets too much to bear.

I worry about you so much. I wish I could keep you and Mum and Dad safe. It's very difficult!!!! I am so aware of everything you do for me and have done for me and I'm thankful for everything we shared as children. For opening the window for me so I could get into the house more quickly after school. For playing Sylvanian Families long after you'd grown out of them. For not telling Mum when I tried to kill you.

I'm always looking back at the past, Otty, but I'm so scared of committing to a future. I had a dream last night that it was 2017, and we had crows' feet and bits of grey in our hair. I dreamt that you were wearing a red beret and you were laughing in that snorty pig way that you do when you're exquisitely amused. You were a famous short story writer and your books had been translated into sixteen languages. You'd translated them all yourself!!! I was curled up like a snail. My lips were blue and I looked bruised and beaten. [*Sticker of a snail, beside which Mina has written 'OUCH'.*]

Imagine, Ottila. Another decade of depression. There's just no way I'm strong enough.

No. Shake it off, Mina!!! How about this for a plan? Ten years from now, me, you, Mum and Dad should go on a big adventure. To a beach in Barbados or something. Mum will be the sensible one, warning us not to eat too many snacks before dinner. Dad will be telling us a joke, dripping mint choc chip ice-cream all over his beard. I'll have a child by then, a son called Spike, and I'll tell him off every ten minutes for being cheeky. But not horrible telling off. Just mapping out his boundaries. And you'll be back with Reatha, making gigantic, Turner-Prize-winning art installations together. As well as getting your Carver-esque short stories regularly published in the *New Yorker* and *Paris Review*, of course.

((((((Tilly)))))). You are the best sister I could ever have hoped for. And don't apologise for things you apologised for years ago. All is forgiven: but really, there is nothing to forgive. Consider the whole lot forgotten.

Hugs and kisses,
Your piece of pencil crayon sharpening (turquoise colour),

Mina. x x x x x x x x x x x x x

Then

On the thirteenth of July 2007, Mina took an overdose. It was Dad who found her. Lying at the top of the stairs, the washing-up bowl beside her, splashed with sick.

When Dad called the emergency services, I'm not sure why he asked for the police before an ambulance. Both turned up. All that fuss for one unconscious girl.

I was in Glasgow at the time. Mum texted me. 'Bad news I'm afraid. Mina in intensive care. No need to come back yet but stay on red alert.'

It was four days before Mina woke up, and a week before they told us there were no early signs of brain damage. Her throat was bruised from the tube they'd inserted into her, but apart from that, she was okay. Sadder than I've ever known her, but okay.

Dad didn't visit her in psychiatric hospital. Not once. He was too upset. Mum and I got angry with him for that. Then, when Dad ended up in hospital, after the cancer diagnosis, Mina didn't visit him. *She* was too upset. They weren't so different, Mina and my dad. It's just that my dad didn't want to die. And Mina did.

Mum never quite managed to wash the vomit stains off the carpet. Every time any of us used the stairs, we'd see the faint purplish splatter, a Rorschach test.

'It's like blood,' Mum said, on her way to bed.

'It's some kind of creature,' said Dad, going down for breakfast.

'It's Mina's heart,' I said, frozen.

Mina closed her eyes. 'It's just the beginning,' she murmured.

When we had the house valued, after Dad had died and Mum was thinking of selling up, the estate agent wrote something on his clipboard when he saw it. 'Shame,' he said. And we all felt it, in different ways.

Maggie's Centre

It's been two days since the relapse, but I still don't feel right on Monday morning. In fact, when André passes me, he says: 'God, you look rough, Ottila. Everything okay?'

I didn't read Mina's letter until late last night. I was unable to sleep, and told myself that if I just got it out of the way, then I'd be able to stop obsessing over it and drop off. Of course it didn't work like that. I began raking over old memories. Thinking about how guilty I felt the day Mum told me Mina had tried to kill herself. How self-absorbed I must have been not to notice the warning signs. Mina's words: *You are the best sister I could ever have hoped for.* Did she believe that someone as flawed as me was all she deserved? I don't know. She said I have nothing to apologise for. I should probably use her words to help me find a way to forgive myself and move forward. But I'm not ready for that yet. Today I'm desperate to cry. When I lost my watch on Saturday night I cried, yes, but those were drunk tears. Drunk tears don't make you feel any better. The alcohol must destroy the natural painkillers. I need real, sober tears. Yesterday I tried replacing the feel-good TV programmes with *Call the Midwife*, *Happy Valley* and *EastEnders*. They definitely made me feel worse, but my eyes remained dry.

Before bumping into André, I was planning on heading to the kitchen to get a glass of water for my third Berocca. I don't know if three Beroccas in one morning is within recommended limits, but each time I take one I feel a tiny bit less guilty. Hearing André tell me how crap I look, however, makes me duck into the quiet room and collapse on a sky blue pouffe.

'Hello, Ottila,' says a familiar voice.

I look towards the window and see a silhouette. Maude. The sun is blazing and it illuminates the dust particles around her. I try to remember what the view is out of that window. I think it's a small patch of wasteland next to the car park, opposite the Brachytherapy Unit.

Maude comes over and takes a seat on the pouffe next to me. She offers me a Polo, then asks: 'How's your day going?'

'Fine thanks, Maude,' I reply with as much cheer as I can muster. 'How are you?' I take a mint and balance it on my tongue. When we were little, Mina and I used to compete with one another, see who could make theirs last the longest. Mina always won.

'Me?' Maude says. 'Oh, I'm fine. But then I'm not the one who just walked into the quiet room crying.'

'I'm not crying.' I touch my cheeks, to make sure.

'Aren't you?' Maude grinds her Polo into pieces while she looks at me, her eyes flecked with gold. 'You're sad,' she says. 'It's written in every feature.'

'It's nothing serious. Family problems. Silly stuff.'

'How's that *chłopak* treating you? The Greek boy?'

I try to smile. It's more of a grimace.

'It is still the Greek boy, isn't it?' Maude nudges me in the ribs.

'Ow!' I yelp, almost spitting out my mint. And then . . . I don't know why it happens. Maybe it's because I've been desperate for a hug since the relapse. It might just be a jab, but it's human contact.

The important thing is, I feel what I've been waiting for. My throat tightens, and an urgent pressure builds up behind my eyes. Gratefully, I succumb to it, and the tears spill out of me, each one more soothing than the last.

Email to Thales

From: Ottila McGregor
To: Thales Sanna
Date: Mon, 21 July, 2014 at 19:35
Subject: Re: Argh

Thales,

This is crazy. We've been living apart for more than a month, but you haven't moved out yet. When are you coming back to finish packing those boxes? I'm feeling pretty pissed off that you're behaving so childishly about all this. You called me a sociopath a few weeks ago, so why don't you just get in touch and we can end things properly?

Furthermore (and yes, I am using a stuffy, argumentative word like 'furthermore'), you blame me for never telling you about Reatha, but I'm not the only one with secrets. What about you and Eleni? I found a letter you wrote her at the start of the year, just a couple of weeks before you and I started hanging out. Oh yes, I found out all about your gorgeous ex-fiancée. A Greek goddess, and with a sense of humour to boot? I don't know why you didn't send the letter to her in the end. Maybe you had to draft a new one because you forgot to tell her how out of your league she was? Oh no, wait, you said that. In that case, maybe she was just too dreadful to

hang on a sec, you've just come online –

Gchat with Thales

Thales Sanna   _ ↗ ×

thales. you're here

hello?

hi ottila

was writing you an email

read it before we chat

just sent it

read it yet?

I wanted to tell you about eleni

it's not the same as you fucking my sister though, is it?

um

pretty much

come on, that's not fair

come here and get your boxes

I'm sick of them

I hate you

I hate you too

I miss you

ok that was awkward

forget I said it

I still hate you anyway

I miss you too

MON, 7.49 PM

Happiness is a
form of courage.

Holbrook Jackson

Letter to Mina

Hey Teenio Meenio,

I'm just writing to say I hope you're okay. Don't worry about replying; I know you're not in the right frame of mind. Mum says you ate a sandwich and two satsumas last week. That's great. I hope you can start eating even more soon. I know: I'm a nag!

Things are good with me. Work is going fine. A woman called Maude brought in some *chruściki* today, which she said she'd baked especially for me. *Chruściki* is Polish for *little dry twigs*. Something like that, anyway! They're basically ribbons of deep-fried dough: delicious.

Mum and I had a long chat on the phone the other day, and we talked about Dad. Did Dad ever tell you he used to hear voices? Mum says she thought I knew, but Dad never mentioned it. Apparently the voices told him to do bad things. Mum is scared to talk to you about it in case you get upset, but I thought you might actually be quite pleased to hear it. Then you'll know we don't think you're making it up. You're just the same as Popsicle!

I heard you tried to hang yourself again on Friday. Mum says your eyes are bloodshot and you're finding reading difficult at the moment. I hope you can read this sometime soon, but I understand if it's a struggle. Mind you, you'll either have made it this far or you won't, so I'll shut up!

Ottila xxxxxxxxxx

Recovery Meeting Transcript

PATIENT: I'm terrified of it happening again.

THERAPIST: Terrified that you'll drink?

PATIENT: Now that it's happened once, the spell is broken. All that hard work, all those days of sobriety – one hundred and ninety-one days – were wiped away in one mouthful. It's like that whole period of time, from January to July, is now meaningless.

THERAPIST: You've done your body the world of good. Your fatty liver has completely cleared up.

PATIENT: So what's to stop me drinking again, if I'm back to being a normal, healthy person?

THERAPIST: The likelihood is that you'd –

PATIENT: I don't want to drink. I really don't. These last few months I've been a different person. I feel like I'm only just starting to discover my real personality. The non-drunk me. I like myself more.

THERAPIST: That's wonderful.

PATIENT: I got my white belt last night. Apparently my roundhouse kick is 'exemplary', but my uppercuts need work. I could show you some of my moves, if we put that table over by the door.

THERAPIST: I don't think we're allowed to do that.

PATIENT: I guess it might be dangerous. I could kick you.

THERAPIST: I'm sure you wouldn't do that.

PATIENT: There's so much anger inside me. I never realised until I started going to these classes. The carpet stinks of old sweat. It's full of scabs and athlete's foot, but standing there, in that room, makes me feel great. There's this big red punch bag hanging in one corner, which the teacher calls Jeremy. I feel like if I could just have half an hour in that gym, just me and Jeremy, I could really blast my negative thoughts into oblivion.

It's funny. I got a tiger tattooed on my ribcage at the start of the year. I wanted it to symbolise the force I felt on the inside. I knew I had strength back then, but ... this is different. I can see now that the kind of strength I had before was just a toughness, a resistance, an endurance. It was so passive. Now I've got some real *fight* in me. I sat at the back of the bus the other day. On the top deck, where the badasses sit. I wedged myself between two big-bicepped men and sat with my legs stretched out and my eyes half-closed, scowling, and I swear I could've *beaten* anyone who got in my way. Actually, one of the men next to me asked me if I'd mind not treading on his Fine Art portfolio, and I apologised and crossed my legs. But I still had the scowl of a lunatic.

THERAPIST: Should I be worried about this?

PATIENT: I wouldn't hurt a fly.

THERAPIST: I've noticed you use the language of madness a lot when you talk. Words like lunatic, crazy, insane. Is it something you worry about? That you might be insane?

PATIENT: No. Of course not. Why? *Should* I?

THERAPIST: What about Mina? Do you worry about her?

PATIENT: I worry about her, yes, but not that she's insane. Even if she was, I'd still love her. I don't know . . . they're just words. I suppose I'd think twice before using them in certain situations, in case I offended someone. Are *you* offended? Mina wouldn't mind. I'm sure she's called me a lunatic plenty of times.

THERAPIST: Let's get back to your anger issues.

PATIENT: You'd tell me if you thought I was insane, wouldn't you?

THERAPIST: I don't think you're insane.

PATIENT: Hearing voices doesn't make you insane, does it?

THERAPIST: A surprising number of people experience auditory hallucinations. Up to a quarter of us. Do *you* experience them, Ottila?

PATIENT: Not that I know of. I'd know, wouldn't I?

THERAPIST: I think I've led us down the wrong path here. Tell me about how important it is for you to feel strong. You want to feel like you're capable of winning a fight, is that right?

PATIENT: I would never hurt anyone, like I was saying. But it's good to know I *could*. I think I finally understand my old flatmate, Laurie, now. *Kanabō* club. Mythical weapons. This is no different, I suppose. Maybe I understand Ben's criminal impulses too.

THERAPIST: How are things with Thales?

PATIENT: He's back at the flat, finally. We're talking things through. He says he's learning to accept the fact that I went out with his sister. It was a shock seeing him again. I thought he'd have put on weight being at his parents' so long, but he's actually looking quite slim. Gaunt, in fact. He's got black circles under his eyes, and he's developed this new habit of jiggling his legs up and down when we're sitting at the table. I had no idea the toll all this was taking on him.

Anyway, the main thing is Thales is back, and he's taking me to Jodrell Bank for my birthday next week. We're going to look at the Lovell Telescope, which has been scanning the cosmos for over half a century.

THERAPIST: Communication is important.

PATIENT: It was so weird reading that letter he wrote to Eleni, but I'm trying to learn from it. Since he moved back in, Thales has been working on the script for his short film every night, sometimes until one or two. The old me might have asked him to come to bed, but the new me isn't going to be controlling. All I want to do is help.

THERAPIST: Sounds like you really are getting stronger.

PATIENT: Thales mentioned in that letter that Eleni had stopped him from seeing friends. You know, he's never mentioned having any friends to me. That's strange, isn't it? I've been too wrapped up in myself to realise that until now. I took the plunge and sent a text to my old flatmate, Laurie, asking if he fancies coming over for a coffee sometime. He was a bit of a nightmare to live with, but I think he might be okay as a friend.

THERAPIST: As long as you're not trying to rush everything at once.

PATIENT: Nope. Slow and steady wins the race. Ooh, maybe I'll get a tortoise tattoo.

Text Message from Thales

> **Thu 31 July 16:41**
>
> Sorry for the moodiness at breakfast. I didn't sleep a wink last night!

Email from Mum

From: Alice McGregor
To: Ottila McGregor
Date: Tue, 5 August, 2014 at 3:51
Subject: Fwd: Fever

---------- Forwarded message ----------
From: Alice McGregor <alice.mcgregor54@mcgregormail.com>
To: aart@aartjonckers.nl
Date: Tue, 5 August, 2014 at 3:50
Subject: Fever

Mr Jonckers,

At the risk of you thinking something along the lines of 'mutton dressed as lamb', there's something I have to tell you: I'm wearing a silver minidress. Me! In a silver, sequined minidress from New Look! And I've just been out in said minidress, dancing the night away to songs I've never heard of, in a nightclub called Fever. Well, I say songs. They're more like a series of electronic bleeps, but by golly you can wiggle your hips to them.

Some of the young girls I was with, Sharon and Lydia, snorted some white powder to keep them going for longer. I don't know whether it was coke, crack or ecstasy. I haven't done drugs since I had a bad trip with my husband, Bernhardt, when we were much, much younger. I ate half a gram of magic mushrooms and ended up head-butting a mirror, thinking I was stuck in a void.

It's an unusual feeling being the oldest person in a nightclub. You get some funny looks, even some appalled ones. But there are a few, a select few, who seem to love it. One young lad pressed his crotch against mine and tried to lick my throat! Can you believe it? Of course, I pushed him away, the filthy little sod. I am in the market for a boyfriend, truth be told, but not under those circumstances. Nightclubs are for boogying the night away, not for cheap thrills.

I've signed up to an online dating site but I'm having trouble getting my profile right. I can't work out how to talk about myself without sounding depressing. It's so hard to know what to say to a perfect stranger. Unless that stranger is *you*, Mr Jonckers. Ha. I almost snorted out my hot chocolate. Can you imagine that?! The two of us, walking along the canals of Amsterdam, me in my silver minidress, and you smoking a pipe, trying to dream up new ways to support autistic people. It's so crazy it might actually work.

On a different note, do you ever prescribe medicine to family members of autistic people? I was thinking maybe a little something to calm me down in the evenings before bed. I don't know, nothing too addictive, and of course it must be legal. I'd talk to my doctor about it but she is (pardon my French!) a Grade-A bitch. She wouldn't even give me a prescription for some cough medicine last time I asked.

Ah well, time for me to lie prostrate on my mattress for three hours before finally succumbing to sleep. Goodnight, my handsome hero. Don't worry, I'm only messing about. Life's too short not to have a joke now and then.

Seriously, though: any thoughts on Mina???

Regards,

Alive

Little Book of Happy

LBOH,

I just ripped a crappy old Albert Einstein quote out of you. Einstein might have invented the general theory of relativity, but he knew eff all about happiness. All you need to be happy, he says, is a chair, a table, a musical instrument and some fruit. Pah. You need much more than that, I'm discovering. One thing you definitely need is hope. And now Thales and I are back together, and my therapist has talked me through the relapse, and given me an acronym to help stop it happening again, and I've ditched Ben from my life, and I've managed to cry and cry and cry some more, I am left with a moderate amount of *hope*. It's a sweet, sweet feeling.

Since Thales and I reunited, I'm pleased to say we've ditched our old rota and have a new plan that involves spending more time on our own individual projects, and more time with friends. Delyth and I went to the Cornerhouse to watch *Ramanujan* – a biopic about a maths prodigy who travels to England from India and becomes a Fellow at Cambridge University. Delyth said she'd have preferred the story if he'd ended up at a different university, like Bangor or Lincoln or 'anywhere but bloody Oxbridge', but I liked it.

Also, Laurie accepted my invitation and came round for a coffee. When I'm not living with that guy, he's fine. He and Thales hit it off as expected, and were flicking through the Dungeons & Dragons *Monster Manual* in no time. Before he left, Laurie invited Thales to join *kanabō* club. I tried not to snort with laughter and I'm glad I didn't, because Thales said yes.

Two days ago, it was my birthday. It was weird not celebrating with a bottle of fizz and a night on the town. We watched three episodes of *Battlestar Galactica* and had an early night. Well, *I* had an early night. Thales stayed up working on his script, throwing screwed-up balls of paper across the living room floor.

What else is going on? André has been talking to me like a human being. I've started training for my white-and-yellow belt in kickboxing. I've even started to get the hang of meditating, and managed to do it for a whole hour yesterday. Admittedly I fell asleep for some of it, but it recharged my chakras no end.

O

Email from Mum

From: Alice McGregor
To: Ottila McGregor
Date: Mon, 25 August, 2014 at 23:10
Subject: Fwd: Fever

Darlingf,

Dads anversarys coming up on Wednesday.. I'm goingto take a pilgrimage up to scotland and light a candleforhim. I'll be back by end of the week.Probvably stay in a trekker hut somewhere along the West Highlaned Way, and lose myself in the wildernesss for a while,, with a great big battle of whisky.

Make sure Thalees looks after you. Your time together is so precious you know.?

Love you oodles, noddle,
Mum x0x0o

Text Message to Mina

Wed 27 Aug 20:31

A good old-fashioned SMS for you. No more stinky old Snapchat! Hope you're getting on okay. I'm eating smørrebrød in honour of Dad. x

Viking Death

Viking Mania <http://www.vikingmania.com>

Viking Death

What happened when Vikings died? Did they have funerals? Did they believe in the afterlife? How did they pass on their possessions to future generations? Find out everything you need to know about Viking deaths right here!

Grave

For Vikings, the way you were buried was dependent on how rich you were. The lowest ranking Vikings, <u>thralls</u>, would generally be dumped in a hole in the ground with nothing but worms and soil for company. Sometimes slaves were sacrificed with their masters, to serve them in the afterlife. On the upside, these slaves had a grander funeral than they might have had otherwise but, on the downside, they were burnt or buried alive.

<u>Karls</u>, the free workers and warriors of Viking society, were given <u>grave goods</u> to carry with them into the afterlife. A man may have been given farm equipment or weapons. Women were presented with jewellery and household items.

<u>Jarls</u>, the aristocrats of the Viking world, had the most elaborate funerals. They were given the most expensive and varied grave goods, and perhaps even a slave or a pretty girl to help them along the way. Sometimes they were burnt on a pyre and sent out to sea. Other times they were buried in stone 'ships'. This worked a bit like a standard ground burial, but the burial site would be surrounded by stone slabs, marking out the shape of a sailing vessel. Follow <u>this link</u> to take a look at the remains of the Jelling stone ship in Denmark.

Ceremony

Viking funerals helped serve two purposes. The first purpose was to aid the living. Having a loved one die is a painful process, and rituals surrounding death can help those left to cope with the transition they must make going forwards. A ceremony enables people to grieve properly.

The second purpose was to give the dead a smooth passage into the afterlife. If the funeral was not carried out properly, a dead person could end up roaming the earth as a <u>draug</u>: similar to what we might think of as a ghost or zombie nowadays. The appearance of a draug was believed to be an ominous portent and a danger to its living relatives, so best avoided.

There were many rituals involved in preparing a corpse for the funeral. An interesting example is that corpses' nails were cut, to prevent them from being used to construct the mythological <u>Naglfar</u>, a ship made out of the finger and toenails of the dead.

Inheritance
On the seventh day of mourning, a special ale called Gravöl ('grave beer') would be drunk at a feast called a <u>sjaund</u>. This signalled that the inheritance could now be claimed. It not only related to material goods, but also applied to the passing on of positions of power.

Afterlife
The Vikings had varying opinions on the afterlife, and surviving evidence of their beliefs is somewhat conflicting. On the whole, however, it seems as though Vikings believed the following . . .

For those who died in combat, there were two possibilities: half were chosen by the god <u>Odin</u> to go to a majestic hall called <u>Valhalla</u>. Soldiers here were able to drink and feast, but in return they were expected to protect Odin from the wolf <u>Fenrir</u>. The other half of dead soldiers would go to a field called <u>Folkvang</u>, governed by the pleasure-seeking goddess <u>Freya</u>.

If you did not die in battle, but you were an honourable soul, then Vikings believed you would end up in <u>Helgafjell</u>, known as the 'holy mountain'. This mountain was believed to be so sacred that you could not look at it without washing your face first.

The least advantageous place for the dead to end up was Helheim. Ruled over by the gigantic goddess <u>Hel</u>, accounts of this place vary considerably from text to text. What we do know is that it was cold, dark and underground. Chances are, if you found yourself here, you'd had a dishonourable end. Apparently, for many Vikings, dying of old age, curled up in bed, was considered one of the least honourable ways to go.

Text Message from Mina

Wed 27 Aug 23:09

What's SMS?

Letter to Dad

Dad,

Ottila, your little 'Hun' here.

It's three years today since we got the phone call from the King of Norway telling us you'd died in battle. You lived like a Viking, and died like one, Dad. I hope for your sake you're in Valhalla now. I can picture you there, drinking ale out of a cow's horn, an enormous plate of wild berries and smoked meat in front of you. Sounds more like your kind of place than that other option: a big field. If you are in that other place, though – Folkvang – just watch out for Freya. She sleeps with everyone, even her own brother. Don't fall for her charms.

Mum misses you. She's gone to visit your ashes this year, but I couldn't really handle travelling up to Scotland with her. Too many memories. I hope I can visit you sometime soon. In the meantime, I thought I'd write this letter instead. I'll put it on the lake in the park opposite my flat and set fire to it. Give it a water burial. Maybe somehow the charred words will float into the afterlife and you'll be able to read them.

Mina is okay.

Well, to be honest, Dad, that's a bit of a lie. She's not okay. She's worse than before. Things are deteriorating by the day. She hasn't managed to go back to work since you died. She's signed off permanently now. She attempts something awful at least twice a year. I can't even see the skin on her arms because there are so many scars. How can you make a person's mind better?

I feel a bit upset that you never told me you heard voices. Why did you feel you couldn't confide in me? I might have been able to help. And if not me, why didn't you tell Mina? It would have made her feel so much less alone. Opening up like that was never your thing, though. If you were here you'd probably want to give her a big cuddle, buy her a chocolate bar, and tell her everything will be fine. But what happens when she starts refusing ice-creams? Stops accepting cuddles? She's been in hospital more often than she's been out lately. We're not even allowed to bring her food or books without having them checked first. I'm beginning to think that hoping she'll get better is pointless. It's tiring as well.

Perhaps it's best to accept the likelihood of it never changing. But how can I accept it when it upsets me so much? Every time she tries to kill herself, it's like she's killing off a little bit of me.

Why does everyone assume dead people have all the answers? You didn't know what to do about Mina when you were alive. Why should losing your sinoatrial impulses give you clarity?

I never really spoke to you about my love life. You called me a 'slut' once, while we were painting the kitchen walls. We were doing it to surprise Mum when she came back from a weekend at Granny's. I must have been about seventeen. I screamed at you and threw the paintbrush onto the kitchen counter, leaving a trail of Tangerine Twist that never quite disappeared. You told me to go and look up 'slut' in the dictionary, assuring me it meant 'a dirty or lazy woman'. I was so upset I went out and had sex with a fifty-five-year-old man. He called me his *precious girl*.

I'm seeing someone now. His name is Thales. His parents are Greek. We've had our problems, but we're sorting them out like grown-ups. I can do that now. Sort things out without a blazing row. Nothing wrong with a bit of conflict now and then, but I find it helps to have the sort of arguments that *don't* involve ripping pictures off the walls and hurling out slurred profanities until I puke up on the rug and pass out by the front door. The good old days, eh?

Turns out I enjoyed my mead a bit too much, just like you. Even Mum seems to be in on the act nowadays. Bloody booze. Thales is the first person I've ever been out with sober. I think that before him I chose people to go out with who helped enable my drinking habits. Party animals. Married men. People in bands. Worst of all: poets. Thales serves coffee for a living. He makes films too. He made one film, *Tractor Boy*, which ended up getting shown in Keswick, which is honestly a bigger deal than it sounds. Do you remember when we went to the Pencil Museum in Keswick? The world's longest coloured pencil! We couldn't stop laughing in the car park afterwards.

Thales is the first man I've allowed myself to love since you. *Properly* love. Not the sort of lust and shame I felt with Ben and André. Do you know how scary it is? Real love? Letting someone into your heart, when they might die on you at any second? I'm trying to spend at least five minutes a day imagining he's dead, grieving for him, just to prepare myself.

Don't worry, I'm seeing a therapist.

Once I'd gotten over the initial shock of your diagnosis, Dad,

I spent a good few months hating your guts. I couldn't believe you'd smoked for so many years. If you'd really loved me, and wanted to spend as long as possible with me, why hadn't you quit years ago? That made me so furious. I would chain-smoke four or five menthols after every phone call, just to get at you.

Of course, the hate didn't last. When you died, I planted an apple tree in the back garden. *How beautiful*, I thought, *to watch something be created out of destruction. One day, I might be able to pick an apple from the tree, and bite into the fruit that's grown out of my misery.* Every time I went back to see Mum, I'd check on the tree. I took measurements, to see how many centimetres it had grown. I talked to it, pretending it was you.

Have you ever heard of apple canker? The bark on the tree begins to die. Around the affected area, there's a cracked, swollen ring, and there are pustules in it. They're small and creamy to begin with, then they grow big and red, releasing some sort of slime. The fruit is affected too. At first, the rot appears on the bottom of the apple, turning it brown and soggy. Eventually, the fruit becomes dry, like powder, and it disappears in a puff of putridity. That's what happened to your apples, Dad.

You know what species of tree I'd planted for you? A James *Grieve*!

Everything has become a metaphor these days.

I hope you know I'm alright. I'm being good for you, like you asked. I stopped smoking. I stopped drinking, apart from one hiccup, which my therapist informs me is nothing to beat myself up about. I've stopped cheating on people too. It's just another form of self-harm. Can you believe I once slept with three people in a day? One of them was my boyfriend, one was a girl in my Anglo-Saxon class, the other was my friend's cousin, who helped move furniture into my new flat. Two of them even passed each other in the stairwell. I used to take a quick shower, check the flat for stains, and then move right on to the next one.

Is it inappropriate to tell you this stuff, Dad?

Not really, because you'll never read this. You don't exist. You're just a set of memories that will one day be forgotten. But not for as long as I can possibly help it. Happy deathday, Dad. I'm off to set fire to you now. Give Odin my best wishes.

Your eldest dóttir, Ottila xxx

Memory of Dad

Every night, after I'd done my homework and finished my piano practice, Dad would come into the bathroom with me and Mina. He'd keep his eyes on his watch, and then he'd sing:

Brush, brush, brush! Brush those teeth, on the top and un – der – neath. Brush 'em in the day. Brush 'em at

night. Brush, brush, brush, to keep them white!

He'd repeat the song over and over again, with key changes, for exactly two minutes. When the two minutes were up, we'd know that we were allowed to put our toothbrushes away and go to bed.

Going to bed was the best bit. Before lights out, I'd crawl into Mina's bunk, and Dad would read us some *Teddy Robinson, Just William* or *The Faraway Tree*. More often than not, he'd nod off before he reached the end of the chapter, and we'd wait patiently for him to wake up and finish.

After story time Dad and I would kiss Mina goodnight, and then Dad would tuck me up in my bunk and test me on my times tables. The two times tables and the five times tables were always fine. On the nights we had to do the threes, the fours or, worse still, the sixes, I'd get frustrated.

It's like my brain turns to jelly, I told him one night, quietly so Mina could sleep. *I try to think of the right number, or any number, but my mind goes wobbly.*

It's just practice, he replied. *You'll get there.*

Dad?

Yes, Ottila?

I know it sounds strange, but sometimes I think I might be magic.

In what way, sweetums?

I just . . . I don't know. It doesn't matter.

Go on, you can tell me.

Mina was already snoring so I decided to talk. I told my dad that even though I was terrible at times tables and arithmetic, I knew that I had mysterious powers. I told him that I could fly, and that I was partially psychic, and that I could see invisible creatures. Dad smiled when I said those things. Not the smile of someone laughing at me, or someone thinking what a cute kid I was. It was a much more complex, adult smile, a smile that I didn't understand. It was a smile of regret, of guilt, of sympathy. Then, when the smile stopped, he said: *You're so similar to me, Ottila.*

You feel special too? I asked, screwing up my nose and thinking very hard. *Is it because you were born in another country?*

Now I watched him do a different smile. It was one of the smiles I knew. In fact, it was a smile that was both laughing at me *and* thinking I'm cute. *Maybe that's one of the ways I feel special,* he said.

Because Grandma and Granddad were Scottish, and you were born in Denmark, but you speak like me, like you're from England. I think that means you've got superpowers.

Dad kissed me on the forehead. *My, you're doing a lot of thinking for a little girl that's got to go to sleep.* He pulled the covers over my shoulders, how I liked it, and then walked to the door. There, he turned, and opened his mouth, like he was about to say something, but he paused. His gaze remained fixed on the floor and then quickly shifted up to me. *Five times six,* he whispered, switching off the light.

I don't care because I can fly, I whispered back.

FIVE

Email from Reatha

From: Reatha Sanna
To: Ottila McGregor
Date: Wed, 3 September, 2014 at 21:12
Subject: bloodbath

Well, well, well, Miss Mc. You caused quite a sensation at my parents' house over the summer. I'm guessing Thales has filled you in on the details of what's happened since your fateful visit, but in case there's anything he neglected to tell you:

1. I moved out of my parents' house in August.

2. My mum has begged me to introduce her to all my girlfriends, forevermore.

3. My dad has thrown away his lesbian porn collection. That my dad had a porn collection (at his age!), let alone lesbian porn, is not something I had the pleasure of knowing, until I – quite literally – stumbled upon it, thereby swiftly leading to number one on my list.

It felt fucking nuts to see you after all these years. I'd made such a point of avoiding you for so long. I used to think you moved to Manchester after your Masters to get at me: invasion of my home turf. That's partly why I buggered off to East Asia for a year. I was hoping that by the time I got back you'd have moved even further south, nearer your parents . . . I had no idea about your dad. I'm sorry.

When I realised it was *you* who was walking through my front door, at my brother's side, I quickly made a wish. I wanted you to have wrinkles and bad teeth and to still do that clicky thing with your jaw when you ate. Turns out the crows' feet around your eyes make you look like you've spent the last decade smiling, and your teeth haven't turned into tusks. You *do* still do that clicky thing with your jaw, but it's not enough, goddammit.

In fact, learning about how you've stopped drinking, and seeing a healthy glow in your cheeks, and the way you looked at my brother . . . urgh. All I could see was how *happy* you are! And honestly, Til, I'm over us now. You and me happened in a different lifetime. Shit, I was still calling myself Reatha *Mavros* back then, using my grandma's maiden name after a stupid falling out with my parents. Thales was off at film college, being golden boy with 'perfect' Eleni, who was a witch by the way. My parents wanted to introduce me to some Athenian jerkwad who was on an Erasmus Exchange. Things blew up between us all. Maybe if I'd talked more openly about my family to you we wouldn't have ended up where we are now.

But you and me . . . it was so long ago. It's like you had sex with my twin sister. Oh wait, I mean brother! Can you even remember how it felt to touch me? I've no idea about you. Christ, I barely even remember *myself* back then. I've put on weight and lost weight and changed my hair and had so many tattoos over the years. How often do the cells in your body regenerate? Ninety-nine per cent of the atoms in your body get replaced, don't they? So I'm literally *1 per cent* of the person I was when you and I were together. You've been intimate with 1 per cent of me, Til, and not a cell more!

What I'm trying to say is that it's okay that you're with Thales now. Honestly. You're you, and the past you was *her*. She was mine, and you are my brother's. I have a girlfriend, anyway. Her name is Nora, and we've been together for three years. In fact, this whole saga has propelled us into moving in together. I was staying with Mum and Dad to try and save up for an MFA, but I can do that, albeit more slowly, living with Nora. The main reason I never wanted to tell Mum and Dad about her is not because she's a woman. She's actually a communist, and that is *way* worse. One of my great-grandparents' children was taken away by insurgents in the Greek Civil War, and even today my grandmother refuses to wear red.

But now Mum is intent on becoming a part of my life. She wants to meet Nora, and teach her how to make dolmades. When Mum and Eleni first met, they made dolmades together, and now she's got it into her head that it's some kind of bonding ceremony for mothers and their potential daughters-in-law. Hey, perhaps *you* should suggest a dolmades session with her? Send her some grape leaves as an olive branch. Seriously, though, Mum is trying so hard it's heart-breaking. She's sent us four bottles of olive oil this month as a 'housewarming present'. I'll have to introduce her to Nora sooner or later, but I have a feeling she's not gonna be super keen on Nora's stretched earlobes or Spider-Man neck tat.

I'm not trying to make you feel bad, Ottila. Fuck, you weren't to know how secretive I've been. I've never even used my real name in my paintings or online in case my parents find anything out about me. But it's about time my parents got to know who I really am. Obviously I wish it had *come from me*, and that you hadn't got mixed up in it, but hey, what are ex-girlfriends from eight years ago for?

In my strange, roundabout way, all I'm trying to say is this: I hope you and my brother stay together. Listen up, though: something's not right with Thales. That's part of the reason Mum urged him to stay at ours for so long over the summer. I don't know what it is, but he's not himself at the moment. Watch him closely. Look after him. As long as you do that, we can be friends.

Peace,

REATHA ^_^

Script

[*I rescued this discarded draft of Thales's script from the dustbin. It's got baked bean juice on the corner, but other than that it's not too noxious, I promise.*]

INANIMATE OBJECTS
by Thales Sanna

FADE IN:

EXT. TERRACED HOUSE - DAY

An overcast day in Salford. Zoom in on a red brick terraced house with a blue front door.

INT. LOCATION KITCHEN - DAY

In a simple, modern kitchen, we see appliances in unusual places. The kettle is on the sofa. The toaster is on a chair. The bread maker is on a doormat, by the back door.

BREAD MAKER
Wish I could go out today.

TOASTER
You've got cabin fever.
(pause)
I like it in here.

KETTLE
I remember the outside.

(shifts from one side of the sofa to the other, towards the back door)

TOASTER
No you don't.

BREAD MAKER
The boxwood smells like cats' wee.

                    KETTLE
I once knew a girl called Rebecca. Things got a little
                    steamy.
(boils and clicks, with a small belch of steam escaping
                from its mouth)

                    TOASTER
        You didn't date a girl called Rebecca.

                    KETTLE
            I might have. I don't remember.
                    (pause)
            I don't remember anything.

                    TOASTER
At least all your bits and pieces are still in working
            order. My left grill has gone.
    (button pushes down and grill only glows red on
                    one side)

                    KETTLE
It's no biggie. You've got another. At least you can
    remember what it feels like to have a left grill.

                    TOASTER
        I bet that's where she's gone, you know.

                    KETTLE
                    Who?

                    TOASTER
Her. I bet she's gone out to buy a new one. She's going
                to replace me.
                (all appliances gasp)
                I'm defective.

                    KETTLE
            That's not true, mate.
    (shifts back to the other side of the sofa, to be
                nearer the toaster)

BREAD MAKER
There are people out there watching Samuel Beckett.

TOASTER
I'm going to live in a dustbin.

BREAD MAKER
I miss the smell of rain.

KETTLE
The smell of what?

TOASTER
I used to have such big hopes and dreams. One day, I
thought, I'll warm up a nice big slice of sourdough.

BREAD MAKER
That had better not be a dig at me. I do as I'm asked.

TOASTER
I barely had the chance to get started. I'm only one
and a half.

KETTLE
Calm down, everybody. How about a nice cup of tea?

TOASTER
Okay.

BREAD MAKER
Okay.

KETTLE
Now if I can just remember how to do it . . .

FADE OUT:
'*Failure*' *by Swans plays as the credits roll.*

Text Message to Thales

Fri 05 Sep 15:42

How about some *Divinity* tonight? Let's do a two-player co-op. We can eat elven stew and pick up magical crystals and cure each other's wounds while burning the Midnight Oil. x

Text Message from Thales

Fri 05 Sep 16:10

Thanks, but I'm going to head to the library and pull an all-nighter. T

To be happy, we must not be too concerned with others.

Albert Camus

Email from André

From: André Marsh
To: all-staff
Date: Thurs, 18 September, 2014 at 09:52
Subject: sad news

Apols for the group mailout guys. I've just had some sad news about one of our longest-running service users. Old maude who made the cakes has gone to a better place. She bravely battled with an anaplastic astrocytoma for two years, but passed away last night with her family at her side.

I was thinking that in honour of everything maude did for the Centre we could hold a cake sale next saturday. We could use the money we raise to get her a plaque in that patch of wasteland out back next to the car park, maybe even plant some flowers or something in her honour. She always loved the outdoors here and she'd have liked the thought of our garden expanding, and some kind of commemorative thingmajig in it. What do you think? It's a shithole out there at the moment, so might be good to brighten it up a bit.

There'll be a card going round for you to sign later on, and I'll send it to maude's family this afternoon. If anyone can think of a good limerick (maude loved limericks, didn't she? Or was that tony?) to put in it then get cracking. Answers on a postcard!

Oh yeah. Anyone who wants to go to the funeral email me for the deets.

André

Maude

There was a brave woman called Maude,

Who baked babkas and pink petits fours,

But we should not forget,

Cakes were just one asset,

Of this great human being, who ~~soared~~ roared.

Little Book of Happy

Dear Little Book of Suddenly Impossible All Over Again,

I feared this day would come: when someone I know and like at the Maggie's Centre dies. But Maude. She'd had a double mastectomy. Radiotherapy. Chemotherapy. The works. She just went on and on. I thought she'd keep going forever.

And the fact that all anyone seems to remember about her is that she liked to bake. Can people really forget each other that quickly? What would remain of *me* if I died tomorrow? *Ottila: she used a fountain pen.* Shit.

I don't think I can face the funeral. The last one I went to was Dad's. Mina refused to go, because she was too sad. Mum shook hands with everyone and reminisced and joked, and even read out a Maya Angelou poem: 'When Great Trees Fall'. It was painful watching Mum stay strong that day. Even more painful than seeing her collapse afterwards. I saw two great trees fall that week.

I can't bear losing people. I'm afraid I'll lose Thales if I'm not careful. He's been so unsettled since we got back together. I really hope it's nothing to do with Reatha. He says he's fine with it, but I know it'll take time for him to adjust. I think the main reason for his mood is that he's been feeling like a washout ever since he got that rejection letter. I've tried telling him it's no big deal – I've had loads of the bloody things – but the dark circles under his eyes are growing.

I wish everyone who ever walked into your life would stay healthy and happy forever. I'll miss seeing Maude walk into the centre on a Tuesday morning, beaming because she's heard a brilliant fact on the Discovery Channel that she can't wait to share. I'll miss her wicked laugh and her generosity and her boxing stories and her Polish words. I'll miss feeling like I have a secret grandma.

I'm not brave enough to work at Maggie's any more. I can't allow myself to make friends with cancer.

Ottila

Email from André

From: André Marsh
To: Ottila McGregor
Date: Fri, 19 September, 2014 at 14:09
Subject: Re: Limerick

Ottila,

Thanks for this. Nice idea. not sure I quite grasp the ending though. why would Maude roar? She was such a sweet old biddy! Don't want to confuse her family. Went with Pete's poem about maude's delicious victoria sponge in the end, and found a card with a pic of a cupcake on it. you signed it yet?

André

Job Application

22 September 2014

Dear Sir/Madam,

I would like to apply for the post of Arts Grants Assessor.

Currently I work in marketing, but I am also a writer/ theatre maker, and am extremely experienced at writing grants applications. I have now written thirty-two applications for arts grants in the UK. Given that I have had a zero per cent success rate in receiving any money, I thought I might stand more of a chance getting paid to *read* the applications, rather than writing them.

Please find enclosed a copy of my CV and references. I look forward to hearing from you.

Best wishes,

Ottila McGregor

Post for Thales

[*This was on the doormat when I got home from work, in a jiffy bag addressed to Thales. I've never opened his mail before. Thing is, though, I'm looking out for him. So it's different.*]

*** Thank you for your ePills order of:

50 x Brain Buster Pills

Remember to read the label carefully before consumption.

ePills will not be held responsible for any improper consumption or adverse effects following product use.

Warning: contains Adrafinil.***

Email from Delyth

From: Delyth Hughes
To: Ottila McGregor
Date: Tue, 23 September, 2014 at 12:24
Subject: Re: Dilemmas

Matey, let's go for a burger sometime this week and talk it over. Personally, I think you did the right thing by putting them back in the envelope and not saying anything. I'm not being funny, but opening other people's mail is a no-no. Could've been anything in there. If that was my post, I'd be tamping. Can see why you did it, mind, and now you know you've got to address it, no pun intended.

Taking weird pills off the internet is perfectly legal. Don't quote me on that! What's important here is the root cause: why's he taking them? Can you help him deal with his problems without medication? If not, maybe you need to have a serious think about whether being together is good for you. You've got your own struggles to be getting on with at the moment, lady. Don't want to be dragged down by somebody else's shizz. You know I like Thales a lot, and he makes the best coffee in the hospital, but . . . just be careful, alright mate? Having said that, I've been single for nearly three years, so might not be best placed to give relationship advice! The single life rulez ok.

Re: Maggie's, you're braver than you think you are, and you can definitely handle this job. In fact, you're corking at it. But you'd be a great asset to those arty-farty grant people too. Stop thinking too hard and go where the heat is. That's how you'll keep burning bright.

Righto, I'm off to give a Tarot reading to an elderly woman's Dalmatian. Wish me luck.

Chi blessings, Delyth x

Text Message from Mina

Wed 24 Sep 05:04

I know you're probably asleep, Tilly, but I just wanted to say I've named my ladybird toothbrush holder after you. Ottila the Ladypillar!!!!

Little Book of Happy

LBOH,

I know, I know: me again already. Sticking another piece of paper inside you, making you alarmingly close to coming apart at the seams. But truly, LBOH, I've been feeling like I'm coming apart at the seams too. First Maude dies, then I find out Thales has been taking brain pills.

I've already told you the last thing my dad said to me: *Be good for me*. But do you know what Maude's parting words were? *You're a good girl, Ottila*. I was in the kitchen, washing up, and I handed her a clean spoon. Is it some kind of sign? I've transitioned from naughty to nice. If that's the case, why is Thales taking mental stimulants? Don't I make him feel clever enough? Or is it egotistical to place myself at the centre of his crisis?

I don't know. It's tempting to think that Maude was giving me an important spiritual message when she said those words to me. But the truth is she was no more magical than I am. She was one human being, saying to another human being: at this moment in time, for what you've just done for me, I think you're a good person. And that's all you ever can be: good in the moment. Until recently, I didn't know about Thales's pills. Now that I do know about them, I have a choice. I can hope that the problem goes away by itself, or I can try and do something about it.

Delyth told me I have to go where the heat is. Sometimes that feels like a warm embrace, and at other times it's walking on hot coals. That doesn't mean I can't do it.

Ottila

Your work is to discover your world and then with all your heart give yourself to it.

Buddha

Email to André

From: Ottila McGregor
To: André Marsh
Date: Wed, 24 September, 2014 at 10:52
Subject: making the shithole rock

You know that land at the back of the centre? The bit you call the shithole? There's something I think my (clear-skinned) boyfriend, Thales, could do with it. He once mentioned to me that he'd like to build a rock garden. He's keen to work outside and I reckon he'd do a really great job. What do you think? Everyone loves a rock garden. I'm sure Maude would have approved.

By the way, if it's not too late, I've decided I'd like to go to the funeral on Friday. The people at Maggie's mean a lot to me. Working here means a lot to me too.

Ottila

Email from Mum

From: Alice McGregor
To: Ottila McGregor
Date: Thurs, 25 September, 2014 at 08:12
Subject: Men

Why do they have to be such pigs? Yes, I *know* that's a generalisation, and of course men aren't actual porcine creatures, and some of them are in reality very nice indeed, but still. Why don't they all go and eat *swill*?

Safe to say: my date went badly. Wes – that was his name – Wes! He was a perfect gentleman to start with: kissed me on the cheek, held the door open for me, said he liked my dress. It wasn't the minidress, by the bye. It was a flowing, purple number. Eminently respectable.

We had a couple of vodka tonics at The Stable in Cirencester. He lives in Oxford so it's halfway. To begin with, we made the usual small talk. Job? Retired fishmonger. Ambition? Chess Grandmaster. So far so good.

But then, when I asked him if he had any children, do you know what he said? He said he had three. One of them works in finance, another is volunteering in Peru and the youngest lives at home. When I asked what the youngest one did, he got this horrible look in his eye, and said: 'Scrounges off the government'. Ottila: his son has Down's syndrome! Well, needless to say my third vodka tonic ended up on his shirt, which was actually rather lucky, because it meant I was still able to drive home. I'm trying to be stricter with myself about drink–driving, you see. Even if I *do* feel sober enough to drive after way more than two piddly little drinks. Silly old rules.

The worst thing was how outraged I felt on his son's behalf. When I was a party planner, I once organised a leaving do for a chap with Down's. He'd been working for the council for twenty years, but he was one of the lucky ones. Do you know how *difficult* it is for people with that condition to find work? This wasn't just about that though. I felt angry because of Mina too. You know how hard she tries. And you know what that hospital she's at is like: there are so many people there who couldn't even begin to hold down a job. But to think for one minute that people might see them as *scrounging*. It makes me furious.

Oh, who am I kidding? The problem isn't with men. It's with bigots and bullies. I think I'll leave the Internet dating scene for a while, try and meet Prince Charming in real life. All I want is someone who looks and acts exactly like your father. Is that too much to ask?

I haven't told you much about my trip up to Scotland, for Dad's anniversary. After I visited the beach at Largs and said hello to Bernie's ashes, I took myself off to Rannoch Moor for a few days. I decided against the trekker hut in the end, and took a tent with me. Much more adventurous, although the midges were a nightmare. It was probably about two days into the trip, after many hours of walking around what's essentially a desolate expanse of boggy moorland, when it hit me: a change of scenery is sometimes all you need!

Speaking of which, I've got enough to keep me occupied, what with the clubbing scene and my paintballing group. I got a bruise the shape of Africa on my bicep last week. Come to think of it, it blended in with my dress very well on that date.

How's Thales?

Mum xoxo

Maggie's Centre

Something momentous is happening: Thales has started building a rock garden. I'm standing at the window in the quiet room, spying on him. He's got a day off from the cafeteria, and he says autumn is the perfect time for it. He says rocks are in his bones. He says they're his destiny. He's wearing scruffy tracksuit bottoms, a paint-splattered sweatshirt, and a big smile.

I'm so relieved that André said yes. And that Thales said he'd do it. He didn't seem peeved with me for meddling – just gave me a big hug when I brought it up. 'Thank you, Ottila,' he said. 'I'll do my very best.'

Delyth made a valid point when she asked me if I was able to be in a relationship with an addict. I'm in a vulnerable position right now. So is Thales. But actually, I think I'm good for him, and he's good for me. My relapse is starting to feel like it happened in another lifetime.

At the moment Thales is doing the work for free, but André is going to have a word with *the powers that be*, as there might be a job coming up for a new gardener, permanently tending to all the plants and flowers out front. It'd be three days a week, which would mean Thales could fit his film writing around it.

As I stand here watching my boyfriend happily digging up tree roots, it's hard not to convince myself that the pills are no longer a problem. That now he's got a project to get stuck into, he's miraculously cured. Of course it's not going to be that simple. While we were eating our toast this morning before work, Thales said, 'I hope I don't mess this up.'

'Why would you do that?' I asked, licking strawberry jam off my fingers.

'Just a habit of a lifetime,' he answered.

Not wanting to go down a dangerous route so close to the start of work, I steered the conversation back to rocks. Thales explained he'd get Carboniferous sandstone from the Pennine foothills, and in the north Cheshire Basin he'll acquire the more weatherable Permo-Triassic mudstones.

The quiet room feels quieter than ever now Maude is gone. I'm glad I decided to go to her funeral. André gave a surprisingly good speech. I had no idea Maude had worked as a nurse in Ireland or that she liked swimming. I didn't know she was religious either. When the coffin was lowered and the priest said 'We commit her body to the ground', I started to cry. I was crying for Maude, of course, but I was also crying because of the strange formality of it all. The rigid backs, the meticulous order, the decorous language. All that stuff is there to give you a structure to hold on to while you fall apart.

It made me think about the other rituals I've been part of this year. Burn's Night. Lupercalia. Meeting my partner's parents for the first time. These ceremonies and rites of passage have been performed by so many people, so many times before, but that doesn't make each instance of them any less important. And every time they feel completely singular.

To build a rock garden, Thales says, you start by putting down the keystones. You dig a hole in the soil for the bigger rocks, and you can prop up the smaller stones with even smaller ones, to get them all at the right level. There's a science to it. The rocks are meant to tilt backwards, with the layers running the same way. Once they're in place, you sprinkle topsoil and grit into the gaps. That's how you make something that lasts.

Ottila's Proposal

Name of Activity
Asking Thales not to marry me.

Amount Requested
A relationship full of love, commitment and passion, in sickness and in health, etc. But for god's sake, please, *no marriage*.

Proposal
Let's face it. The institution of matrimony was created by a patriarchal society looking to crush the female population into submission. It intensifies social inequalities, enables violence, excludes sexualities and identities deemed as Other and, on an existential level, is an extremely fucking weird thing to do. Legally binding yourself to another human being? Pretty sure that's called indentured servitude.

Did you know that 40 per cent of marriages end in divorce? What a waste of time and emotion. And then there are the complexities of sorting out distribution of property, child custody, division of debt.

I probably don't need to convince you on this subject, Thales. You were due to marry Eleni this year and it was making you miserable. As for me, I've been proposed to six times, and I have no doubt that all six of those people ended up feeling relieved that I said no.

So how about we skip all the hassle and socio-political injustice, and forgo the nuptials? Because honestly, Thales, I don't want to be your *other half*, your *ball and chain* or *her indoors*. I don't want to be your *little woman* or *wifey chops* or *the boss*. I don't want to send out invitations made of doilies, or draw diagrams of tables and chairs, and I don't want to wear a scrap of white. I don't want anyone to feel obliged to come, I don't want Mina to say she's *not* coming, and I don't want to be walked down the aisle by anyone who's not my dad. I don't want your family to hate me, and I don't want to have your surname or a marzipan cake. Above all, I don't want to become Bridezilla.

What I *do* want, Thales, is you. I know we've had our fair share of troubles, but in spite of all of that, fuck what they say about addicts being bad for each other; I think we're a good team.

So I'm not going to ask you to marry me, my friend, but I do want to ask you this: shall we just skip the rest of the vulnerable, will-they-won't-they beginning part, and simply agree to be together forever? I know we're already boyfriend and girlfriend, so maybe this is a moot point, or an impossible question, but will you be my long-term, non-violent, socially equal, sexually progressive, feminist lover for the rest of time? Let's just make it work, now and always. Okay? Say yes, and you'll make me the happiest human being on the planet.

Little Book of Happy

LBOH, I did it.

Not the proposal. I haven't found the right way to ask Thales about that yet. I asked him something else.

'About those pills,' I said last night, while we were doing the washing up. 'I don't judge you for taking them and, as you know, I'm hardly one to preach, but do you really need them?'

For a moment I thought Thales was going to throw the tea towel on the floor and run out of the flat, but he stayed put. 'Um,' he said quietly.

I directed all my focus onto the oven dish, really making it gleam.

'I have to take them, Ottila,' he said, 'because if I don't, I'll stop.'

'Stop what?'

I waited for the words 'this relationship'.

'Writing, making stuff, achieving. I'm no good without them.'

I threw the dish down on the drying rack and embraced Thales with wet hands. 'You're *very* good without them.'

In retrospect, that might not have been the best choice of words. I didn't mean to suggest that Thales wasn't any good *with* the pills. As I write this now, I'm biting the insides of my cheeks, twisting my mouth into awkward shapes. You know how far I've come: I'm thinking about someone else's addiction, instead of my own.

Tonight Thales is at Laurie's for *kanabō* club with the two Davids. It's great that he's gone out socialising. Turns out mythical weapons *are* powerful, even in the real world. Actually, that's got me thinking. André mentioned at last week's team meeting that we have a gap in the schedule on Wednesday afternoons. He wanted ideas for new classes. Bear with me, LBOH, I need to do some research before we take this thing any further. Looks like I'm off to read a *Monster Manual*, which is a phrase I never saw myself writing.

Ottila the Dragonslayer

Favourite Creatures in the *Monster Manual*

- Displacer Beast (a six-legged puma with tentacles)
- Roper (catches prey by disguising itself as a stalagmite)
- Drider (elf on the top half, spider on the bottom)
- Otyugh (dung-eater)
- Rakshasa (these creatures are humanoids but their palms are on the 'back' of their hands)
- Efreeti (part flesh, part fire)

Email from Thales

From: Thales Sanna
To: Ottila McGregor
Date: Thurs, 23 October, 2014 at 15:00
Subject: Brain dump

O,

Sorry I didn't get to see you again this lunchtime. As usual, I'm hiding in the work toilets to write you this email. My colleagues are growing increasingly concerned about my intestinal health. Naomi made me drink a fennel and turmeric tea earlier, which was truly putrescent. I can't wait to leave the coffee shop and become a proper, bona fide gardener! To be honest, I don't think my boss can wait either. She said it's not appropriate to keep turning up for my afternoon shift covered in rock dust. Spoilsport.

I was foolish to start taking the Adrafinil, Ottila. I'm sorry for being so stupid. This morning I only took half a tablet. You're right about me not needing them. It's not like they've been making my film scripts any better. They just make me obsess over them. If there was such a thing as a creativity pill, or a talent pill, then maybe . . . I jest. Partly.

Thank you for looking out for me, even if you did open my post without my permission. The truth is these tablets are toxic to my liver in the long run, and taking them could end up killing me. I suppose I'll always struggle with medication. I hope you're okay with that.

Give me a little time, and I'll try to wean myself off the tablets completely. Expect brain fog, depression, weird food cravings and a very tetchy boyfriend. Business as usual, then, amirite?

T

Twenty Things to Do Instead of ~~Drinking~~ *Taking Brain Pills*

1. **Read a book** – *I've left a hefty tome of logic puzzles on your bedside table*

2. **Go for a drive** – *you can buy Euro Truck Simulator 2 for the PC if you want?*

3. **Exercise** – *sexercise*

4. **Dance like no-one's watching** – *but please, please, please can I watch?*

5. **Stroke your cat** – *I'm not going to make a rude joke here*

6. **Call your mom** – *tell her how great I am and that I'm sorry*

7. **Read to a child** – *or a childish girlfriend*

8. **Visit someone in an old folks' home** – *we work in a hospital for Chrissake so I'll let you off this one*

9. **Speak in rhyming couplets for an hour** – *60 minutes of rhyme / guarantees a good time*

10. **Scrub the limescale in your bathroom** – *I'm starting to really like this list; there's an old scourer you can use under the sink ;)*

11. **Make marmalade** – *or buy some*

12. **Take a hike** – *Heaton Park is lovely this time of year*

13. **Listen to music** – *ever heard of The Mozart Effect? Classic FM makes you brainy, baby*

14. **Have a bubble bath** – *in our case a frothy shower*

15. **Make pickles** – *OR BUY SOME*

16. **Visit a friend** – *do you fancy inviting Laurie over for dinner tonight?*

17. **Do your nails** – *all this gardening has made them very dirty so don't skimp on this one*

18. **Write a poem** – *just a 39-line sestina, comprising 6 stanzas of 6 lines each, plus a 3-line envoi will do*

19. **Do some laundry** – *well one of us needs to do it, it's spilling out of the basket*

20. **Develop** ~~a new crush~~ *an everlasting bond with your current girlfriend*

Text Message to Thales

Thu 13 Nov 12:33

Hope the grit is going on a treat. To celebrate you finishing your rock garden today, be sure to take a look under the northernmost lump of Carboniferous sandstone before you leave.

Fortune sides with him who dares.

Virgil

Email from Mum

From: Alice McGregor
To: Ottila McGregor
Date: Fri, 14 November, 2014 at 19:05
Subject: Xmas

I've been thinking about Christmas, love, and I reckon you should do your own thing. Mina will be in hospital, and I'm not really in the mood for festive cheer. Every year seems to get worse, not better. I'm actually thinking about taking a city break.

Do you remember how much booze your father used to insist on putting in the brandy butter? You'd be his official taster, and you'd get squiffy after just a few mouthfuls. Sometimes I think about that Christmas we spent, the four of us, plus your friend Ghaaliya, the one who ended up at the women's refuge. The smell of that poor girl's feet! It made your sister cry. And then we got that phone call to say your uncle had the accident. Your dad and I had a blazing row, and he went to the pub for his Christmas dinner.

I'd give anything to relive that Christmas.

Perhaps you and Thales would enjoy doing something together this year, anyhow? I can drive the tree up to you. And the tablecloth and napkins. Thales can wear your dad's Santa costume if he wants, too. Kinky! I was very pleased to hear about Thales's gardening, incidentally. If he ever wants to chat about all things green, he knows where to find me. Not today, though, I'm too tired.

Aren't hangovers rotten? I managed to swallow a teaspoon of that milk thistle you recommended, but I don't think it's helping. It tasted a bit like breast milk, if you don't mind me drawing the comparison. I mean, how do they milk the thistles?

Sorry. Dad joke.

Right, I'm off to have a look at the lastminute.com website. If I end up booking anything, I'll be sure to forward you all the information. Mustn't let you think I'm running off again!

Mum xo

A Recent Memory

Our arms go *whoosh*, *whoosh*, *whoosh*. Our ears tingle. Our mittens grow wet with snow.

'I'm an angel!' cries Mina.

I look up at the sky, imagining for a moment that things are upside-down. That the sky is the ground and I'm high in the air, making patterns in the clouds. It's the first Christmas after Dad's death. I'm not wondering if he's up there, looking down on us. In fact, he's right here. I scattered his ashes on the same patch of ground my head now rests upon, in the spot where he once dislocated his shoulder chasing a duck around the garden. I'll never know where that duck came from, or why Dad was chasing it. I'll never be able to ask him now.

Whoosh, whoosh, whoosh.

I didn't scatter his ashes here because of the duck. I did it because it's the central point of the garden. When you're standing here in the summertime, you can see the vegetable patch to the left, poplars to your right and blue cornflower fields straight ahead. Maybe the duck had just come here to take in the view.

'My fingers are freezing,' says Mina. The euphoria of making snow angels over Dad's grave is beginning to wear off.

'Let's just do one more thing,' I reply. 'Let's make the angels hold hands.'

I hear Mina's legs moving wider apart, vigorously brushing the snow left and right, scared to stop, in case it breaks the connection we've just made with our dead father. 'Angels don't have hands,' she says as she swipes chunks out of the ground. 'They have wings.'

I nod, solemn. 'You're right. We'll make the tips of their wings touch.'

Mina's legs stop swishing. 'Okay,' she whispers.

I reach out until I find her left mitten and we wave our arms back and forth, holding hands in the snow, until it feels right.

'Now get up carefully,' I say, wondering why I order her around so much. 'Don't ruin the pattern if you can help it.' We stand up, our feet planted carefully within the boundaries of the angels' skirts, and then we leap forwards as far as possible, so we don't leave a trail of footprints.

Then we turn and look at what we've done.

Two muddy, egg-timer shaped indents, with slush and grass and mud in their centres, and one giant uber-wing between them. Siamese snow angels.

'It's us,' giggles Mina, 'when we die.'

Whoosh.

Text Message from Mina

Sat 15 Nov 10:24

Tilly!!! I'm making you something in craft. It's a monkey made of felt. Hope you like it. :)

Little Book of Happy

LBOH,

Thales hasn't replied to my proposal yet. *Two whole days* have gone by, and he hasn't said a word. Did he even find the note? I sealed it in a sandwich bag and then squeezed it into a crevice. Is it possible I pushed it in too far? Is it lying there in its gravelly bed, lost for all eternity? Worse still, what if he *has* read the note and is so embarrassed by it that he can't find the words to tell me? I almost managed to bring it up with him in bed last night, but then I wimped out and suggested we listen to a podcast. We lay side by side, holding hands, while a man called Ira talked about the debris in outer space.

It's taking Thales longer to get off the pills than anticipated. I've been keeping the fridge stocked with gherkins and chocolate cake and smoked cheese, to keep him distracted, but he's barely touched them. He said that once the headaches disappear he'd like to start a healthy eating regime. Said we need to think harder about what we're putting into our bodies. I'm definitely up for that, right after I've finished all this cake and cheese.

The rock garden looks great. Maude's plaque is in pride of place, nailed to the largest rock. I think she'd have been chuffed to have her name attached to a lump of earth over three hundred million years old. André let me choose what to put on the plaque, so I went for a picture of a gecko. I felt it was important not to make it too serious.

André's been in a generous mood all round, actually. I mentioned to you a while back that I was going to read Thales's *Monster Manual*. Well, LBOH, I not only read it, but I loved it! It's a compendium of imaginary creatures from the fantasy role-playing game Dungeons & Dragons. Before I met Thales, I thought D & D was just some gross thing that geeks played in basements, but I must be a geek myself because I'm quickly becoming a fan. The thought came to me while Thales was out with Laurie. Maybe I could run a role-playing game at the Maggie's Centre? Perhaps orcs, elves, gnomes and mages could help in the fight against cancer! Amazingly, André said yes. I'm free to leave my Marketing post one afternoon a week and run a D & D session instead. André didn't even make any lewd comments about *role-playing*, which I see as a step in the right direction.

So, I've done my research and created an eerie underwater setting where the game will take place. It's a bit like writing a story. I have to think about the starting point, and then create obstacles, normally in the form of terrifying monsters, such as the dung-eating otyugh. The players have to fight these creatures using a sort of Top Trumps style dice roll system.

Does that sound complicated and off-putting? I promise it's a lot of fun! I've had four people sign up to play already, and we've started building characters. We've got Lena (Moonwitch), Nettie (Norg), Charlie (Glookgrumble) and Rajesh (Pogwimp). Charlie is the shyest, and Rajesh is recovering from a partial colectomy, so we're being gentle with him, but they're all getting into the swing of it brilliantly. Even annoying Pru wants to get in on the action, and you know what? I'm looking forward to having her. I'm glad I never got funding for that rubbish theatre piece. And I'm glad I didn't get an interview for another job. Not that I'd have gone in the end. This feels like real life, here, with these people, now.

There's a party happening in the flat two doors down. AC/DC are booming through the walls. At the end of the last song, Brian Johnson screeched out 'Have a drink on me' nine times in a row. Guess what? I don't even feel a tiny bit jealous.

Ottila

Text Message from Thales

Mon 17 Nov 13:51

I'm waiting until I'm completely off the pills before I say my piece, but a response to your big question is forthcoming.

Email from Mum

From: Alice McGregor
To: Ottila McGregor
Date: Thurs, 20 November, 2014 at 21:13
Subject: Fwd: Fwd: Ryanair Travel Itinerary

---------- Forwarded message ----------
From: Alice McGregor <alice.mcgregor54@mcgregormail.com>
To: aart@aartjonckers.nl
Date: Thurs, 20 November 2014 at 21:12
Subject: Fwd: Ryanair Travel Itinerary

Mr Jonckers,

I've made up my mind, and I'm heading to your fair country for Christmas! I've heard the festive season in Amsterdam is rather lovely, plus there's a Nazi history trail I'd just love to do.

I'm forwarding you my flight details in case you fancy meeting me at the airport. It's a long shot, but I figure it's a public place, so I'm probably safer meeting you there than in my hotel room! Lol!

I've no idea whereabouts in the Netherlands you live, and whether Schiphol Airport is within striking distance, but if you do fancy hooking up and putting our heads together over this Mina business, then I'm all yours. In fact, discussing Mina is something of a matter of urgency, as the hospital have just moved her back to the medium security wards. They say they're thinking about discharging her in the New Year. But how will that work, Mr Jonckers? How will I protect her?

Merry Christmas! (Almost.)

Alice x

Text Message to Mum

Thu 20 Nov 21:42

They're thinking about letting Mina out? That's great news. Are you sure about Amsterdam? Thales says he'd love you to join us. He's planning on cooking a whole goose.

Note Inside Egg Sandwich Container

Today is my last day making latte art. I couldn't find a way to attach this note to a hot drink topped with a heart, so I'm sending it to you the old-fashioned way, in a sandwich container. Hopefully I can enlist Naomi to sneak it to you during her afternoon break.

I don't have long to write this – Kerrie's about to hold me a little leaving do. There's a carrot cake with my name on it. Literally. Tomorrow I'll be joining you at Maggie's as Official Gardener no. 2 (title yet to be confirmed). In the meantime, I wanted to tell you that I think you are cool. I'm sorry it's taken me this long to say so. A request to *not* marry someone is worth taking seriously, and I've been wanting to make sure I get the words right.

When it comes to marriage, what you say about the high probability of divorce, and so on, makes absolute sense to me. It's not just that there's no point to matrimony, but it's actually *damaging* for some people. I find the sense of ownership implicit in marriage to be deeply worrying. I'm not surprised so many people prefer cohabiting.

What I was wondering, though, was . . . in spite of all that, in spite of our strong beliefs, would you object to giving it a go?

Is there any world in which you might consider having me, a snivelling wretch, as your husband? What I'm saying, inside this egg sandwich container, is: Ottila, will you marry me? I know it's antiquated and stupid and more than a little ethically dubious and definitely way too soon to be remotely sensible, but the truth is, this time, I actually *want* to do it. Nobody's forcing me into it. You are a superlative woman, Ottila, and I want to sign an antediluvian government document that proves I said so.

I'm aware that by asking you this question I am joining a long line of similarly snivelling wretches who have been desperate to marry you (my sister included) but, tell me, have any of them asked you with such panache? Surely the fact I have used the phrase *high probability of divorce* is enough to make your heart race with desire.

Well, what do you think? If the answer is yes, then put a paper clip in this container (with or without eating the sandwich first, it's up to you) and get Delyth to bring it back to me. If the answer is no, then of course we'll do the other thing: the long-term, non-violent, socially equal, sexually progressive, feminist relationship. But if you send me a paper clip, I'll do a cartwheel outside your office window.

Love always,

Thales x

P. S. Sorry I'm still fat.

Text Message to Delyth

Fri 21 Nov 14:42

Mate, would you mind popping over here and doing me a quick favour?

Receipt

the hellenic deli

Market Place
Stockport
SK1 1ES
0161 429311

JAR GRAPE LEAVES... 4.25
LONG GRAIN RICE... 0.99
ONION LOOSE.. 0.16
LEMON LOOSE... 0.86
PINE NUTS... 3.99
DILL FRESH.. 0.75
PARSLEY FRESH.. 0.75

Items: 5

TOTAL DUE..11.75
VISA DEBIT from customer..................................11.75
Balance due.. 00.00

06/12/14
13:37

Thank you for shopping at **the hellenic deli**.
Please retain for your records.
VAT NO. GB 4923857

Rocks

His hand on my back, my hand on his arm, his breath on my cheek, my breath on the glass. We're looking into a display case at H. Samuel. It's a nine carat gold ring, with a cubic zirconia. It's to last us forever. It's thirty-nine ninety-nine.

'Forty pounds,' Thales says. 'I'd happily get that for you, my raging ocean.'

'Thirty-nine ninety-nine,' I say. I try on a two-hundred-pound white gold and diamond solitaire ring.

The woman in the shop is the first person to know about our engagement. I've dropped hints to Delyth, but this woman here is the first to know that we are serious. We look at her name tag: 'Rhona'. Rhona knows.

'How does it feel?' she asks.

Fabulous! I want to tell her. *We're in love!*

'Not bad.' My fingers are too squat for an attention-seeking rock.

Out in the shopping centre, a blond boy runs up to the H. Samuel window and sticks his nose against it. He makes a pig face at the eternity rings.

'Yeah, it's okay,' I continue, wondering how one person is meant to wear one ring for the rest of their life. I think about my old friend Sadia, the one I did that teaching course with for a while, and the story she told me about walking down the street and catching her ring on a lamppost, her whole finger tearing clean off, having to get it sewn back on at A&E. Was that story true? The blond boy sticks out his tongue and licks the glass.

I hand the ring back to Rhona, desperate to tell her our wedding plans. That we're going to get married in Gretna Green on Burns Night, that we'll be addressing the haggis as man and wife.

I look at Thales instead of the diamonds. *I love you*, my eyes say to him.

I want you, his eyes say back.

Rhona waits politely.

I point at the display case, and then try on the thirty-nine ninety-nine pound ring. I see my whole future wrapped in a band around my finger, and I say, slowly, quietly, uncertainly, desperately: 'I like it.'

'I can get it for you today if you want,' Thales says. 'I can afford it. I was saving the money for an evening out, to celebrate or whatever, but we can stay in and have beans on toast for dinner. If you want something more expensive, though, I'll happily get that for you too. I'll get whatever you want. It'll just take longer. We can wait.'

I wonder what cubic zirconia is, whether it has anything to do with cubism. It does actually look like a Georges Braque painting if you look at it close up. What makes a diamond so much better than this? The stones are practically identical.

'Will this one last?' I ask Rhona, wondering whether to add the words 'a lifetime' to the end of my sentence. *I'm in love, Rhona, and I plan to be in love with this man for a lifetime.* I don't say that. You don't say things like that in H. Samuel.

Rhona assures me that the ring will last a long time, but says we can buy three years' worth of insurance for seven pounds if we want it. I tell Thales I'll pay for that bit. I bought the dolmades ingredients at the deli earlier, the ones I'm going to charm his parents with, so we're trying to keep things fair. There's something about Thales buying the actual ring for me though that turns me on. Maybe the patriarchy has infiltrated me more than I thought.

Thales gets out his debit card. We look at each other, all jumpy, and know that this is it. I'll never take his surname, and I won't wear white, and we won't make table plans, but we're doing this. He puts his PIN into the machine, then I pay for the insurance and it's done.

Rhona smiles mechanically, telling us to enjoy our day, and we head out of H. Samuel. Another historic moment, to be celebrated with baked beans. My own piece of the universe for forty pounds.

Christmas Card to Thales

[*The front of the card contains a rudimentary sketch of a stable, with straw lying on the ground, but no animals or baby Jesus. There is an arrow pointing to the stable, and next to the arrow it says: 'me'.*]

Καλά Χριστούγεννα!

I feel stable. I know it's an ongoing project, but thank you for helping me get here.

This will be the first Christmas I've ever spent without my mum or sister, but it's nice to be with my new family: you. Look forward to eating sprouts in our pyjamas and all that festive jazz.

Ottila xxx

P. S. Don't worry about not being able to get us a wedding booked at Gretna Green. I've got a better idea.

Email from Mum

From: Alice McGregor
To: Ottila McGregor
Date: Thurs, 25 December, 2014 at 1:24
Subject: Fwd: 1,753 bridges

---------- Forwarded message ----------
From: Alice McGregor <alice.mcgregor54@mcgregormail.com>
To: aart@aartjonckers.nl
Date: Thursday, 25 December 2014, 1:22
Subject: 1,753 bridges

Joncky Wonky Me Ol' Mucker,

The clock has now well and truly struck midnight, and Christmas morning is upon us. I'm sitting in the lobby of my small, Dutch hotel, on an old dinosaur of a computer, and I'm writing this to you while Anouk, a pretty girl with asymmetric hair, snoozes behind reception.

The hotel is not too shabby, considering the price. My only complaint is that I asked for a double room, but I've been given two single beds smushed together, with a sheet covering them. Don't you just hate that? Not that I'm planning on having anyone else in there with me. This isn't a festive booty call, good sir. (Hello, Ottila! As ever, I'll be forwarding this to my daughter after I've pressed send.) Actually, I'll be passing out soon, I expect, because I'm really rather piddled.

I'm going to tell you a secret now, Mr Jonckers. Ready?

I used to be a big drinker. Ottila doesn't know this, but before I got pregnant with her, I was a mess. Bernie, my husband, drank a lot too. That's one of the things that brought us together. Gradually, Bernie eased off the drink while I kept easing *onto* it. I had a terrible time trying to give it up. Finally, around the fourteenth week of my pregnancy, the morning sickness got so bad that I couldn't so much as sniff a glass of wine, and I stopped. After that, I stayed happily teetotal for years. It wasn't until a few months after Bernie died that I broke my abstinence. (Ottila, you remember the week I went AWOL.) I didn't tell a soul where I'd gone, but I'll reveal the location to you now, if you like. It was *Leicester*, Mr Jonckers. For the simple reason that I didn't know anybody in that city, so I was unlikely to be recognised. I checked myself into a Travelodge and spent seven days getting blottoed. To begin with, it felt magnificent. As if Bernie was back at my side. But by the end he felt further away than ever. So, I pulled myself together, sobered up, and I went back home to be the stoic widow and mother that I knew I had to be.

You are an astute man, Mr J. You can probably see where the problem lies. The fact is that I never found a way to get that grief out of my system. Yes, there was the sensible, grown-up grief that I was allowed to feel. The kind of grief that let me quietly get on with my day. That enabled me to say 'Don't worry' to my children, that allowed me to shed an acceptable amount of tears on anniversaries, that let me sit thoughtfully among the seedlings in my garden, remembering happier times with a gentle smile. But there's a different grief, a *wild grief*, that's been welling up inside me. A grief that snarls and bites. A grief that wants revenge on humankind. And it's only in these last few months that I've started to let that grief escape.

You must think I'm a terrible mother, Mr Jonckers. But do you know how hard it is to keep it together when your husband dies against his will and your daughter repeatedly tries to commit suicide? I take my hat off to anyone out there who can manage it. I think I might have given up entirely if it wasn't for Ottila. She doesn't know how much of a help she's been, but honestly, she's my anchor. And when I get back from the land of brown cafés (that's not even a marijuana thing ... I made that mistake yesterday, much to my own embarrassment), I'm going to put myself back together again. But this time it's going to be the real me. Warts and all. I'm going to tell my children when I'm upset or angry, and I'm going to let them worry as much as they want. There's nothing wrong with worrying, you know. It's suppressing it that kills you.

I can hear sleigh bells out in the street. Or maybe it's a ring tone. Either way, it's annoying. I used to find this time of year so magical. Partly because Bernie and I met on Christmas Day. We both went to the same beach in Whitby, and ran into the freezing cold sea: a Christmas morning tradition. I was visiting my mother, and Bernie had been on some kind of excavation in York. He was an excellent archaeologist at one time, my husband. And then he decided to give it all up to pretend to be a Viking. He was excellent at that too, as it happens. The morning we met, we were the only two on the beach dressed as Santa. That's what got us talking. He told me my beard was better than his. It was, incidentally. I miss that silly, old, unshaven fool.

There's a leaflet in my hotel that says there are 1,753 bridges in Amsterdam. That's quite a lot, isn't it? I'm guessing that when the first one was built nobody had any idea there'd end up being 1,752 more. They just built one, and then someone else built another one, and, before they knew it, they were joining up dots all over the city, forging new pathways until they reached the sweet spot. Come to think of it, I'm sure they haven't finished. There'll be bridges popping up all over the place for as long as people live. As well as older ones falling down.

Well, I'm sending this to you as a witness: I've had my last drink of 2014. A juniper berry gin on Christmas Eve. I know you won't believe me when I say this, Mr J, but I'm honestly not a full-blown alcoholic. Even so, I'm going to stay off the booze for a while. Nobody ever built a decent bridge while they were on the sauce. A lot of people have jumped off bridges in that state, but not built them. I'm sure of it.

(I'm so sorry you got your boozing gene from me, Ottila. When you first quit drinking, part of me felt a little jealous, because it seemed so much easier for you than it was for me. But I know that's plain silliness, and I'm extremely proud of the way you've taken control of your life this year. I know how close you were to your dad, and to be honest I was always rather envious of that too. You've always said you take after him but, deep down, I've always felt that you and I have a lot in common. I apologise if you feel like you've inherited all my bad bits. I think the world of you.)

Now, Mr Jonckers, all that's left for me to say to *you* is goodbye. You've been of no help to my youngest daughter whatsoever, but you've been a real comfort to me. If you ever *do* feel like giving me some advice on Mina, my inbox is always open. But if not, then consider yourself fully unsubscribed from my irregular little family newsletter. I'm off to build some bridges of my own.

Yours, architecturally,

Mrs McGregor

Text Message to Mina

Thu 25 Dec 10:13

Hello, Mina. Thales here. I've heard lots of nice things about you. Your sister says you like birds. Here's a photo of a starling that landed on one of my mudstones the other day. Hope to meet you one day soon. Merry Christmas.

Head Nurse's Report

The patient, Mina McGregor, is to be discharged from her stay on the Simiel Ward tomorrow morning. Her mother, Alice (nearest relative), will be collecting her. The patient will stay with her mother in Trowbridge for two nights, before returning to her home in Oxfordshire.

Despite continued incidences of self-harm, the patient asserts that she stands a better chance of recovery in her own home, rather than in the psychiatric ward, and Dr Okoro (Responsible Clinician) is inclined to agree with her. Her suicidal ideation appears to have worsened since being admitted to the ward, and it is possible that this will diminish once she leaves the potentially triggering environment of the hospital.

Dr Okoro has agreed a care plan for Mina, and is looking into the possibility of providing her with 17 hours of support from the Kingsand Trust, who would visit her at home and help her with daily tasks, shopping, activities, etc. We will pass on any relevant information to Mrs McGregor.

Mina has been moved from section three to two, and will remain this way for twenty-eight days (until 26th January), at which point she will no longer be detained under the Mental Health Act, providing she does not break the conditions listed overleaf.

Glenda Cross, Head Nurse at Simiel Ward

Letter from Mina

Dear Ottila,

I bet you weren't expecting this: a letter from little old me!!! It won't be very exciting. My brain can't concentrate like it used to. But I will try to do something. Here is a picture of us. [*Picture of two messy, hand-drawn stick men, with facial features only vaguely fitting over the heads. They were clearly drawn without looking at the paper, in the style Ottila and Mina call 'cherubs'. Under the picture, Mina has written: 'cherubs of ourselves'.*]

I am enjoying sending texts to Thales. Please thank him for being so nice to me. I hope I can meet him one day, when I feel up to it. Maybe we can play Bananagrams together. Thank you for sending me my own set for Christmas.

On the subject of Thales, I am very pleased for you finding someone you are comfortable with. You deserve it, kiddo!! And so what if he's Reatha's brother? Life is weird, and the sooner we all accept that the better.

This letter has already become much longer than I meant it to be. It is early in the morning but I can't sleep so I am going to try and do some craft now. I was going to knit, but I've completely forgotten how to cast on.

I'm relieved it's the last day of the year, because 2014 has been really rubbish for me. I am really annoyed that having my brain electrocuted didn't help me feel any better. Another woman in my ward had it, and after her fifth session she laughed for the first time in a year. Never mind. Little old Meeny's mind is very resistant to help. But I'm going to try, Tilly. I'm going to do my best to feel better again.

Wub you!!!!

From Mina. xxx

Text Message to Thales

> **Thu 01 Jan 00:01**
> happy new year. you're snoring in bed next to me. fuck the hootenanny.

New Year's Resolutions

1. Keep up the good work.
2. Spend more time with Mum.
3. Eat broccoli.

Card from Thales

[*The outside of the card displays a picture of a grey wolf, its head tilted up into the sky, lips parted mid-howl. Above the wolf's head is a bright, full moon. A caption beneath the wolf reads 'Who's Afraid of the Big Bad Wolf'? The inside of the card is written in green biro.*]

8 January 2015!

O,

You are certainly not afraid of the big, bad wolf. You made it! One whole year since you quit alcohol.

Despite your protest this morning, it honestly doesn't matter in the least that you slipped up and drank alcohol once this year. The point is, you moved on from it. And I am so, so proud of you.

From your fanged friend,

T x

P. S. Can't wait to get married. Hope you like the windowpane waistcoat I've picked out at Moss Bros. Don't worry, windowpane is just what they call it. It's not see-through. It's made of polyester.

Email from Mum

From: Alice McGregor
To: Ottila McGregor
Date: Tue, 20 January, 2015 at 9:40
Subject: Happily Ever After

Hello, sweetheart. I hope work is going well, and that you and Thales are not too bogged down with preparations. I'm awfully excited, you know. I think having a Lupercalia-themed wedding is a marvellous idea! And I don't blame you for snapping up the Friday 13th booking. Yes, of course it was a bit of a shock to hear you're getting married when you've only known Thales a short time, but you always were a romantic, like me.

Obviously, I had no idea what Lupercalia was, so thank you for sending me those links. I remember seeing an RSC production of *Julius Caesar* in Stratford. Someone tells Mark Antony to give his wife a smack in order to make her fertile. I finally understand what that was all about now! I'm glad Thales won't be hitting you at your wedding, darling. But a cake shaped like a sacrificial goat sounds like such fun.

I'm so sorry I haven't met Thales yet. Somehow I've never thought to suggest a visit. I'm going to try harder from now on. I'm your mother, and I'm here for you. I'm looking forward to meeting Thales's parents as well. I've even used Google Translate to teach myself to say 'How do you do' in Greek, although I'm not sure whether it translates literally. It's great his sister can make it to the wedding. You and her used to be friends, didn't you? It's a shame you won't have *your* sister there on your special day. It's awfully tiring for Mina, going to family events. You do understand, don't you?

Any thoughts on what I should wear for the ceremony? I don't have any animal skins but I saw a nice leopard print maxi dress on ASOS earlier this morning. That's right, Ottila: ASOS! I haven't been on a seed website for weeks; I'm an ASOS girl now. I also set up an eBay account and sold that wobbly old chest of drawers of your father's for fifty quid. I got five out of five for customer service! I might sell the kitchen table next. Get something funky and modern instead. When you get ten thousand positive feedback ratings, you get a shooting star. Can you get ten thousand ratings in one lifetime? If some old Italian guy can paint the ceiling of the Sistine Chapel, my dear, then I reckon anything's possible! Perhaps that will be my (belated) New Year's resolution; that, and capturing the flag at paintballing.

Well, I had better be off. Mina's getting the train over for lunch. It's the first time she'll have used public transport in over a year. Poor thing has forgotten so much since her ECT. Said she couldn't even remember how to buy a ticket. I've sent her an email talking her through it. She phoned me three times yesterday to cancel, but I've rallied her round and I think she's looking forward to it now. I'm a little worried about the fact she says she hasn't eaten anything for three days, so I'm going to tempt her with an indoor picnic. I've got strawberries and Laughing Cow. Wish me luck!

Lots of love,

Mum xoxoxoxoxo

P. S. I feel ghastly for forgetting about Christmas presents. You'll get a little something from me in the post any day now.

Text Message to Mum

Thu 22 Jan 17:51

Yay! I love the fact you got me a watch with Wonder Woman on it. She's a badass warrior, just like you. Thank you for the watch, and for everything else you've given me.

Recovery Meeting Transcript

THERAPIST: So we can probably think about discharging you soon.

PATIENT: Really? Will I make it on my own?

THERAPIST: You've been making it on your own this whole time.

PATIENT: I could spiral out of control.

THERAPIST: What might that look like?

PATIENT: Drinking. Cheating on Thales. Falling apart.

THERAPIST: And then what?

PATIENT: [*Panicky.*] I don't know, I . . .

THERAPIST: You could come back here if you wanted.

PATIENT: I'm allowed to come back?

THERAPIST: That's what we're here for.

PATIENT: I didn't realise I could just come back.

THERAPIST: Any time you like. [*Laughs.*] Via your GP, of course. Remember it's okay to make mistakes.

PATIENT: I'm not going to use that as an excuse to drink. Or cheat.

THERAPIST: Good. The potential for a fresh start is not an excuse to mess up in the first place. It's a way of moving on when necessity strikes.

PATIENT: I keep thinking about how awful that hangover felt. Mentally, even more than physically. [*Pause.*] I almost quit therapy that week.

THERAPIST: I'm glad you didn't.

PATIENT: [*Small exhalation, perhaps a laugh.*] I know that marrying Thales isn't some sort of happy ending, you know. And it's a *symptom* of my happiness, not the cause.

THERAPIST: It can be whatever you want it to be.

PATIENT: I'm just relieved I can make plans again. And trust myself not to screw them up.

THERAPIST: And if you do . . .?

PATIENT: I start again. [*Patient laughs.*] I've been making a kind of scrapbook about my quest for happiness.

THERAPIST: That sounds nice.

PATIENT: It's been really good recording all the stuff I've been doing. A sort of reminder: even when you're determined to be the most fulfilled and content person on earth, life gets in the way. But that doesn't make what you *do* experience any less special.

THERAPIST: Sometimes the process can be just as important as the product. I think we've explored that idea before.

PATIENT: Do you remember when I started seeing you I told you I wanted to be happy? It was like a prayer for me. I whispered it under my breath as I did the washing up, as I took the bus to work. *So happy it hurts. So happy it hurts. So happy it hurts.*

THERAPIST: I think I remember you –

PATIENT: I didn't know what I was talking about back then.

THERAPIST: No?

PATIENT: I didn't even know what happiness was. What I was hoping for, I think, was to find myself in some kind of manic state of euphoria, where I felt so good it actually, genuinely, physically pained me. You know when you work in retail, and your jaw aches from smiling so much throughout the day?

THERAPIST: I –

PATIENT: I got it all wrong! True happiness means something totally different. It means *accepting* pain. Messing up. Suffering. Sometimes, happiness hurts.

THERAPIST: It's not quite that –

PATIENT: It's all about balance. I can see it now. It's *everything* that's happened over the past year, not just the good bits, that's led to me being happy.

THERAPIST: It's healthy to embrace the full range of emotions.

PATIENT: Do you think I could get copies of the interviews we've had? From your dictaphone?

THERAPIST: You think you'll find more answers that way?

PATIENT: Actually, they're just for my scrapbook. If I'm allowed.

THERAPIST: I'll see what I can do.

PATIENT: That would be amazing. Thank you. [*Pause.*] Can I just ask one more thing?

THERAPIST: Go on.

PATIENT: I've never dared mentioned this, I'm so sorry if it's rude, but I keep looking at your arms, and . . . am I allowed to mention the scars on your wrists? Did you ever try to . . .?

THERAPIST: I don't mind telling you my story. But I'll switch the dictaphone off for that.

PATIENT: Only if you're comfortab

[*There's a loud rustle and the dictaphone switches off. This is the last audio file on the pen drive.*]

Say Hello to a Brand New Chapter

The workbook is coming to an end and you have done so well. Since you made the decision to stop drinking, you have begun to write a whole new chapter in the story of your life. You have developed your personal relationships, you are spending time and money on things that matter and looking after your physical and mental health. You'll be surprised how different this chapter turns out compared to all that have preceded it.

But remember, if you find that you are making mistakes, then it's never too late to get editing. This story is yours, and no one else's, and your story is beautiful.

Note

[*The following is written in fountain pen on the lid of a box. The box contains a white cube made of felt.*]

Thales McSanna,

Ta da! Here's a gelatinous cube for you on our wedding day. That *is* your favourite creature in the D & D *Monster Manual*, right? I commissioned Mina to make it specially.

I'm glad this is happening, and I'm even gladder we decided to meld our surnames together into a monstrous hybrid. Thank you for *not* agreeing to *not* marry me. Even though I absolutely stand by my view that marriage is one of life's great tragedies, it feels like the best thing I've ever done. And you're good for me.

x

Little Book of Happy

Dear Little Book,

I'm afraid our time together is coming to an end. It's been lovely getting to know you, but you are very cumbersome now and I'm ready for something new.

Maybe I'll buy a proper diary from Smiths. I kept one religiously when I was a kid. I remember one of my earliest diary entries, when I was seven. 'Found out no adverts on BBC 1 and 2.' To the point, and completely honest.

But I haven't always shared my revelations with you, I'm afraid, LBOH. Sometimes I've told you what I've wanted you to hear. Wanted myself to hear. There are so many things I've done that I haven't told you about.

I haven't cheated on Thales, if that's what you're wondering. 'It's okay if you have, Ottila,' my therapist said to me once, 'it doesn't make you a bad person. Our actions can surprise us, because they express something we've been feeling without realising it, and we just need to start listening to ourselves again.'

I mean, yes, I've thought about cheating a few times. I do this thing where I'll be having a brilliant time with Thales, and then I'll suddenly stop and look at him, and fixate on something ridiculous, like, one of his eyebrows is slightly more arched than the other, and then I'll convince myself I need to try being with someone else instead, someone with symmetrical brows. Or we'll have an argument and I'll tell myself that's a freebie, that I deserve a night off: a passionate encounter with a hot, sadistic kickboxing instructor, for example. But when I think about it for too long, it makes me crumple up with sadness. I'd be missing out on so much. So I find a new kickboxing class.

I'm sorry for keeping this stuff from you, LBOH. I want us to be close. That's why I'm going to end by telling you this.

Yesterday I married Thales. We had a great day. Does that sound impressive enough? Well, I mean it: it was really great. The best day of my life? Probably not. I was nervous and dry-mouthed around Thales's family. If I was going to label any one day of my life as the best, I'd much rather pick the day Thales and I went to Manchester Museum and learnt about plate tectonics and isinglass. That was when Thales first told me he loved me. Or I'd pick the day Mum and Dad told me and Mina we were allowed to get a cat, and we went to get Cloud. Or the time we all jumped in the car and travelled to the Welsh border on a whim. Had a cup of tea in Hay-on-Wye then played the number plate game all the way back home.

I enjoyed my wedding day in a different way to those days. It was more quiet and considered. I felt such a rush of sincerity when I said my vows, like I suddenly realised what the phrase 'rest of my life' really means. Thales wore odd socks, and I kept looking down at them, thinking how lucky I am to have found my match.

I'm glad we decided to keep the whole thing non-alcoholic. I'd have killed for a glass of champagne, but that's life. The sacrificial goat cake was delicious. Halfway through the meal, I nipped out of Thales's parents' dining room and went to the toilet. I took my phone out of its hiding place in my right (borrowed and blue) stocking, under my ill-fitting but still very fancy yellow dress, and I wrote a text.

Miss you, it said.

Then I deleted it. I closed my eyes, and I whispered six words under my breath: 'Decide to be okay with it'. I flushed, washed my hands, and went back into the dining room, taking my seat next to Thales. My cheeks were glowing with good intentions.

'You look happy,' Thales said.

And I was. I am.

Yesterday is dead, tomorrow hasn't arrived yet. I have just one day, today, and I'm going to be happy in it.

Groucho Marx